Death
on
Tour

Critical Acclaim for Janice Hamrick and *Death on Tour*

"*Death on Tour* is fun, romantic and delightful, and full of fascinating bits about ancient Egypt." —*Cleveland Plain Dealer*

"Hamrick does a good job capturing life on an exhausting budget tour as her snazzy if snarky amateur sleuth . . . investigates some fishy fellow tourists." —*Publishers Weekly*

"The cozy mystery was once limited to adorable English villages and the like, but it long ago outgrew its traditional boundaries. Janice Hamrick's *Death on Tour* is a charming example." —*Seattle Times*

"A classy whodunit, *Death on Tour* also offers a trove of Egyptology and a wealth of humor—Christie's characters were never this smart-alecky. Hamrick plays fair with clues, and the alert reader has a fighting chance of identifying the culprit from among the cast of suspects." —*Richmond Times Dispatch*

"Janice Hamrick's debut mystery is highly recommended for those who love a charming, suspenseful, hilarious cozy with a happy, fairy-tale ending. (It's the perfect cozy for taking on vacation.)" —*Gumshoe Review*

"Hamrick's character-driven debut is a good mystery and a charming travelogue." —*Kirkus Reviews*

"Murder, possible smuggling, a colorful array of characters and what could be the start of a romance are vying for top billing with the wonders of Egypt in this funny and expertly plotted debut, introducing high school teacher Jocelyn Shore. Readers can only hope that Hamrick's next installment is as much fun as this one." —*RT Book Reviews*

Death
on
Tour

JANICE

HAMRICK

St. Martin's Paperbacks

This is a work of fiction. All of the characters, organizations, and events portrayed in this novel are either products of the author's imagination or are used fictitiously.

DEATH ON TOUR

Copyright © 2011 by Janice Hamrick.
Excerpt from *Death Makes the Cut* copyright © 2012 by Janice Hamrick.

For information address St. Martin's Press, 175 Fifth Avenue, New York, NY 10010.

ISBN: 978-1-250-01311-8

Printed in the United States of America

Minotaur edition / May 2011
St. Martin's Paperbacks edition / June 2012

St. Martin's Paperbacks are published by St. Martin's Press, 175 Fifth Avenue, New York, NY 10010.

10 9 8 7 6 5 4 3 2

To my parents
Joyrene and James Pope
and to my daughters
Jacqueline and Jennifer Hamrick
who have always been there for me
and who always believed I could

Acknowledgments

Writing might be a solitary activity, but thank goodness it is never done in isolation. My heartfelt thanks go to my wonderful editor, Kelley Ragland of Minotaur Books, for her meticulous work in editing this manuscript and for believing in it in the first place, and to St. Martin's Minotaur and the Mystery Writers of America for sponsoring the First Crime Novel Competition and giving me this opportunity. My gratitude also goes to the following wonderful people at Minotaur Books: Matt Martz, who kept me on track and answered my millions of questions with unfailing patience, Anna Chang for her awesome copyediting skills, and David Baldeosingh Rotstein and Ben Perini, who designed and illustrated the coolest cover art ever. My thanks go to my agent, David Hale Smith, for taking a chance on me and for his much-needed advice, encouragement, and guidance. And finally, I would like to thank Cindy Marszal for reading my first drafts, for saying all the right things even when those things were hard, and for sharing the writing adventure with me.

Sunday, Cairo

After a restful night in your luxury hotel, join your Egyptologist and traveling companions on a short ride to the necropolis at Giza where you'll see the enigmatic Sphinx and marvel at the awe-inspiring great pyramids. Travel by luxury coach to ancient Memphis to admire the 40-foot statue of Ramses II and the Alabaster Sphinx. Next, a quick stop at the Step Pyramid at Saqqara, followed by a demonstration of the making of world-famous Egyptian silk carpets. No visit to Cairo would be complete without a visit to the Egyptian Museum, where you will see the treasures of King Tut and the most famous mummies in the world.

—WorldPal pamphlet

Chapter 1

DEATH OF A TOURIST

The body lay facedown in the sand beside the giant stone blocks of the great pyramid of Khafre. Overhead, the blue sky flickered dimly through a haze born on the khamsin winds whistling relentlessly from the desert. The morning air was still cool and very dry, but full of the promise of heat to come. Men wearing head cloths and flowing tunics ran back and forth like ants, shouting in Arabic, while camel drivers stood beside their indifferent animals, craning their necks and talking excitedly. Policemen carrying automatic rifles guarded the perimeter of the crowd, looking alert and dangerous, when only a few minutes before they had been sleepy and bored.

Our tour group stood huddled together in a little knot a few yards from a brightly colored heap of clothes that had once been Millie Owens. Every few seconds, one of us broke from the herd, caught a glimpse of the body, and hurried back to the safety of the circle. It seemed impossible that the body was really there, that it wasn't some horrible mistake, and that

Millie wasn't really just resting and would soon bounce up and start annoying us again. I wished she would.

Almost, anyway. I'm a high school history teacher, and I'm well acquainted with the full range of human behavior, but I'd never seen anyone who grated on the nerves of an entire group like Millie Owens, not even in PTA meetings. To be honest, the sight of her dead body lying at the base of the pyramid was not nearly as disturbing as it should have been. I glanced around at the faces of my traveling companions of the last two days. Everyone looked worried, but no one was crying, unless you counted a pair I called the ditz duo, who were wailing and whirling around like the dervishes we were supposed to see at dinner tonight. Our guide, Anni, was halfheartedly trying to calm them. The rest of us stood in shocked silence. Shocked, yes, but not grieving.

What bothered me the most was that it seemed that no one had seen what had happened, or at least no one was admitting it. Granted, the morning light was barely kissing the stones of the pyramids and the inevitable tourist hordes had not yet descended, but literally scores of people milled about. The hawkers with their postcards and plaster statues of Horus. The dozen or more carriage drivers with their unenthusiastic horses. The tourist police, managing to look both incompetent and frightening at the same time. Our own group of twenty-two, now down by one.

So how was it that no one had seen a fifty-five-year-old woman climb onto a pyramid and fall to her death? Our group could probably be excused because most of us spent a good deal of effort staying away from Millie. A buffer of twenty paces was the minimum required to avoid interaction. Just

4

last night, I'd been scouring through my Egyptian phrase book for the correct phrase for "pepper spray." Not that I'd have really used it on the old bat, but it would be nice to have, just in case I could take no more. Millie was one of those intense, pushy women who seemed to be in constant motion. Her mouth moved in an unending stream of fatuous observations, idiotic questions, and catty gossip. While the rest of us were still making introductions, she somehow knew everyone's names, and a great deal more. She had a way of weaseling out details and then making rather shrewd guesses to fill in the gaps, and she wasn't above snooping. I'd caught her going through my backpack on the bus during the very short trip from the hotel to the pyramids, less than an hour ago, and she'd just gazed unblushingly at me and handed it back.

"Diarrhea already or just playing it safe?" she'd asked loudly, an embarrassing reference to my Imodium.

I'd glared at her, unable to think of a snappy retort quickly enough. I suppose I should be grateful I hadn't been carrying anything worse. And I was pretty sure she'd stolen the new strawberry lip balm I'd bought the day before at the hotel gift shop.

Millie was . . . or had been . . . living proof that no one ever really changed after high school. In a school the size of the one in which I taught, I saw a dozen Millies every day. She was the kid who bounded into a group of pretty, popular girls like a slobbering stray, oblivious to the discomfort she caused, clueless to the social cues that might have allowed her to join in. The nicer girls tolerated her for a few moments before suddenly remembering homework or prior commitments. The meaner girls were openly rude, cutting her with razor-sharp

5

tongues before flouncing away in disgust in the face of her hurt incomprehension. The Millies of the high school world broke my heart, but that didn't make them any easier to tolerate in the adult world.

Not surprisingly, our Millie had been traveling alone. She had droned on at great length about her traveling companion's attack of appendicitis striking only hours before their plane was scheduled to take off. I decided that this "traveling companion" was either fictitious or had burst her own appendix with an ice pick. My own traveling companion, my cousin Kyla, backed the former because she contended that no one would have agreed to come with Millie in the first place. My money was on the latter because, as I pointed out, there's no explaining how one chooses one's roommates. It took her only a second.

"Bitch," she said admiringly.

But that was all yesterday. Today, the March sun was brilliant even through the haze, and poor, sad Millie Owens was dead, which no one could have wished for her. And something had gone seriously wrong with our beautiful trip to Egypt.

I leaned against the stones of the pyramid, cool in the morning air, and wondered how many others had done so throughout the millennia since they had been carved. Maybe not many. Had the Egyptians spent much time in their cities of the dead after the pharaohs had been laid to rest? The huge necropolis had been a thriving community, almost a small city during construction, but what about afterward when the work was finished and the new pharaoh was far away fighting wars or building new monuments? I imagined an unearthly silence enveloping everything as the wind pushed the sand higher around the stones until they were all but swallowed by the desert.

Pretty much the opposite of what was going on now. The police were now moving among the vendors. I'd never heard so much shouting to so little purpose. Even after two months with my Pimsleur CDs, I could not understand more than two or three words of Arabic, but I could tell that they were getting nothing out of the bystanders. Wild gestures, head shakes, points and shrugs, but not one coherent statement as far as I could tell. Somehow, impossibly, Millie had climbed up onto one of the gigantic blocks of the pyramid and then fallen to her death.

It just made no sense. Large though the blocks were—and they were far too big for an out-of-shape tourist to climb without help—they just weren't that tall. A fall of five or six feet at most. Far enough to break an arm, or a hip, I thought, glancing at the wizened, ancient figures of Charlie and Yvonne de Vance, but a neck? Maybe if she'd managed to get up to the second layer and somehow bounced off the first.

One of the policemen beckoned to our tour guide, Anni, who joined him a few paces away. Anni was a lovely and interesting mixture of traditional and modern Egyptian. A little younger than me, probably in her midtwenties, she had large dark eyes made to seem even larger by kohl eyeliner and thick mascara. She wore a lightweight turtleneck shirt carefully pinned to her headscarf to ensure that no part of her neck or hair showed, but over that she wore a t-shirt with an I ♡ WorldPal logo. Jeans and tennis shoes completed the outfit.

In one hand, she held a pink Hello Kitty umbrella, which she used, not for protection from nonexistent rain, but as a beacon for gathering her small flock around her. Everywhere we went, we followed Hello Kitty like a row of ducklings following their mother.

Now she began a rapid torrent of Arabic with the policeman. The only word I understood was "la," which meant "no." She said it a lot.

My cousin Kyla joined me beside the stone, looking worried. She is far too careful about her clothes to lean against a dusty pyramid, but today she stood stiffly upright a pace away, looking striking as always. Her long dark hair, the exact color and texture of mine, was pulled into an elegant twist, gleaming in the sun. I'm not sure how she managed it, but her tan slacks and lemon shirt still looked crisp and pressed. And now, while the rest of us fretted, she looked perfectly cool and composed.

A façade. I could tell she was as worried as anyone.

"What do you think is going on?" she asked under her breath.

"I think they're going to arrest us all and throw us into Turkish prison."

"Besides that."

"No idea."

She gave me a look. Kyla may look slim and elegant from a distance, but she is basically a pit bull without the fur. Back home in Austin, she leads a team of software developers with a great deal of organization, energy, and blunt speech. She also deeply believes that she is fully capable of handling any situation at any time, which I am happily and constantly pointing out to her is just not true. In return, I'm pretty sure she considers me

8

weak and cowardly, mostly because she has called me both to my face. Still, there was no one I would rather have with me on any kind of adventure, and when I invited her to join me on a tour of Egypt, she said yes almost before the words were out of my mouth. Of course, she then spent the next six weeks trying to talk me into skipping the tour group and going about on our own, which was completely crazy. I'd wanted to go to Egypt my whole life. The pyramids, the mummies, the Nile. A dream trip, the fulfillment of a childhood desire. But go without the protection of a group and a guide who at least spoke the language? In a country where guards with machine guns stood on every corner and escorted every busload of tourists? No way. And if Kyla thought I was a coward, I could live with that. Of course, it seemed that even tour groups couldn't protect you from everything. Millie's death could hardly be considered part of the normal WorldPal package, but I knew if it interfered with our trip, Kyla was never going to let me hear the end of it.

I turned my thoughts back to the accident. The whole thing bothered me, and not just because a lonely middle-aged woman was dead.

"How do you think she got up there?" I wondered aloud.

She glanced behind me at the huge blocks. The top of her head barely cleared the upper rim of the stone. "I could get up there if I wanted to," she announced.

"So could I, if a lion was chasing me. But not any other way. And she was a lot older than we are."

Kyla considered. "She was pretty wiry," she said doubtfully. "I mean, look at Flora and Fiona. They must be about a hundred, but I've seen Fiona tossing suitcases like a teamster."

I ignored this. "And even if she did climb up and fall, how could that kill her?" I eyed the sad little heap from where we stood, but there was no way I was going over to check.

"Stranger things have happened," she answered.

Maybe, I thought. But I couldn't think of any.

One by one, the rest of the group joined us against the side of the pyramid. The youngest members of the group, two teenage boys called Chris and David Peterson, gave a hop and hoisted themselves onto the blocks, demonstrating how easy it was if you were a teenage boy. I could see their plump little mother open her mouth to call them back and then think better of it.

A few paces away, the Australian woman, Lydia Carpenter, dug in her purse for cigarettes and moved downwind to light up. Her husband, Ben, joined her, and the two of them stood with their heads together, conversing quietly. I watched them with interest. Lydia always carried a little metal box into which she dropped her ashes, even here in the desert, with nothing but sand and dust at her feet. Which didn't seem to be good enough for some people. Jerry Morrison, a lawyer from somewhere in California, gave a snort of disgust and muttered something about a "filthy habit" in a stage whisper. He was traveling with his adult daughter, who joined him in moving away and turning their backs. Lydia and Ben stared at them with contempt.

One of the men in our group, a dark-haired giant with a booming voice, began talking about Millie a few paces away, and Kyla and I both perked up our ears and moved forward a step or two to listen.

"No, she is definitely dead," he said, speaking to a young Asian couple, who were looking worried. Noticing our interest, he gave a small shrug. "I'm a doctor. I checked her pulse before the police pushed me away."

"I don't understand how she could die from a fall like that," I said.

He nodded. "She may have caught her head on the stone and broken her neck. They wouldn't let me examine her more thoroughly, but there was blood on the back of her neck, at the base of the skull. A tragic accident."

I wished I could remember his name. Subdued now, he was ordinarily an exuberant personality with the dark skin of his Indian ancestors and the kind of voice that needed no microphone. He could easily have been obnoxious, but somehow instead managed to be extraordinarily likable.

Kyla held out her hand. "Kyla Shore. Sorry, I've forgotten your name."

He beamed at her, forgetting to be somber. "DJ." His huge hand swallowed hers. "DJ Gavaskar from Los Angeles. And this is my wife, Nimmi." He beckoned enthusiastically and his wife joined him.

Nimmi was a small woman, slim and catlike. Gold gleamed from her ears and throat, her shirt was of beautiful raw silk, and her bag was a large Louis Vuitton that probably cost two week's salary—mine, not hers. Dressed to impress. She was the kind of woman it might be fun to dislike at first glance, but her eyes and smile were as warm as her husband's, and I found myself returning her smile. She held out her hand and gave me a ladylike fingertip handshake. Her fingers were cool and small, like a little bird. I instantly felt large and clumsy.

"Of course we have met, but it is difficult to learn so many names at once," she said with a smile.

"Jocelyn Shore," I told her.

She smiled and glanced from me to Kyla. "And are you twins?"

I didn't dare look at Kyla, although I could sense the sudden arctic chill coming from her direction.

"No. Actually we're not even sisters. We're first cousins."

"Really? Well, the family resemblance is striking. You are both beautiful girls."

I gave a polite smile, feeling my face redden a little. It always puzzled me how people could say such extraordinarily embarrassing and personal things right to your face without a hint of self-consciousness. And Nimmi was not nearly old enough to get away with calling me a girl.

DJ broke in. "I was just telling Keith and Dawn that I'd examined the body."

Nimmi gave a delicate shudder. "So tragic."

I glanced at the other couple. I didn't know much about the Kims yet, other than they were from Seattle and either one or both of them worked in a lab researching food additives. I liked the way they held hands whenever possible, and kept their eyes on each other when it wasn't. I suspected they had not been married very long.

Another half hour slipped away and the group attitude changed subtly from horrified shock to annoyed boredom. I've noticed it often, the development of a group personality, completely independent of the personalities of any of the mem-

12

bers. I saw it in my classes. Somehow one period of world history became fascinating and enjoyable, while the next was complete agony and I struggled to keep the kids awake. A group of adults is the same. After only a few hours together, we'd already gelled into a single entity with its own needs and agenda. Looking around, I could see that while any one of us would claim we were filled with concern and sorrow, the group as a whole was tired and bored and wanted to get on with the day. After all, we had only a week in Egypt, and no one was exactly brokenhearted that Millie Owens wouldn't be monopolizing our guide's attention, snooping through bags that didn't belong to her, and asking the most painfully brainless questions ever asked in the history of human speech. The group was ready to move on.

At last, Anni rejoined us, looking appropriately somber and concerned. She did a quick head count in Arabic under her breath.

"Where are Flora and Fiona? Does anyone see them?" she asked.

We gave a collective sigh and glanced around unenthusiastically. The ditz duo had never yet been on time for a rendezvous. During our meet and greet yesterday, they'd said they were sisters, but they didn't look alike at all. Flora had short gray hair, cropped like a man's on the sides, but with a ridiculous fluffy puff on top. She had a way of staring through her glasses as though they were fogged, and she couldn't focus very well. Fiona was tall and thin, with impossibly black wispy hair, worn long and untamed as God intended. Unlikely bits of it stood at attention at different times, making it hard to concentrate on anything else. Her glasses were racy cat's-eye

13

horn-rims, her hands large and clawlike. I admit I'd searched surreptitiously for a hint of an Adam's apple when we'd first met.

DJ spotted them at last near a police officer on a camel. Both camel and officer appeared to be watching them somewhat incredulously. They were looking at a map, which was flapping in the wind, and gesturing to each other wildly. DJ shouted at them and waved Hello Kitty, while Anni hurried forward to retrieve them.

They rejoined the group all in a dither. "We couldn't find you. We were afraid you'd left," said Fiona breathlessly.

"Yes, we were hiding behind the big pink umbrella," said Kyla under her breath.

"Well, we are all here now," said Anni. "And Mohammad is coming," she said, referring to her counterpart who had met most of us at the airport and whisked us through customs with speed and efficiency. "He is going to handle everything about . . ." she hesitated.

I could tell she didn't know how to refer to the body. She went on gamely, ". . . about Millie. I have told the police that we know nothing at all about how the accident happened, and we are free to go. Now, what does everyone want to do? We can return to the hotel and rest," she suggested.

The group howled a protest. We were in Cairo. We were standing against the sun-drenched side of the four-thousand-year-old pyramid of the great pharaoh Khafre. Twenty paces away, a deep and mysterious tunnel guarded by dark men clad in flowing tunics plunged sharply downward into the heart of the pyramid itself. Nearby, just upwind in fact, waited a caravan of camels led by enigmatic denizens of the desert who had delved the secrets of point and click digital cameras. Go to the hotel? The only dead body that could have made that seem attractive was my own.

Alan Stratton spoke up. "I think we'd all like to carry on as planned," he said firmly.

I looked at him speculatively, noting again the absence of a wedding ring. He was tall, in his early thirties, and traveling alone, which by itself would have made him the most interesting person on the trip, even if he hadn't also been very nice looking. Kyla and I had noticed him right away and were dying to learn his story and figure out why he was by himself, but so far we hadn't had a chance. He seemed to linger quietly on the edge of the group, but was never quite part of the group, which was actually something of a feat in itself. While the rest of us huddled together in shock, he'd been one of the few to hurry to Millie's side after the initial discovery, and I'd seen him talking to the police and then to Anni. Now he was acting as our spokesman, saying aloud what we were all thinking.

Anni looked around at the rest of us, who were nodding like bobblehead dolls on the dashboard of a semi.

"Then that is what we shall do. Now, who said that they wanted to go inside the pyramid?" she asked, spreading a stack of colorful tickets like a deck of cards.

Half an hour later, we hopped back on the bus and took a very short drive around to the western side of the pyramids, where a veritable herd of camels waited for us. This was one of the advantages of being on a tour—we never had to walk very far and we didn't have to haggle for our own camels. Anni kept us on the bus an extra moment to give instructions

15

about tipping while we pressed our noses to the windows like a pack of Pomeranians.

The scene outside was chaos. Dozens of camels lay in the sand, long bony legs folded beneath them. Small patches of brilliant green fodder were sprinkled through the herd and contrasted sharply with the barren ground. The camels' humps were covered by the kind of quilted pads used by movers to protect furniture, and those in turn were covered by enormous saddles with very high horns in front and back. Patterned multicolored blankets covered the saddles. These wild desert camels wore coats that were almost white, instead of the sandy color preferred by ordinary city camels in zoos, and managed to looked sleepy and mildly annoyed at the same time.

On the edge of the camel herd stood about ten horses in a variety of colors, looking oddly small and almost apologetic by comparison. It was obvious to all concerned that real men rode camels and only pathetic losers or possibly elderly nuns would stoop to riding around on mere horses. The camel drivers were as exotic as their charges. They wore the traditional Egyptian galabia, a long-sleeved blue, gray, or black tunic that fell to the ankles, and most of them also wore white or red-and-white scarves wrapped about their heads to protect themselves from the sun.

We spilled off the bus in great excitement, only to be met by a squadron of shouting camel drivers. The front-runners shied like startled deer. Dawn Kim actually turned and tried to get back on the bus, but she was blocked by rickety Charlie de Vance, who was still trying to bend his knee replacement far enough to make it down that last step. Anni smoothly turned us over to the one driver with whom she had an arrangement, and the others shuffled off dejectedly.

We followed our camel driver eagerly. The redheaded Peterson boys raced ahead while their mother shouted warnings about staying away from the camels. Fiona and Flora clutched each others arms like hens and kept repeating that they wanted to share a camel. Jerry Morrison held back with his daughter, looking disdainful.

"Filthy," he said. "I bet they've got fleas."

"Oh, Daddy," said the daughter. I was pretty sure her name was Kathy, and I was absolutely sure she was way too old to call her father "Daddy."

I hoped they were just experiencing some temporary culture shock and weren't intending to complain or bicker the entire trip. I also hoped Jerry was wrong about the fleas.

I stooped to tighten my shoelaces, willing to be one of the last to board a camel rather than be too close to the Morrisons. Or the ditz duo.

"Hurry up," said Kyla impatiently, tapping one polished leather shoe in the sand. It was already covered with a light coating of dust, which did not entirely displease me. I rose and joined her.

The camel driver beckoned to us impatiently, and we followed, picking our way gingerly past a few recumbent cud-chewing camels to join him. Our driver was immensely fat, the giant beach ball of his stomach making a tent of his galabia. I imagined dozens of small desert creatures sheltering under the folds and then gave a little shudder. One of his front teeth was gold, the other missing, and his swarthy skin was covered with a light sheen of sweat.

"Here, you two ladies. On this camel, please." He gestured to a bored creature. I had to admit, up close they did look a little flea-bitten.

"Oh no," said Kyla. "I want my own camel."

"No, no. Very strong. No problem for two," he nodded emphatically.

Kyla shot him a glance that should have made him stagger back. "I want my own camel," she repeated.

He appealed to me with a look, but I just raised my eyebrows and stared coldly. It worked on seventeen-year-olds and it worked on him. His shoulders slumped a little. "This way." And he led Kyla to another camel.

The young man who held the lead rein of my camel gave a small private smile, then helped me into the saddle.

"Hold here very hard and lean back very far," he said and waited for me to obey.

It was good advice. I gripped the saddle horn and leaned back just in time as the camel's back half rose sharply in the air, throwing me forward. Then the front half rose, throwing me sharply back. I settled back into the saddle some eight feet off the ground, pleased not to have fallen.

Alan Stratton came and stood beside my camel, looking up at me and shading his eyes with his hands against the brilliant morning sun. His eyes were the most remarkable color, a soft green that changed subtly from sage to gray depending on the light. His hair, cut short and therefore clearly not as curly as it could have been, was a soft golden brown that had probably once been blond. It made a very attractive little swirl at the crown of his head.

"Having fun?" he asked. His voice was as attractive as the rest of him, deep and ever so slightly gravelly.

I realized I was staring like an idiot. "I had no idea they were so tall," I said inanely and immediately wanted to kick myself.

He gave a little grin. "Ever ridden one before?"

"No."

"Me, either. You look like a natural."

I was trying to think of something devastatingly witty to say when a different camel herder beckoned to Alan and led him away to one of the larger camels. I watched as the animal lifted its hind end straight up and tossed Alan forward like a rag doll. He held on gamely and then gave me a little wave of triumph. I waved back.

The fat camel driver gave a shout, and we were off. Camels take huge, slow strides, swaying from one side to another. Ahead of me, the rest of the group, singly and in pairs, plodded forward across the sand toward the pyramids. I could not believe I was actually here. I wanted to shout with excitement, to grab someone and jump up and down laughing. Kyla was too far ahead to share my exhilaration, but she would have understood. We hadn't grown up together as kids, but my family moved to Austin for my high school years, and except for one or two quarrels, Kyla and I had been inseparable ever since. During our sophomore year, we'd both become obsessed with Egypt in the way that only teenage girls can obsess about anything. We saw every Discovery Channel special and conned our parents into driving us four hours each way to a special exhibit at the Houston Museum of Natural Science. Saturdays were spent renting every mummy movie ever made. Of course, obsessions don't last forever, and we'd eventually moved on to boys and clothes, but when the King Tut exhibit arrived in Dallas a couple of years ago, Kyla and I had attended the opening weekend, waiting in line for what seemed like forever in quivering anticipation.

Now I was actually here, on a camel, riding across the sands of the Sahara toward the great pyramids of Giza. Directly in front of me, Kathy Morrison perched stiffly in the saddle, but I didn't think I could share my excitement with her. I glanced back. Alan Stratton rode the last camel in line, a pensive look on his face. I gave him a huge grin. He met my eyes and relaxed into a smile.

"This is the best!" I called, and he started laughing.

Behind him, the camel herd dotted the sand like toys scattered by a child while the immense desert rolled away to the horizon until it blended seamlessly into the hazy sky. It was a perfect picture and without thinking I raised my little camera and snapped. For an instant, I thought his smile faltered. I wondered if I should apologize, but the next moment he was smiling again.

"You look good on a camel," he said teasingly.

"Likewise," I answered, then turned around quickly before he could see any signs of the warmth I felt rising in my cheeks.

What was wrong with me? I was as bad as any high school student, feeling all hot and bothered just because an attractive man was being pleasant. To distract myself, I began wondering why he hadn't been pleased to have his picture taken. Maybe he had a hidden past. Maybe he was hiding from the law. Or from a crazed wife. Or from the mafia. Or he was a spy. Or maybe he was just camera shy, I told myself sternly. More importantly, did I really look good on a camel? How good?

Fortunately, before my own thoughts could drive me crazy, the boy leading my camel stopped and reached up for my camera. It was my turn to have my picture taken. On a camel. In front of the pyramids of Giza. With a great-looking guy just out of frame who might or might not have been flirting a little. If it wasn't for that pesky woman's terrible death, it would have been a perfect morning.

The Sphinx was another two-minute bus ride away. We rode in air-conditioned lumbering comfort around the far side of the pyramids and came out on a road that sloped downward, running along the Sphinx's left. We all craned our necks to get a view, those lucky enough to be on the right side of the bus pressing against the windows like kids at Christmas. Above their heads, I caught a glimpse of the battered, enigmatic face, noseless but serene. Just as the pamphlet said, the massive figure truly rose from the sands in majestic splendor, but what the pamphlet could not convey was its sheer size. The tourists standing behind the barricades at its base looked like tiny dolls.

The bus pulled to the side of the road. We all jumped to our feet, waiting for the doors to open, but Anni waved us down again to give us our instructions.

"As you can see, the authorities do not allow us to approach too closely anymore. Restoration is still ongoing and there has been too much damage done over the years by tourists as well as invading armies. So we stop here. And I will tell you that this is the best place to take your photographs. Even though you will go closer, you will not have as good an angle when we go down the hill. We'll stay here just a very few minutes and then walk together down to the front so that you can see that I am right." She gave a little smile. "The bus will meet us down below in the parking lot. Ordinarily, we would have some free time here, but since we are running a little later than planned, I will ask you to stay with me throughout the visit."

We all nodded our complete understanding and pledge of cooperation. Anni made a gesture to Achmed, our bus driver, who obligingly opened the doors. The Peterson family was off the bus first. By the time the rest of us had streamed off, the boys were halfway down the path and their plump little mother was puffing along behind them, yelling futilely for them to come back. Their father resignedly put the lens cap back on his huge camera and prepared to follow.

Kyla watched their figures getting smaller in the distance. "Dear God. Is that what you put up with day after day?"

"Basically."

"What was that line about tigers eating their young?"

I grinned and took a perfectly framed picture of the Sphinx. "Those are pretty good kids. You watch, they'll be the first ones on the bus at the other side."

She just shook her head. "What a nightmare. And look— there go those batty old ladies."

I turned. Sure enough, Fiona and Flora were now tottering down the path in the Petersons' wake, apparently confused about whom they were supposed to follow. Fiona's wispy black hair was sticking straight out in back. Anni

22

caught up with them after a few paces and gently steered them back, helping them with their cameras and pointing them in the direction of the Sphinx, which they had apparently not noticed up until then, because they lit up and started pointing excitedly.

"A hundred bucks says Anni loses it before we get to the ship," said Kyla.

"That's what, three more days?" I considered. "I think she can hold out until then. Make it fifty and you've got a bet."

"Fine. I win if she snaps during the first half. You win if she snaps during the second half. And if she doesn't snap at all, we'll put an extra twenty-five each in her tip envelope."

I nodded agreement. Casually, I looked around to see where Alan was and if he was possibly looking for me, but he stood several paces to the right, taking a photograph of Charlie and Yvonne with a camera that looked almost as old as they were. Charlie kept stepping forward to give Alan pointers on focusing.

Kyla and I took turns taking pictures with the Sphinx in the background and then followed the group down the sloping road. Anni led the way, the pink Hello Kitty umbrella open and held high.

Nimmi Gavaskar passed us to catch up to the Australians, Ben and Lydia Carpenter.

"I meant to ask you earlier," she said to them in her pleasant singsong accent. "How is your niece feeling this morning? Is she any better?"

"Not bloody much," said Ben. He and Lydia were in their early forties, open and funny. His hair was a little long and thinning on top, his scalp very brown beneath the blond wisps. "She looked like she'd been rode hard and put away wet."

"Ben!" snapped Lydia, but without any real annoyance. "She had an unpleasant night. That's all you need to say." Lydia had sandy blond hair, bright blue eyes, and the creased leathery skin of a devout smoker.

"Sorry, love," he answered, unrepentant. "She's got your basic Mummy's Revenge, that's for sure."

"That must have come up suddenly," I said without thinking. "She looked so great at the airport."

Ben gave a little jump. "You saw us at the airport?" he asked.

I nodded. "Our plane was a bit ahead of yours. We were just going to our car when you were heading to the baggage carousel. She's very pretty," I added a little uncertainly. I wasn't sure why he was staring at me.

"You should let DJ examine her. He would be very glad," Nimmi offered. "He specializes in pediatrics, but he is fully qualified to look at adults too. He would be most happy to be of service."

"That's very kind of you," said Ben. "I'm sure she'll be feeling better in a day or so, but we'll take you up on that if she's not."

"Please don't feel it would be an imposition. These things are better caught early. DJ could come to see her when we get back to the hotel."

Ben shot Lydia a questioning look, and she gave a quick negative shake of the head. I'm not sure Nimmi even noticed, but I did. Personally, I would have taken Nimmi up on the offer if I were sick so far from home, but maybe this young woman was a private person.

They hurried on, and we dropped back. Kyla gave me a puzzled glance. "What was that about? Did you really see them in the airport?"

"Yes. I only noticed them because their niece looks just like a student I had last year."

"Hmph. Well, it's too bad she's missing all this today. She must have been sick when she landed, since she missed dinner last night, too. At least that means the rest of us are probably all right. Nothing wrong with the food." Kyla seemed satisfied.

"No, the food's great," I agreed.

"Well, I'm still not going to eat the salad, no matter what they say."

"You wouldn't have eaten that anyway," I pointed out. Although you couldn't tell by her perfect figure, Kyla was strictly a meat, dessert, potatoes, dessert, and dessert kind of girl.

She just grinned at me. "Yes, but now I have an excuse."

We reached the bottom of the hill and rounded the corner. To our left, a row of makeshift stalls full of brightly colored scarves, shirts, and assorted knickknacks were manned by dozens of Egyptian men, all clad in the traditional long tunics. Tourists who approached too closely were quickly swarmed, sort of like one of those Animal Planet specials where the foolish cricket ventures too close to the ant mound. Kyla and I veered away before they could spot us.

As we started walking back toward the Sphinx, we realized Anni was right about the angles. We had been closer and higher where the bus let us off beside the road. It didn't matter though. I heard zoom lenses whirring into action. My own tiny Canon only had a 3x zoom, which was better than nothing, but I admit to a strong feeling of lens envy when Tom Peterson pulled out his big Nikon again. That baby could capture the crow's-feet around the Sphinx's eyes.

Nimmi caught up with DJ, and both of them handed their camera to Keith Kim, who obligingly snapped their photo, then handed his camera over for them to return the favor. The small electronic click was still hanging in the air as DJ made a beeline for the row of shops that lined the street, Nimmi trailing reluctantly in his wake. I watched him a little incredulously, but within seconds he was haggling for all he was worth, appearing to enjoy the shouting and commotion. I don't know how he could even see what he was attempting to buy.

Not that I was watching, but Alan Stratton was the last one down the hill. He'd been the last off the bus, lingering a moment to talk to Achmed, our driver, and hadn't hurried on his way down. Now, he strolled up behind Kyla and me.

"Picture, ladies?" he offered, holding up his camera.

Kyla gave him a blinding smile, and he blinked a little in the professionally whitened glare.

Have I mentioned that I'm just a little jealous of Kyla? People say we look alike, and we do, to an extent, because both of us resemble our fathers, who are identical twins. My eyes are brown, hers are blue, but they have the same shape, and we both have dark wavy hair and the Shore nose, thank goodness, small and straight. My own mother's nose looks like a little potato in the middle of her face. Kyla and I are often mistaken for sisters, although no one would seriously take us for twins, regardless of Nimmi's comment. Like me, Kyla was slender, but she was also fine-boned, whereas I had the sturdier build of some distant farm-working peasant ancestor. I could open my own peanut butter jars, but that was cold comfort compared to being asked to the prom. Not that I was all that bad. On most days, I could even admit that I probably wouldn't shatter mirrors, but Kyla transcended basic prettiness into real beauty. Going to the same high school with her had been wonderful, and we'd been closer than sisters, but every once in a while things had gone south in a hurry. The current situation was a perfect example. In the presence of a single, attractive man, Kyla transformed from a fun-loving, foul-mouthed buddy into Princess Siren. She couldn't help it, and neither I nor Alan Stratton had a prayer in hell. I sighed and prepared to become invisible.

"Hard to believe that thing was once buried up to its neck in sand," Alan was saying, as he snapped our picture.

"Would you mind taking one of us with my camera?" I asked, holding it out. Everyone promised to share pictures at the end of a tour, but most of them did not follow through.

"Oh, let's mix it up," said Kyla. "Alan, you come stand by me, and Jocelyn can take the picture."

I almost laughed out loud. Alan bemusedly followed orders, and I took a very good picture of the two of them, Kyla's dark hair streaming in the wind, her head resting on his shoulder, her arm linked casually through his.

Even before I lowered the camera, she was strolling away with him, arms still linked, chattering away. To my surprise, he looked back at me over his shoulder, his expression a perfect mixture of embarrassment and guilty pride. He almost seemed to be pleading with me to rescue him, but I decided that was just wishful thinking on my part.

I looked around to see where the rest of the group had scattered. Tom and Susan Peterson had finally caught up with their boys and were taking pictures directly in front of the Sphinx. The boys' bright red hair exactly matched their mother's in the sunlight, and they were laughing and making rabbit ears behind each other's head. Near the street, the enormous figure of DJ Gavaskar still stood outside a tiny stall, surrounded by hawkers—none of whom even reached his chin—who were pushing a variety of goods in his face and all talking at the same time. He was laughing and gesturing wildly, in his element, while his wife, Nimmi, stood a few paces away with an indulgent look on her face. To my right, father and daughter Jerry and Kathy Morrison had found a low rock wall where Kathy was posing suggestively while her father took a few unenthusiastic pictures of her. I suspected she was trying to look like some sort of international supermodel posing for a fashion photographer in front of a fabulous international location, but she mainly came across as a cheap porn wannabe. Her father kept glancing around as though hoping no one was watching. For a minute, I felt almost sorry for him.

I walked slowly, taking a few pictures, but mostly thinking about Millie. Here, undistracted by camels or handsome men, the tragedy of it all began to hit me. Millie was dead, laying on a stretcher or in a drawer somewhere, covered by a sheet, never to open her eyes again, while the rest of us were carrying on as though nothing had happened. Our scheduled time at the Sphinx would be cut short by a few minutes, but that was all. The show must go on. I took a deep breath of cool air, aware of the sun on my face and the breeze in my hair, very grateful to be alive. It was a little chilling to think that it could so easily have been me instead. Well, not really, because I wasn't foolish enough to climb onto a high place and fall, but if I had died, the tour group would have gone on just as it was doing now. Maybe Kyla would have dropped out. But the rest of them would be doing what they were doing now. And then what? A call to my parents and to my school to let them know I wouldn't be back. A few people would be sorry. My mom would probably claim my fat little poodle from the kennel. And that would be that. Life would go on, just not with me. I wondered who would be mourning Millie and hoped there was someone. Feeling sorry for Millie and maybe a little for myself, I turned around, looking for Kyla, who never, ever, had morbid thoughts and who would provide a much needed kick in the pants.

Kyla was still strolling with Alan, but our guide, Anni, held court a few yards away, talking about the Sphinx and its long and mysterious past, so I decided to join the group. Anni was far more than the average tour group leader. She was, in fact, a legitimate Egyptologist with a degree from Alexandria University. She had a lovely carrying voice, and she was talking about the Turks using the Sphinx as target practice in the late 1700s to a riveted audience consisting of Ben and Lydia Carpenter, Dawn and Keith Kim, and the octogenarians Charlie and Yvonne de Vance. Charlie had one hand cupped around his ear and was leaning forward at a precarious angle.

"The facts about the Sphinx are fascinating enough, but there is a mystery told as well. Some archaeologists have said that the erosion that you see, particularly on the body, was not caused by wind and sand, but by water. It is true that Egypt was not always a desert land. This would mean that the Sphinx is far, far older than the pyramids themselves and was not built as a guardian of the tombs, but rather that the pyramids were built here because of the protection offered by the Sphinx." Anni looked at us with a sparkle in her eye.

"But you don't believe that, surely?" asked Charlie, not quite certain whether she was joking or not.

"No, of course not, but it is still interesting, is it not? And it is true that for many hundreds of years, the body of the Sphinx was buried by the desert where it could not have been eroded by either water or wind, so how did it become so worn?"

We all looked up in silence at the enormous, weather-beaten figure, with its high cheekbones, stiff headdress, and serene expression. The face was pockmarked with bullet holes, the cheeks crumbling and scarred, but it still exuded the power its creators originally intended.

Anni smiled, then glanced at her watch. "And now, we should return to the bus." Running her eyes over our group, she handed Hello Kitty to Keith Kim. "Will you hold this and stand just over there? I will try to gather the others."

As soon as the pink umbrella unfolded in the crisp air, the group began gathering. Which meant Anni only needed to round up Flora and Fiona, who were nowhere to be seen. As I'd predicted, the Peterson boys were the first on the bus, happy and out of breath from racing each other to the steps. Kyla was one of the last on the bus, and she flopped down beside me with a pensive look on her face. I followed her fixed gaze and saw that Alan had stopped to speak with Anni. I'd fully expected to have the seat to myself while she joined Alan in his. Had he purposely given her the slip at the last minute, or had random circumstances separated the two of them? I began digging through my purse when he finally climbed the steps of the bus. For some reason, I didn't think I could bear seeing him staring like a faithful puppy at Kyla.

when I left the part, my apartment developer the mayor the few minutes, or had vanished continuation of separated the crew of them. I organising up through his pace when he finally, who had the shop of the bar. For some reason, I didn't think I could hear something strange like a sink of a dampish light.

Chapter 2

CARPETS AND CREEPS

A couple of hours later, after visiting the Step Pyramid and the Alabaster Sphinx, we stopped to see a demonstration of the making of hand-knotted silk carpets. This type of thing was part of the price you paid for being on a tour. Under the guise of a learning experience, the tour company ensured we were a captive audience for a very persuasive sales pitch. I was immune by virtue of previous tour group experience and the fact that I had no money.

By scrimping on everything for two years, right down to the shampoo I used and the brand of peanut butter I chose, I'd managed to save just enough from my teacher's salary to cover this trip. I knew it was a luxury I really couldn't afford, but it was my reward to myself for making it through the divorce, a spectacularly cliché event that could have come right out of a Dear Abby column. Boy meets nice girl. Boy marries girl. Boy meets slut. Boy turns into giant asshole. Nice girl throws giant asshole out. End of marriage, end of story. She wasn't even younger or prettier, but she was definitely sexier, from the low-cut silk blouses to the tramp stamp at the base of her spine. I had been devastated, stupid me. But I wasn't a pushover, and Texas is a community property state. So, when things got surprisingly ugly, especially considering we had no children, I promised myself that when it was all over, I would do something just for myself, and traveling was one of the many things Mike had vetoed during our short marriage. I chose Egypt because I'd wanted to see the pyramids since I was a kid and because Mike had once said he would rather get an ice water enema than go. And now here I was in Egypt, and I could only hope that Mike was getting his wish too. Multiple times. But there was definitely no room in my budget for expensive handwoven carpets.

We stood in a distressingly modern building that would have been unremarkable in a corner of a Walmart parking lot. Fluorescent lights blazed overhead, illuminating the multicolored rugs that lay in enormous stacks on the floor, like giant limp decks of cards. In one corner, two very young girls tied knots onto the warp threads of a giant loom. Their hands moved with breathtaking speed as they tied the shimmering strands into place. The colors could have come from the Nile itself, pale blues, delicate greens, pearly grays. The owner of the shop, a lean older man with quick smug eyes, explained that they learned this craft after school, and it would bring a very good income to them when they were certified. Watching them critically, he added that they were judged on the uniformity of their knots and the speed at which they worked. Looking at the tense lines of their small shoulders, I wondered how they could bear the combination of stress and tedium.

As the presentation began winding down, a pack of young Egyptian salesmen began circling like wolves, and by the time we were told to meet back at the bus in half an hour they were already beginning the process of cutting the weak from the herd. A very handsome young man watched Kyla and me with an unsettling intensity, and we purposely lingered beside the loom, hoping he would go away. As a cover, we pretended to be interested as Yvonne de Vance asked some technical questions about the weaving. She was about a hundred years old and her rickety little husband, Charlie, was even older, so I'm not sure why she cared enough to waste some of the few minutes she had left with esoteric questions.

Charlie de Vance gave a huge chuckle. "Which ones fly? I want to see one of them magic carpets."

The owner of the shop threw back his head and let out the hearty guffaw of someone who has heard a very weak joke for the thousandth time. I felt my toes curl with embarrassment, but he seemed quite unfazed.

"All of our carpets are magical, but you must take them home with you before they will work," he said with a wink.

Charlie looked delighted. "Good line, son. What do you say, Yvonne? Want to see what they've got?"

Interrupted in her interrogation of the young girl, Yvonne gave him a sour look that rapidly softened into affection as she noted his eager expression. She took his arm and they tottered willingly into the clutches of an overeager young salesman.

The owner, a large man in western dress, stopped beside Kyla and me. "I hope you are enjoying your visit to Egypt," he said.

"Yes, very much," I smiled.

"You are sisters, yes? I noticed the likeness right away. Very beautiful sisters."

"Not sisters," Kyla said shortly. "Cousins."

"Ah, cousins," he beamed. "Very nice indeed." He moved on.

Kyla glared after him. "Sisters!" she snorted. "I will never understand it. We don't look anything alike at all."

We did, of course. However, Kyla knew deep in her soul that she was unique, and it was one of her pet peeves to be compared to me. If pressed, she would admit that a stranger might be induced to believe that we shared a distant relative on some obscure branch of the family tree, but only if he were blind or drunk or probably both.

From long experience, I knew the right thing to say to stave off a full-blown rant. "He was just making conversation, and after all, we're about the same age and height. Although you are far prettier and more stylish and better in every way than I am. I'm sure it was just a natural mistake, and he should be allowed to live."

Kyla turned a cold eye on me, but then grinned. "All right, but it better not happen again."

The boyish salesman with the intense eyes was circling ever closer. Kyla took one look at him and darted away, leaving me hesitating alone just one moment too long. He pounced.

"Do you not like our carpets? They are very special. No one else in the world makes them like we do." His English was accented, but otherwise almost perfect.

I smiled and shook my head. "They are very beautiful, but I am not able to buy anything today. You would be much better off finding someone else to help."

"No, no," he assure me. "It does not matter if you buy. We are delighted to have visitors learn more about our beautiful carpets. You do not need to buy. It is an honor to see such a very pretty lady in our shop. Very pretty. Tell me, are you married?" He smiled and looked directly into my eyes.

"No," I answered, puzzled. If I didn't know better, I'd swear he was flirting. Without thinking, I touched my thumb to the inside of my left ring finger where my wedding bands had been for so long. They now rested at the bottom of Town Lake in Austin, Texas. I could have sold them, but watching the way they flashed in the sun just before they vanished into the blue water had been worth any price I could have obtained. Moreover, Mike had been trying to get them back in the divorce to make some sort of point, and I wanted them beyond his reach forever. After he knew they were gone, he actually claimed they had belonged to his grandmother and had priceless sentimental value. That fell apart when I pulled out the receipt from Zales. He had always kept good records.

The salesman was still talking. "That is impossible. A beautiful lady like you. Well, if you are not married then that is my good fortune. Will you marry me? I assure you, I would be the happiest man in the world."

I started laughing. Of all the ridiculous things. A thirty-second courtship. It had to be a world record. And he was almost young enough to be one of my students—one of the more brazen ones. He smiled a very charming smile.

"At least allow me to show you the difference between the finest silk rugs and the less costly wool," he said quickly and started herding me away. "Even if you do not buy, you will know what to look for when you return."

I gave a smile and tried to escape. "I would love to look at your beautiful rugs, but we aren't going to be coming back. In fact, we're leaving tomorrow. You really should find somebody else to help."

"Ah, no, no. I do not care if you buy. One day you will return to Egypt and you will remember." We stopped beside a huge pile of rugs resting on the floor, and he pulled one off the top. "Look at this one. Do you see the colors? The rich shades. You will not find anything like this in your country. Tell me, where are you from? Utah, perhaps? I have heard many things about Utah."

Utah? What an odd guess. I wouldn't have thought they'd get many tourists from Utah or at least any who would admit it. And what was there to hear about Utah?

"No. Texas," I answered. I thought he gave me a strange look, but he went on.

"Here, look at this. Do you see how the color changes as you turn it?" He flipped a rug expertly. True to his word, the color changed from a shimmery salmon to a rich peach. I was impressed in spite of myself. I reached out to caress the surface. It was so thin, more like a tablecloth than a rug for the floor. I knew I could not afford it, but I did wonder how much it cost. I was just thinking about asking, when he touched my shoulder.

"You are very late," he said in a lower tone. "Did something go wrong?"

I looked at him, puzzled. He was standing beside me, his face just inches from mine, and I could not think what he

37

meant. Different customs or not, he was definitely invading my personal space, and I shifted away slightly. If we were running late, it could not be by much.

"Yes, there was a terrible accident while we were at Giza."

"An accident," he said thoughtfully. "That is too bad. I hope everything was . . . resolved." He flashed a quick smile that seemed loaded with meaning.

I wasn't sure how to respond to that, so I just nodded and turned my attention back to the rug. "This is very lovely. How much is it?"

"This one? This is a very fine piece, but I think I have something you would find even more interesting. A very fine rug, made entirely by hand in Siwah. We keep it in the back room, just over here." He gestured to a plain metal door in the back wall.

I lifted my eyebrows. Go into a back room with a guy who made used-car salesmen seem blasé? Who made sharks circling a carcass seem soft and cuddly? No way, no how, not even if he was now my fiancé.

"No, I don't think so. What about this rug? How much is it?"

"But this other is made in Siwah," he stressed. His smile faded. The mild enjoyment I'd experienced at his flirting was replaced by a little tickle of uneasiness. I looked around for Kyla and caught sight of her beside DJ and Nimmi, laughing as he haggled for a rug. Ridiculous to be nervous in such a public place, I told myself.

"*La, shokrun*," I said firmly. "No, thank you. I can't buy anything, and I need to join my friends now."

38

He gave me a very hard look. "You misunderstand. You should come with me now."

I took a swift step back, no longer amused. He stepped forward grimly, but at that moment Alan Stratton appeared beside me. He gave me an encouraging smile and turned an inquiring eye on the salesman. I was so glad to see him that I clutched his arm, which felt warm and hard under my cold fingers. Surprised, he automatically covered my hand with his own. It felt really good. I left it there.

The salesman instantly transformed back into the smiling boy he'd been a few minutes earlier. "Ah, your boyfriend is here. Perhaps you would like to buy a beautiful rug for your beautiful lady, sir?"

"I don't want a flipping rug!" I snapped, my voice sounding shrill even in my own ears.

"Ah, then I thank you very much for your attention," said the boy. And never taking his eyes off Alan, he backed away and then darted off.

I gave a sigh of relief and then reluctantly released his arm. He looked down at me with a little grin. "Flipping?"

"Didn't mean to offend you," I said, hoping I wasn't blushing. I couldn't swear in front of my students, so over the years I'd acquired a slew of milder expressions that occasionally popped out in my real life.

He laughed outright at that, then glanced after the salesman. "He looked like he was getting pretty intense."

"Yes, and thank you for stepping in. Everybody warned me that the haggling here could be overwhelming, but I had no idea. He actually wanted me to go into the back room. It was creepy." Very creepy. Surely that wasn't a normal part of the ordinary rug-buying experience. It bothered me.

Alan didn't seem to think it too strange. "Part of the culture, I suppose," he was saying. "It's just something you have to get used to. Look at DJ. He loves it. He's going to have to buy another suitcase for all the junk he keeps buying."

I couldn't help smiling. DJ apparently was an inveterate haggler. This was the fourth time I'd seen him at it today. While the rest of us scurried past the vendors with eyes lowered and teeth clenched, DJ swooped in with a huge smile and with vigorous gestures haggled for all he was worth. On at least two occasions, a little crowd gathered to watch because DJ was very loud and his performance impressive. He towered over the hapless salesman, as he towered over most people, and a casual observer might think the match was weighted heavily in his favor. But the Egyptian vendors were tenacious and experienced and enjoyed the contest as much as DJ. He always returned in triumph, holding some tacky knickknack like a trophy, but the vendor also seemed quite pleased. Here at the carpet shop, the quality of the objects, as well as the prices, were considerably higher, but the contest was the same. DJ was very loud; Nimmi, tugging at his sleeve and whispering in his ear, was very quiet; and the salesman gesticulated wildly as though in agony. At last, though, DJ gave a triumphant smile, and two men rolled up a large carpet and hurried away. DJ then walked to another pile, pointed to another piece, and the process started all over.

"Do you and your sister travel together often?" Alan asked.

I glanced up at him, surprised to note that his eyes were now on my salesman, rather than on DJ.

"She's my cousin, and don't let her hear you say you thought we were sisters. She doesn't want to believe we look alike."

This was his chance to give me a compliment. Something like, "but you're so beautiful" or "she should be honored to be compared to you" or even "you shine above her like the stars shine above a streetlight." Any of those would have been acceptable. But of course he didn't.

Instead, he said, "Did you notice anything unusual when we were at Giza?"

"Apart from the dead body and the police investigation?" I asked without thinking.

He gave a little smile at that, but went on. "You know what I mean. Just anything you noticed that seemed a little strange. Not anything big—I know you would have said something already if you'd seen anything about the accident. Did you happen to notice anyone strange hanging around Millie? Was she talking to anyone in particular, maybe one of our group . . ." his voice trailed off.

I looked at him, puzzled. "What are you saying? Do you think it was more than an accident?"

He shrugged. "No, of course not. I don't know what I mean. Never mind."

I felt a little deflated. I'd been trying to strike up a conversation with this man for two days now without appearing to be flirting, at least not too obviously, but this wasn't the conversation I'd had in mind.

"What do you do for a living?" I asked. It crossed my mind that he might be some sort of policeman or rescue worker, considering the way he'd run to Millie's side.

"Oh, I'm a, well, basically I'm a financial analyst," he stammered. "With a bank. I work at a bank. Wells Fargo."

I stared at him, watching the way his eyes slid away from mine like those of a guilty pup confronted with a stained carpet. Whatever else he was, he was not a very good liar. He suddenly focused on something over my right shoulder, and I glanced back to see what had captured his interest. Kyla was bending over a pile of carpets, lifting the corner of the top rug to see one underneath. She looked fabulous, cool and elegant in her open-necked lemon shirt and tan pants. She had a knack of making even the most casual clothing seem sexy, whereas I probably looked and smelled like someone who had been on a camel not too long ago.

"I'm going to the bus," I announced, suddenly tired and depressed.

"I'll go with you," he offered with more sincerity in his voice than I would have expected.

"No, don't bother," I said, flatly.

Surprised, he hesitated, but I hurried off before he could protest, even if he wanted. What the hell was wrong with me? My refusal had been instinctive, a knee-jerk reaction to his lie. I was so tired of hearing lies. But it wouldn't have hurt me to continue chatting, to maybe flirt a little, to maybe get to know him and figure out what he was hiding. He was interesting and mysterious, and I'd just passed up a chance to spend some private time with him. I was mentally kicking myself before I had gone three paces.

At the door, I couldn't help glancing back over my shoulder. To my surprise, Alan was still watching me instead of Kyla. I almost turned back, but just then someone called to him and he looked away. Further back, I could see my creepy salesman had turned his attentions to poor hapless Fiona and was escorting her toward the mysterious back room. I felt a little sorry for her, but not as sorry as I felt for myself. After all, I had only myself to blame.

Outside, the afternoon sun was moving toward the western horizon and the winds were dying down. Our driver, Achmed, was standing beside the bus smoking a foul-looking cigarette, but he greeted me with a happy smile and cheerfully opened the door for me. "It is not cool inside. I cannot leave it running," he warned.

"That's okay. I just want to get my water," I reassured him.

The bus was stuffy already, but not too bad. Actually "bus" was something of a misnomer. WorldPal referred to it as a coach, a mammoth vehicle that resembled the inside of an airliner more than the clunky school buses I was used to. The seats were wide and comfortable, with upholstered armrests and levers that enabled you to recline just enough to annoy the passenger behind you. You could pull down a little footrest attached to the seat in front and actually get a fairly comfortable stretch. When the coach was running, icy cold air poured down from the air conditioner vents and soothed your spirit, almost making you forget the heat and dust outside. A coach was an insulated world in itself, not quite a magic carpet, but almost as good and certainly more comfortable.

I found my seat and retrieved my backpack from the overhead bin. I didn't really want my water bottle, but I needed an excuse to be on the bus and water was as good as any. I was really just seeking a few minutes of solitude, the one commodity in very short supply on a tour. I glanced at my watch and tried to work out the time difference between here and Austin. Three o'clock in the afternoon here meant seven o'clock in the morning at home. My ex-husband was probably just waking up. With his new tootsie by his side. I felt a little prickle in my eyes and blinked hard. What was the good of pyramids if I was all alone? Especially if anyone even remotely attractive had his eyes on Kyla and not me. It was exactly like being back in high school. A wave of depression washed over me, one of the aftershocks of the divorce, which I hoped would become less frequent and eventually vanish with time.

I looked around, trying to find something to distract myself before self-pity ruined the day, and my eyes swept across the packs and bags in the overhead bins. On a tour bus, seating arrangements are very important. When first boarding, everyone immediately and inevitably marks their territory by placing some belonging on the seat or overhead. I carry a sweater for that very purpose. On some primitive level, owning your own seat is imperative, and any one of us would have been outraged to climb onto the bus and find an intruder in our personal space. I'd been on tours where the seat you chose the first day became yours for the entire trip. This occasioned discontent for those who were late and didn't manage to nab one of the choice spots. Anni was very wise and made us move to a different place each day, ostensibly to give everyone a fair chance to sit in the front. In reality, she probably wanted to avoid getting continually hammered with questions from the same overeager few. There were always one or two chatterboxes on any tour. Millie Owens had been ours. In fact, she'd tried to nab the front seat for the second time in a row just

44

this morning, and Anni had gently but firmly insisted that she move back. The fact that she'd ended up directly across from Kyla and me had been annoying in the extreme. I was a little ashamed about feeling that way, now that she was dead. Her empty seat seemed to reproach me for my callousness.

Empty. Something about that didn't seem quite right. Where was her seat marker? Nothing was visible on or under the seat across from me. I looked forward to the front seat, the one she'd claimed initially, and there it was. In the overhead bin lay the little pack she'd stowed when she first got on. Anni had collected Millie's purse from beside the body and stowed it somewhere to be sent on to relatives, but she hadn't thought about the pack.

I considered it thoughtfully. I was still convinced that Millie had stolen a lip balm from my bag that first day she'd rooted through it and commented on my Imodium. With a glance out the window to ensure no one was watching me, I stood, retrieved the bag, and quickly returned to my own seat. I don't know what made me do it. Maybe I just needed a distraction from my own morbid thoughts, maybe my teacher-sense was on alert. Something about it seemed significant, and there was no reason I shouldn't satisfy my curiosity. And I definitely wanted my lip balm back.

I held it for a moment, a small navy blue canvas bag with a mesh pouch on the outside for a water bottle and the World-Pal logo in one corner, thinking it was surprisingly heavy. We'd each received one with our information packets and itinerary, although Millie was the only one who brought hers on the bus. For one thing, they were really too small to be useful. Somehow it didn't seem quite right to snoop through a dead woman's bag, even for the noble cause of searching out a stolen lip balm. I reminded myself that Millie herself would not have hesitated, and besides, it wasn't like I was stealing. That did it. My scruples evaporated in the face of such masterful rationalization.

I had to admit, unzipping that bag made me feel like a spy or a crime scene investigator. Or maybe just a common criminal. My heart beat a little faster, and my hands felt clammy. But it was well worth it, because inside was the oddest collection of objects I'd seen in a long time. My lip balm was only the first and least significant of the bunch, but it confirmed what I'd suspected. Millie Owens had been quite the little thief. I saw a silver cigarette lighter with the initials LC on the side, which must belong to Lydia Carpenter. A very nice gold pen that seemed unlikely to be Millie's—probably Jerry's if I were to hazard a guess, although there was nothing to identify it. A beaded coin purse I was almost positive I'd seen in Yvonne de Vance's possession. A whole book of tear-out postcards. I paused. Well, she probably hadn't stolen those. They were available in every gift shop and from every vendor on every corner in Cairo. A miniature red notebook complete with zippered case and miniature pen. Millie hadn't just been a thief. She'd been a full-blown kleptomaniac.

I slipped the lip balm into my own pocket and unzipped the little notebook. Yes, it was wrong, but I hardly hesitated.

The first page or two was just what you would expect. Her own name and address, passport number, and then a list of phone numbers and addresses, beginning with one labeled "Mom." I felt a little pang of pity. Somehow I hadn't thought of Millie as having any family or friends. Yet she'd obviously planned on sending the postcards she'd bought. I flipped forward another page and froze. In Millie's scratchy writing were the words:

Day 1
Meetings at hotel.
Subj. A:
Older than she says she is. Not a day under 45.
Obvious plastic surg.
Lying when she talks about their cars. IF they have
them, then they are either leasing or owe more than
they are worth. Certainly could not afford this trip.
Diamonds are real enough—how did she obtain them?

Shocked, I thought about the group. Who did she mean? It could be Dawn Kim, Lydia Carpenter, or Susan Peterson, I supposed. None of the other women were close to forty-five, at least as far as I could guess. But I hadn't noticed any signs of plastic surgery and certainly no one looked as though they were living beyond their means. In fact, as far as I could tell, I was the poorest person on the trip. I wondered what she had seen or heard.

I turned the page and read:

Subj. B
Wants to be admired, but very rude.
Doesn't like women much. Just a bully or something
worse?
Hasn't been to Paris, no matter what he says.
Is she really his daughter?

Well, that has to be Jerry Morrison. Pretty funny and pretty perceptive, at least about the wanting to be admired. I didn't agree with the last assessment. No pretty young girl like Kathy Morrison would be hanging out with a creepy old man like Jerry, at least not on a G-rated tour like this one, unless he was really her dad.

I flipped the page again and gave a little gasp.

Subj. C and D
Sisters? There's a superficial resemblance if you get past
the makeup.
Probably lesbian.
The older one is hiding something. Must check her
purse to see what she got at the hotel.

Lip balm! It was a lip balm, you old bat, I thought, torn between amusement and outrage. The same tube you stole from me. Who'd have thought that a lip balm from the hotel gift shop would be such a subject of interest to anyone. I hadn't even noticed that Millie'd been around when I went in. I thought about it for a moment, trying to picture the scene. As far as I could remember, there'd been no one but the clerk and myself in the shop, and I hadn't seen anyone from the tour in the lobby, either before or after I went in. I pictured Millie hiding behind one of the potted ferns like a character in a bad movie. And why was I the "older one"? I wished Millie were still alive just so I could give her a piece of my mind.

The sound of voices just outside my window gave me a start. I thrust the items back into the bag as quickly as I could, but the door of the bus swung open and I had no chance to replace it, even if I wanted to. I certainly didn't want anyone to know I'd been snooping through Millie's belongings and extras. Hastily I stuffed the entire thing into my backpack. I'd leave it on the bus at the end of the day, I thought. No one else knew it was there anyway, and it wouldn't be missed. Achmed would find it when he took the bus away to be cleaned, and he could turn it over to Anni.

Chapter 3

MUMMIES AND MISHAPS

We arrived at the Egyptian Museum at about four o'clock, as the brilliant light was finally softening into a mellow afternoon and the shadows yawned and stretched gracefully across the lawns like tired cats. The red brick of the museum darkened to the color of dried blood, contrasting with the white stone columns and carvings that accented the massive front doors. A miniature weathered sphinx waited patiently in the courtyard, surrounded by tourists and palm trees. As the bus rolled to a stop with a squeak of brakes and a loud whoosh of hydraulics, we rose eagerly, but Anni waved us back and picked up the microphone.

"Just a few instructions before we disembark. This is very important. You cannot take your cameras into the museum, not even inside your purses. They are very strict about that here. We will be going through metal detectors and if you have a camera, the guards will make you go back outside to put it on the bus. Achmed cannot park here, so the bus will be gone. You will have to wait for the rest of us here in the courtyard, all alone. Your cameras and anything else you want to leave here will be completely safe because Achmed will stay with the bus the whole time. Do you all understand?" She spoke as though we were children, and not bright children at that.

However, we all nodded obediently and stashed our cameras in our packs or on the seats before following Anni off the bus. After taking so many pictures, the thought of leaving my camera for an hour or two came almost as a relief. I was tired of the distraction of examining each artifact and site more for good photo angles than for its historic interest. I thought of the old days when tourists in white linen suits sat for hours at the base of a monument, sketching curves and angles because there was no other way to capture the image and because time was a commodity in abundant supply. Not like the seven-day dash we were on now.

The grounds of the museum were crowded at this hour. Tired tourists sat on the stone benches lining the walkway and rested aching feet. A few children ran about the fountain, dodging the older pedestrians and laughing. Counting aloud, a harried male tour guide circled a small group, brows creased with concentration. We watched through the bars of the ornate iron gates while Anni bought our tickets, then we followed her through the museum doors.

As Anni had promised, two metal detectors waited just inside the entrance, surrounded by an excessive number of guards carrying small but lethal-looking guns. I eyed the guards warily, but they seemed bored and complacent. Dropping my small purse on the conveyor belt, I went through without incident and joined the others beside a replica of the Rosetta Stone.

The main hall of the Egyptian Museum could hold its own with the finest museums in the world. The ceiling rose two full stories, supported by Greek columns that seemed out of place beside the ancient and massive stone coffins, tables, and statues that filled the hall. In fact, the pieces were so famous, so iconic, that the hall felt more like a movie set than a real place.

A commotion behind us made us turn. Fiona and Flora were blocking the scanning machine, surrounded by guards who were suddenly very alert. The screener was holding up a camera and Fiona was shouting at him. Anni said something in Arabic and flew past us, throwing herself between the ditz duo and the guards. The rest of us stood frozen, our mouths hanging open.

"Tell me that is not a camera," said Kyla in disbelief.

"Those women shouldn't be allowed to travel by themselves. They're a menace," said Jerry Morrison with contempt.

There was a brief silence. Not that he was wrong, and not that the rest of us weren't thinking exactly the same thing, but he was so obnoxious that no one wanted to agree with him about anything.

The Australian couple, Ben and Lydia, moved away from him rather pointedly. Their miniature feud was heating up, which made for some interesting moments. I wondered if another wager with Kyla was in order.

A man in a suit appeared and instantly the shouting ceased. The guards drew back respectfully. The man said something in a quiet tone to Anni and then vanished into an office with Fiona and Flora in tow.

Anni returned, her lips pressed tightly together. For a moment, I thought she was going to explode, but she drew a deep breath and produced a smile from somewhere. Kyla smirked at me.

"She's still fine," I said in an undertone.

"Oh, she's going to snap."

"Yes, but not until Wednesday," I said bravely, although I thought the odds against me were rising dramatically. No one could stand firm under the dual pressure of Flora and Fiona. Mother Teresa herself would be flexing her fingers for a bitch slap of epic proportions.

"We'll wait here a moment," said Anni, and began explaining that the only replica in the entire museum was the Rosetta Stone, the original of which was in the British Museum in London. Everything else was authentic and thousands of years old. We walked a few paces away to a huge stone table, a massive block carved from a single piece of stone. It rested in the middle of the aisle, concave on top, with odd carved channels designed to draw away fluids. I thought I could guess what it was, and gave a little shiver, then poked Kyla to see if she'd noticed. Her grin told me she had, and together we moved closer to look for stains, unrepentantly ghoulish.

Fiona and Flora rejoined us after a few minutes, oblivious to our cold stares. Fiona plunked her oversized purse down on the table. Anni went white and in one smooth moved whisked it off and dropped it back in Fiona's arms. Fiona looked startled and almost dropped it. I could tell it weighed a ton. I wondered what she carried in it and how her scrawny arms could tote it around all day.

"This," said Anni loudly to forestall any protest, "is a three-thousand-year-old funerary table where the ancient Egyptians placed the bodies of the dead to prepare them for mummification. Notice the drainage hole at the foot."

Fiona looked disgusted and began rubbing at the bottom of her bag. I was surprised to see a look of anger pass over Flora's usually vapid face. For a moment, I could swear she almost glared, not at Anni, but at her sister. But the moment passed swiftly, and in another second she began talking to Lydia, who was trying to listen to Anni. Lydia looked annoyed and shuffled away from her.

Anni herded us skillfully through the museum, stopping to point out the highlights, which we dutifully admired. Some of the treasures were surrounded by other tour groups, and we had to wait for our turn to swarm the object. After the grand tour, Anni turned us loose to explore on our own.

"Thirty minutes," she called after our retreating backs. Our life as tourists seemed chopped into thirty-minute segments. We checked our watches and scurried away like cockroaches in a kitchen.

Kyla and I made a beeline for the mummy chamber, completely ignoring three thousand years of history and artifacts along the way. It was the type of behavior I'd expect from a couple of high school girls, which just underscored my theory that no one really matured beyond the age of about fourteen. We paused just long enough to locate the room on a map, then giggled all the way up the stairs.

The Egyptians, no fools, had figured out that tourists thought the mummies were the most interesting thing in the

54

entire museum and were charging an additional fee to go inside. I pulled a wad of crumpled, musty Egyptian pounds from my wallet and paid for a brightly colored ticket. The tickets at the tourists sites were beautiful enough to save for a scrapbook. A few steps away, we showed them to a bored guard who nodded us through, and I stowed mine in my wallet, careful not to wrinkle it. Kyla wadded hers up, looked around for a nonexistent trash can, then stuffed it into her pocket.

The mummy room was small, dimly lit, and absolutely silent, worse than a church or a library. The ceiling was low and the air seemed musty and stale, as though it, like the mummies, had come from inside a crypt. I felt a trickle of sweat slide down the small of my back. As our eyes adjusted to the light, we could see walls lined with display cases and a couple of low glass boxes resting in the middle of the floor. Strategically placed weak lights threw a halfhearted glow on the shadowy forms within. In the far corner, a couple of tourists stood before the glass. They did not turn around as we entered.

We approached the first box on the floor cautiously, steeling ourselves for any number of grisly horrors, and found ourselves looking down into the open coffin of a woman.

"She's tiny," said Kyla finally. "And so . . . dry."

She was, too. Small and brittle and creepy.

"We may have seen too many horror movies," I admitted.

"I swear I saw her on a beach in Florida last year. That leathery skin, those anorexic cheekbones."

We both burst into laughter. The two other tourists turned to look at us with deep disapproval.

The door to the mummy room opened again with a quiet swoosh, and Alan Stratton walked in, pausing for his eyes to adjust to the low light. Kyla brightened visibly, and instantly forgot all about the shriveled bandaged corpses.

"Now that's more like it," she whispered to me with a wink. She immediately went to his side.

I wandered over to another display case so I wouldn't have to listen to the flirting on an empty stomach. I was ready for dinner and my feet and back were hurting. And now I had no one to mock the mummies with. Definitely time to head back to the hotel.

Susan and Tom Peterson burst into the room and looked around wildly, Susan's plump little face frantic with worry.

"Damn it!" said Tom. "Where the hell are they?"

"I was sure they would be here," answered Susan, sounding tearful.

They caught sight of me and hurried over.

"Have you seen the boys?" asked Susan. "They ran ahead of us and we've lost them."

My heart went out to her, she sounded so apologetic. Trying not to laugh, I said, "No. They haven't been in here. Shall I tell them you're looking for them if I see them?"

Tom made a sound like a low growl. "You can tell them we're going to kill them when we see them!"

"Tom!" Susan gave him an outraged glare, then turned back to me. "Don't tell them that," she pleaded.

I did laugh then. "I won't. But if it helps, I'm sure they are fine. Probably back in the King Tut room or looking at the mummification tools. And this will probably be their next stop, so you might as well wait for them and take the opportunity to see what you want to see. You can kill them when they catch up to you."

Tom shot me a grateful look, but Susan just shook her head. "We'll just go back toward Tut's room," she said, and dragged him out.

Kyla still had her arm linked through Alan's, and they were examining one of the pharaohs. She looked very pretty by his side. Tall as she was, her head barely reached his cheekbone and her shoulder rubbed against his arm in just the right place. I felt a sharp pang of jealousy, surprisingly strong. Just because he had spoken to me for a few moments did not make him interested in me, I told myself sternly. I was being all kinds of stupid and I needed to knock it off. Summoning up the strength of generations of Puritan ancestors, I firmly repressed my feelings into a small ball in the pit of my stomach where they could safely churn and burn an ulcer into the lining.

With a small shrug, I turned away. Looking down at the shriveled corpse of Thutmose III, I felt a mix of pity and revulsion. Here was certainly not the burly, menacing monster of countless mummy movies. I wondered if the pharaohs had known what their bodies would become. Perhaps so, especially since they frequently booted out their predecessors and confiscated the better monuments and burial chambers for themselves. Some of the kings made large muscular youthful statues of themselves to be used as a backup in case their mummies were destroyed or lost. The sarcophagi were covered with elaborate texts describing the steps that the dead should perform in order to successfully reinhabit the body or the statue. Sort of an early user guide. No wonder you're still lying there like a dead cockroach, I thought at Thutmose. You wouldn't stop to read the instructions.

* * *

Dusk was falling by the time we returned to the hotel. The Mena House stands in the metaphorical shadow of the pyramids and had since it was built in 1869. Agatha Christie had walked up the front steps into its dim interior in the days when it was cooled only by the desert wind and the shade of the palm trees that encircled it. Prince Farouk of Egypt used to stop by at all hours for sandwiches. World leaders and movie stars, the rich and the powerful, the intrepid and the timid had all come to the Mena House to stay in the one place on earth that provided the comforts of the present and a glimpse into the unfathomable past.

The original building was magnificent, designed with palatial proportions and filled with carved and embossed wood, glittering chandeliers, and gilded pillars. Set like a jewel in the Egyptian desert, the grounds were a garden paradise, complete with palm trees, winding paths, and a turquoise pool forming an oasis in the sand. To the left, the pyramids loomed over the puny buildings of modern generations, giant desert denizens guarding against the coming darkness.

Once off the bus, the group scattered with promises to meet before dinner in the upstairs lounge. Kyla and I returned to our room to shower and change. As peons on a budget tour, we were housed in the newer, modern wing across the grounds from the main building. Our room could have been part of any modern hotel in any city in the world, except that from our tiny balcony, we could see the pyramids on the western horizon. Even from this distance, they appeared immense against the deepening blue of the evening sky, and the crimson glow of the setting sun burnished their sides to a tawny copper. None of it seemed quite real.

Dinner that night was to include belly dancing and whirling dervishes, which I was looking forward to seeing. My shower and primping usually took about a quarter of the time that Kyla's did, so I went first and then pulled on a t-shirt and threw myself on the bed to rest while she went through her elaborate routine.

As soon as the bathroom door shut and the water started, I leaped up and retrieved my backpack. I still had Millie's pack and wasn't exactly sure what to do with it. I should have given it to Anni before I left the bus, or even stuffed it under a seat, but at the last minute I'd decided I wanted to take one more look at the contents. For all I knew, something else of mine or Kyla's might be hidden in the depths, but I knew that was only an excuse. I really wanted to read through the rest of that notebook. As soon as I heard the sound of Kyla drawing the shower curtain, I emptied the bag onto my bed.

The notebook, the lighter, the pen, and the purse all dropped onto the rust-colored floral bedspread, followed by a couple of small items that might have belonged to Millie herself and a hair brush filled with long black hair that certainly did not. Yuck, I thought, picking it up distastefully between thumb and forefinger. Either Dawn Kim's or Fiona's. Who would steal a used hair brush? With a little grimace I dropped it back into the bag so I wouldn't have to look at it.

I picked up a small amulet made of dark green jade hanging on a leather cord. Intricately carved, it had an Arabic inscription in the center, and looked well worn, as though it had been rubbed between calloused fingers for years and years. Not something one could find in a tourist shop, I thought. Almost certainly someone's cherished heirloom. There was no telling from whom she'd stolen it. Anni, Mohammad, even our bus driver, Achmed. I winced. These things would have to be returned.

I turned back to the notebook and flipped through the small pages until I found the entry about Kyla and me. Where did the lesbian suspicion come from? I guess it was inconceivable two women could share a room without something going on. Very catty. And mean-spirited. I did not feel so bad for disliking Millie, alive and dead.

Turning the page, I saw only one more entry remained, so maybe I hadn't missed as much as I thought. I probably could have left the bag on the bus for all I had learned, but then I would have been curious about it for the rest of my life. I might as well finish what I had started. Reading on, I gave a little gasp.

Day 2
Something fishy going on. Smuggling!?
Must verify statue is real.
Contact A or M? Or police?

I sat frozen. Impossible, I thought. Millie had found something that made one of us look like a smuggler? A or M. That had to be Anni, our guide, or Mohammad, our WorldPal representative. How ridiculous. We were a completely ordinary group of tourists, by turns clueless, annoying, enthusiastic, kind, and so on. A pretty standard grouping of random people. In fact, the only thing at all unusual I'd learned about our little group was that most of us were fairly experienced travelers, which I supposed made sense. By the time someone

60

chose Egypt as a destination, chances were that they'd already visited the standard European countries.

So Millie thought one of us was a smuggler. Believed it strongly enough that she was eager to pursue the possibility and turn that person in to the authorities. How ridiculous, I thought again. The unfounded fantasy of a petty mind, not to be given a second's consideration. Except that Millie was now dead. I felt a chill of uneasiness shiver down my spine. A coincidence. Her death had been a freak accident. A simple fall that unexpectedly turned fatal, probably because she wasn't exactly young and her bones had been brittle.

Annoyed with my own suspicious mind, I replaced all the items, stolen or not, into the bag and zipped it. I'd leave it on the bus tomorrow, I told myself sternly, and be done with it. No more thinking about death or smuggling. I lay back on the bed and began thinking about smuggling and death.

After an interminable time, the blow-dryer ceased and blessed silence reigned. I looked at the clock. It would be only 11:30 a.m. back in Austin. Just about time for lunch. I wondered if my ex-husband, Mike, would be meeting his new fiancée back at their downtown condo for a bite and a quickie.

"You're thinking about them again, aren't you?" asked Kyla, emerging from the bathroom.

"Not at all," I denied quickly and guiltily.

"I can always tell. You get this little pinched look around the lips. Sort of like sucking on a lemon, but less attractive."

I gave a groan. "I hate them both so much."

"And rightly so. But you swore you weren't going to think about them on this trip."

"No, I swore I wouldn't *talk* about them on this trip," I

corrected, rising to my feet. It was time to put on the one dressy outfit I'd brought, a flowing black skirt that could be reversed into a flowing black-and-white patterned skirt. Tonight I chose the matching black knit top with the scoop neck. The next night I could go with the white.

Kyla sprayed hairspray on her hair, then slid a pale yellow sleeveless dress over her head and gave herself the once over in the mirror.

I frowned at her, suddenly feeling completely frumpy. "I thought we'd agreed that we shouldn't show our arms and shoulders here?"

Kyla looked surprised. "Well, that doesn't apply in the hotels. They're used to international guests here." She looked at my skirt and blouse with a critical eye. "Don't worry about it. You look very nice. A little conservative maybe, but very nice."

I sighed internally. This explained why Kyla's suitcase weighed almost twenty pounds more than my own. And why no one would be mistaking us for sisters this evening. More like a socialite and her plain assistant, I thought with a flash of amusement. She slipped on a pair of matching yellow sandals that showed off her frosted pink toenails.

We returned to the main building to meet the others, walking along a little path that ran through the hotel grounds, past lush grass, palms, and flowers. Directly ahead we could still see the pyramids, now lit with spotlights from below and the moon above. The moon seemed to float directly over the ancient blunted capstone, almost brushing the top. Overhead, the stars were beginning to grow bright in the clear dry air, undiminished by the glow of the hotel.

Instead of Anni, the tour director, Mohammad, met us

in the lobby as he had done at the airport. He was a big man, almost as bulky as DJ and just as dark skinned with very white teeth. He wore a houndstooth jacket, which had to be hot even in the cooling air of the Egyptian evening. I suspected he kept it on to hide the sweat stains under his arms. I wondered what his day had been like and what had happened to Millie's body. Had he spent the afternoon making arrangements to ship her back to the United States? Had he been the one to make the call to her family? But tonight he seemed completely at ease, the perfect tour host, which was probably the best way to handle the whole ugly situation. Heartless maybe, but there was no point in having what was, after all, just an accident ruin the trip for everyone else. Just an accident, I repeated to myself, trying to push the journal entry out of my mind. Had Millie ever talked to him about smuggling?

"Up the stairs and to the right," he greeted us with a warm smile. "We are having a drink before we go in to dinner."

We walked up a long, beautiful stairway to the elegant bar area, complete with intricately carved wood, domed ceilings, and immense chandeliers. The chairs were oversized, overstuffed, and very comfortable. The whole atmosphere was exotic, a fascinating blend of oriental and Arabic motifs that discreetly but firmly underlined how far we were from home.

The Carpenters were already present in one corner, Lydia puffing away on a cigarette, holding her own little ashtray in her left hand. Smoke or no smoke, they were already our favorite people on the trip, so we plopped down in squashy chairs close to them.

"How's your niece feeling?" asked Kyla.

Ben snorted. "Bloody awful. She's heaving out of both ends, if you get my drift."

Australians. Gotta love 'em. The poor girl would never show her face again if she could have heard that.

Anni overheard and joined us, looking concerned. "Jane is still sick? I will give you some powders. They are better than anything you can get from a doctor. Put one packet in a bottle of water and have her drink the whole thing."

From a little purse slung over her shoulder, she pulled a handful of mysterious paper packets with Arabic instructions printed on them.

Ben gave them the same dubious look he would have given a pouch of possum innards from a faith healer in a revival tent, but then shrugged. "I'll just run these back to her room, then, shall I?"

"Oh, bring my blue sweater when you come back, love," Lydia called after him as he started down the stairs.

Charlie and Yvonne de Vance sat on a nearby sofa, holding hands. I considered them. Even in the soft, flattering light of the chandeliers, they looked about a hundred years old, but I had to admit they got around well enough. I thought I'd overheard them saying they were on their honeymoon. Second honeymoon, I assumed, although at their age it might be the third or fourth. They were certainly snuggling like a pair of teenagers.

The Peterson family encircled a separate table, the boys going through a bowl of nuts like a pair of rabid squirrels. Susan and Tom both looked tired, but Tom caught my eye and gave me a thumbs up.

A waiter with a silver tray appeared with fluted glasses

64

filled with an orange and pink fruit drink and handed them to Kyla and me. Either a daiquiri or a smoothie, I thought, and took a suspicious taste, wondering if the ice was safe here. Smoothie. The Egyptians in general frowned on alcohol, although it was readily available in the tourist hotels. Just as well, I thought, resigned. As tired as I was, a cocktail would have me asleep on my feet. Kyla, however, took a single sip and gestured the waiter back.

"Could you bring me a gin and tonic?" she asked.

"Certainly, madam," he said and glided off.

"You should have one too," she said firmly. "Make it two!" she called after him.

I grimaced. "You know I don't drink that crap."

"You can pour it in your fruity thing. Give it a kick."

Kyla drank the first gin and tonic like water and became extremely cheerful. Without asking, she confiscated mine, which had probably been her plan all along.

The other guests began trickling in. Alan Stratton arrived, saw Kyla and possibly me, and slid into the nearest chair. He looked a bit grim around the edges, I thought, suddenly curious.

"Hello," said Kyla warmly.

She sat up in her chair a little, which showed her figure to full advantage. I wondered whether it was calculated or not, then felt a little ashamed for thinking catty thoughts. Kyla had always liked the boys, and they'd always returned the favor and why not? She made flirting effortless and fun, which was probably exactly what it was supposed to be. The presence of an unattached attractive male on a tour was an unexpected bonus as far as she was concerned.

"I heard some news," he said in a low voice, watching both of us intently. "The police have learned that Millie Owens was murdered."

We both froze. I felt my jaw drop a little and made an effort to close my mouth.

"What?" asked Kyla at last. "You can't be serious."

"I assure you I am. The police are already down in the lobby."

"I thought she fell," I said in a small voice.

"Apparently not."

Had Millie been right about a smuggler after all? And the police were here? I suddenly remembered I still had her blue WorldPal bag inside my room and felt very guilty and a little afraid. What if the police searched my room and found it? The red notebook had Millie's name on the front page. And they'd think I'd stolen it and all those other things as well. How would I possibly explain it? I felt a little panicky.

"How do you know all this?" Kyla was asking.

For some reason, Alan did not take his eyes from my face. "I stopped at the front desk on my way here and saw the police arriving, so I asked Mohammad."

I pictured myself running back to my room and tossing the bag in the nearest garbage can. Going back to my room right now would be the most suspicious thing I could possibly do. I was just going to have to brave it and hope that they either didn't notice it or didn't search the rooms.

"I thought Millie broke her neck?" Kyla was nothing if not persistent.

"They think that she was stabbed in the back of the neck. She died so quickly there was no blood to speak of."

I gave a little shiver, picturing again the way Millie sprawled in the sand.

Kyla shook her head in disbelief. "My God, it could have been any of us then. Anyone who got separated from the crowd for a few minutes. Did the bastards steal her purse?"

"No. Her purse was under her body. It didn't appear to be touched, so it doesn't look like it was a robbery."

"But then why kill her?" I asked.

Alan shrugged. "That's what the police are trying to learn."

"Well, it's very tragic and all, especially for Millie, but I don't see what the police are doing here at the hotel," said Kyla with a touch of asperity. "Tempting though it might have been, it's not like any of us stabbed her."

Appalled, I checked the level of her glass. Sure enough, she was halfway through that second gin and tonic and apparently the first one had kicked in.

Alan looked bemused. "Tempting?"

"Oh, come on. She was a first-class pill. You've been here the whole trip, don't pretend you don't know what I mean. The nonstop talking, the snooping, the unending string of complaints about every single thing. I don't see why we should pretend we liked her just because she's dead." Kyla took another sip and another breath. "And I'll tell you something else . . ."

I cut her off before she could. "So what are the police going to do?"

He shrugged. "As far as I can tell, they're here to collect her things from her room and they want to ask us all once more if we saw anything. Mohammad was trying to dissuade them from interrupting our dinner. He seemed to think they'd already covered all that on site."

"Which they certainly did," agreed Kyla. "That took forever. I know we didn't get as much time at Saqqara as we should have."

And there was more. Kyla gets talkative when she's drinking. "I imagine they want to keep this as quiet as possible. It's the last thing the Egyptians need—a tourist murdered at the pyramids. If you want to know what I think," she went on, merging seamlessly into what I could tell was going to be a long rant.

I was so relieved the police weren't going to search all our rooms that I didn't even try to stop her. But if they were here to collect Millie's things, that meant there was no way I was going to be able to return the bag. I was sure Anni or Achmed the driver searched the bus pretty thoroughly after we got off each day, but maybe I could find a way to stuff it down between a couple of seats. But what if someone saw me? Maybe I should just dump it in the trash somewhere. After all, the items had already been stolen and so were already lost to their owners. But no, that was just being weasely. I suddenly became aware that Kyla and Alan were both staring at me. I could feel my face turning red.

"What in the world are you thinking about?" asked Kyla, grinning. "You look so miserable."

"Nothing. Well, no, not really. I was just wondering why Millie and not someone else." I said the first thing that popped into my head.

Alan raised his eyebrows. "That is actually a very good question."

We stared at each other until Kyla broke the mood.

"Da da dum," she sang in a deep voice. "Dramatic music, cue camera three." We now stared at her. "Oh come on. You two are so serious. I'm not heartless, and I admit that it's terrible and scary and whatever, but the police can handle it, I'm sure. Probably some wacko terrorist or a disgruntled vendor or the curse of the mummy. The point is, it's over. We're safe and it's dinner time and I'm starving. When are we going to eat?"

This last question she called to the group in general, and one of the waiters took note and scurried off. Kyla turned her brilliant blue gaze on Alan and leaned forward ever so slightly. The clingy fabric of her dress succumbed to gravity in a most provocative way.

"So how did you end up on this tour alone, Alan?" she asked.

And there it was. What I'd been wondering for two days, speculating a variety of increasingly unlikely scenarios, and trying to figure out how I could find out, and Kyla just asked.

He hesitated, then shrugged. "I was supposed to be here with my wife," he said quietly. "We made the reservations for this tour almost a year ago. She always loved having something to look forward to. But she died in a car crash six months ago." He stopped for a moment, looking down at his hands. "By the time I remembered the trip at all, it was really too late to cancel, and I had some time on my hands. I just figured I'd do this one last thing we'd planned."

Kyla gently laid her hand on his arm. "I'm so sorry. I didn't mean to bring up painful memories."

He put his hand over hers. "Not at all."

The moment lasted only a . . . well, a moment. But it was there.

When the waiter announced that our tables were ready, we all trooped dutifully through the ornate keyhole doorway to the restaurant, Kyla beside Alan, and me trailing behind, thinking hard. Maybe I did need a drink after all. The shock of learning that Millie's death had not been accidental must be making me paranoid, because what else could explain why something sounded just a trifle false about Alan's touching story.

After dinner, half the group trickled away to their beds while the other half headed purposefully downstairs to the beautiful Sultan Lounge across from the lobby. I joined Kyla and Alan, who were talking and laughing with Ben and Lydia Carpenter. Kyla gave me a half-rueful smile, and pulled me into the circle. I bumped her shoulder with mine and felt a little better.

In the lounge, a low hum of conversation and the clinking of ice in glasses filled the air. Windows hung with slender strings of golden beads stretched from floor to ceiling, offering a magnificent view of the pyramids. A huge bar with an exotic golden canopy sat in the center of the room and along the walls, blue and gold chairs clustered around small low tables. The bar was crowded, but Kyla spotted a free table in a corner and pounced. I took a quick look. Four chairs. This was my cue.

"I think I'll go back to the room," I announced.

"Don't be silly," said Kyla. "Alan can find you another chair. Look, there's a free one at that table over there."

Alan obediently started across the room, but I called him back.

"No, please don't bother. I really am tired and I want to get packed since we're leaving tomorrow." I smiled at them all. "Good night."

With their good nights ringing in my ears, I slipped away, crossed the brightly lit lobby, and escaped into the darkness outside with a sense of relief. I was feeling disappointed and didn't think I could have hidden it for much longer. Petty, I suppose, but Kyla and I should have been laughing together about the amateurish belly dancers or about the whirling dervish who had fallen off the stage after tripping over Chris Peterson's size 14 sneaker. I was dying to talk to her about snooty Kathy Morrison, who had managed to offend the waiter by speaking very loudly with an Egyptian accent when she ordered her food. And what about ditzy Fiona and Flora, who had apparently become lost on the way into the lounge and had to be escorted in by a grim-looking Mohammad. But instead of laughing with me over drinks or on our balcony, she was flirting and having fun with Alan. Which, if I were honest, brought up my second big problem. I wouldn't have minded being separated from Kyla if I were the one chatting with Alan. I kicked a pebble on the path and watched it skitter through the shadows.

The wind had subsided to a gentle breeze, leaving the air cool and clear. Overhead, a full moon rode in a cloudless sky far above the glow from the city in the distance. To the south, strategic lights revealed the golden stone of the pyramid. By contrast, the grounds between the old hotel and the new wing seemed dark and mysterious. The asphalt path was lit by lamps at regular intervals, but their little pools of white light barely made a dent in the darkness. The date palms and shrubs rustled lightly and suddenly I felt just a little nervous. Don't be ridiculous, I told myself. The grounds were walled, and I knew armed guards stood at the gates some distance away, although I could not see them. I quickened my pace, though, hurrying quietly along the path, my flats making only the softest patter against the pavement.

I heard a man's voice as I rounded a bend near the pool, and because the voice was so strained and yet so obviously trying to keep quiet, I slowed and paused to listen.

"How could you? How could you?" whoever it was demanded angrily.

A brief pause and then, "You may have ruined everything. Of course they are asking questions! Of course. And they are not stupid. What am I supposed to do now? They will be watching us. We must cancel the whole thing."

There was another pause. The voice, even at that low pitch, seemed vaguely familiar and I was trying to figure out where I'd heard it. Obviously he was talking on a phone, since I could hear only his side.

"Yes, all of it. You must stop. We can possibly try again in August. Or even next year."

A longer pause this time. "You wouldn't. You can't. Look, it is not too late to back out. No?" After a long pause, his long sigh escaped into the air like a punctured balloon. "You are right. I can't stop you. But it is very risky. For all of us. Fine. We will talk tomorrow."

I heard a sharp snap of a cell phone being closed. Not wanting to be caught listening, I quickly started walking again.

And just in time. A man stepped out of the bushes a few yards away. A big man, although in the dim light, I couldn't see his face. He gave a start when he saw me, then turned quickly and hurried away down a side path.

I walked on toward my room, wondering about what I'd overheard. The words themselves could have applied to any number of things, although the urgent tone seemed to give them added meaning. I wished I could place the low voice. Could the speaker have been Mohammad? I stewed about it for a long time before finally deciding I would probably never know.

Sometime later, Kyla slipped into the room, looking somewhat disgruntled and slightly tipsy. I was already in my pajamas, snuggled under the blankets and rereading my Egyptian guidebook for the hundredth time. Now that I had been to Giza and seen the pyramids for myself, everything I read meant much more to me. And tomorrow we would be traveling to Aswan, and I wanted to be prepared for that as well. In the back of my mind, I was already mapping out a lesson plan for my students, who would be completely unappreciative.

"I didn't expect you back so soon," I said.

"Everyone was tired," she said, kicking off her heels. One flew across the room and smacked into the closet door with a thump. "What do you think about Alan Stratton?"

"He seems very nice," I answered, keeping my voice expressionless.

"Nice?" she snorted. "What a word. Nice and single, maybe. Nice and hot. Nice and . . ."

"Okay, I get it. You like him."

73

"Maybe I do, maybe I don't." She pulled her dress over her head, laid it on the bed, and began carefully folding the shimmery yellow material. "He's certainly interesting though. I just can't tell what he thinks about me."

"I thought you two were hitting it off."

"He just seemed more polite than interested, if you know what I mean." She sounded puzzled.

I didn't answer. I was torn between surprise and satisfaction. I couldn't remember the last time an attractive man, single or not, hadn't been under Kyla's spell within thirty seconds of meeting her. For an instant I let myself wonder what he thought about me.

"Maybe he's just got a stick up his ass. Or maybe he's gay," she mused.

"He's not gay. He was married," I protested.

"So he says."

Time to change the subject. "Never mind about that. Guess what I overheard in the garden."

I told her about the telephone conversation. She lifted her eyebrows.

"Hmm, well it doesn't sound like much, even if it was Mohammad."

"Doesn't it sound like he's got something going on? Something not quite legal? But what could it be?"

"Oh, who knows? He's probably fencing stolen camels or something. Does it matter? We won't be seeing him again anyway—they told us he stays in Cairo while Anni takes the groups south. And you still don't even know it was Mohammad. It was probably one of the hotel employees."

She vanished into the bathroom, and I closed my book

74

and turned off my bedside light. She was probably right. I'd never find out what that conversation had been about. I thought of telling her about Millie's bag, but decided that could wait. I still needed to figure out how to return the stolen things without being accused of stealing them myself. As I drifted off, one last thought occurred to me—hotel employee or not, the conversation had been in English.

Monday, Cairo to Aswan

Travel by air over 500 miles to the desert resort town of Aswan, where you will see the gigantic Aswan High Dam. En route to your luxury hotel overlooking Elephantine Island, stop to view the famous Unfinished Obelisk. In the afternoon, board a launch and visit the island of Agilika with the fabulous Temple of Isis, transplanted from the submerged island of Philae. In the evening, board a felucca and sail across the sapphire waters of the Nile to the lush botanical gardens on Kitchener's Island. End your evening with a gourmet buffet, listening to music under the stars.

—WorldPal pamphlet

Chapter 4

PLANES AND PAPYRUS

On the way to the airport, the bus stopped at the officially sanctioned papyrus factory shop, another of our obligatory learning/shopping experiences. En route, Anni went to great lengths to explain that many places sold fake papyrus and that we should not buy papyrus just anywhere. She made it sound as though, left unsupervised, all of us would stampede away from the bus, cash clenched in waving fists, accosting bystanders and demanding counterfeit papyrus. By the time she had finished, we knew far more about papyrus than we ever wanted to know, but we left the bus with the smug feeling that at least we now had the inside scoop. No one could cheat us and pawn off inferior papyrus like they would to those unlucky schmuck tourists who were not on a WorldPal tour.

The door was located on the side of the building, down a flight of stairs guarded by a rickety metal railing that descended steeply below street level. Seedy hardly described it adequately. Had we not been part of a tour, I most definitely would not have gone into that shop, and as it was I could see Nimmi and Dawn both giving Anni questioning looks. However, the Peterson boys charged ahead, jumping down the last three steps with a loud slap of tennis shoes on concrete and vanished inside. The rest of us followed more slowly, held up by Charlie and Yvonne, who somehow reached the stairs and started down clutching each other's arms. We waited more or less patiently for them to either descend or fall.

Once inside, we found ourselves in a long low room. The floor was covered with worn mint green carpet, the wood-paneled walls covered with dozens of framed paintings. Four relatively young Egyptian men and two young women stood in strategic positions around the room, waiting. They were wearing western clothes, although the women, like Anni, wore headscarves. In the middle of the room, a large flat table held pans of water and a variety of instruments. The fluorescent lighting was overly bright and, reflecting off the carpet, gave our faces an odd greenish cast.

As we drew near enough to get a good look at the papyrus paintings, I couldn't help feeling a pang of disappointment. The paper itself was made of light tan strips of reed that reminded me very much of the bamboo shoots that came in a dish of almond chicken. They were pressed together in the way that kids wove strips of paper together at Easter to make little place mats. Of course, the Egyptians had figured out some way to press the reeds together strongly enough to form a solid sheet, but the strips were still visible. More surprising, the paintings themselves were in the most garish colors imaginable, and although there were many pieces with traditional Egyptian cartouches and icons, more than a few were painted with westernized subjects, including kittens and little birds. Some of it would have been right at home in a Gas 'N' Go in Arkansas.

"Thank God this is the authentic stuff," Kyla whispered to me. "Just imagine what the cheap crap would look like."

She slipped away while the rest of us approached the table to watch a small middle-aged man demonstrate how to soak and pound papyrus reeds. After whacking on a piece of reed the size of a broom handle, he made a cut with a lethal-looking knife and then peeled off a long strip of wet fiber. The faint remnants of enthusiasm fluttered around his movements, but it was either too early or he'd repeated this performance once too often to summon anything more. Listlessly, he held out the mallet for one of us to try. Chris Peterson leaped forward and took it. In another instant, he was hammering away as hard and fast as he could. Bits of reed flew in all directions. Showing a good deal of bravery, his mother grabbed his wrist and twisted the hammer out of his hand before he could mash the reed or someone's fingers to a pulp. Reluctantly, he handed the mallet over to Yvonne and stepped back, his mother hissing something in his ear. I was trying not to laugh out loud when Alan came up beside me.

I glanced up at him. He looked good, even in the sickly glow of the fluorescent lighting, which made his eyes more gray than green. His lashes were the same light brown color as his hair.

"So what do you think?" he asked, tipping his head to where Yvonne was slamming the mallet down with impressive force. The fact that she missed the reed altogether did not deter her in the least.

"Very interesting," I lied. Certainly not as interesting as

81

talking with him. I glanced around to see where Kyla was, but she was not paying any attention to us.

"Really?" He lifted his eyebrows.

"No."

He laughed out loud, causing the Peterson boys to turn around eagerly. Susan pinched an arm with each hand and forcefully turned them back to the demonstration.

"Sorry, boys," he said under his breath. He grinned at me. "So I guess you won't be making some sales guy happy today."

"Unlikely. Although actually, I might buy a little one, just to have something to show my students. It would be nice to find something that didn't look so . . ." I searched for the word.

"Hideous?" he supplied helpfully.

"I was going to say modern, but hideous works too. The colors seem too bright."

"To be fair, I think this may be the way the paints looked on the real deal when everything was new. We're so used to seeing everything faded by three thousand years of sun and wind that bright colors seem fake."

I considered. "So you're claiming that ancient Egypt looked like Munchkinland in the pre-Dorothy era?"

"No, that is not what I am saying. I . . . oh, never mind." He suddenly realized I was messing with him and gave me a look that made me laugh.

Pleased with each other, we moved a little to the side, viewing the pictures that lined the walls. His shoulder brushed mine as we walked, and I wondered if it was on purpose. I gave him a sidelong glance to check, but he was still focused on the papyrus paintings. A little disappointed, I dutifully directed my attention to the wall.

Alan stopped in front of a particularly large papyrus depicting hundreds of small figures floating around a very large cobalt blue scarab. "I bet that would look good in your living room," he said.

"It would certainly complement the overall dung-beetle theme I've got going on," I agreed.

He had no chance to respond. A skillful saleswoman stepped between us and began extolling the virtues of the paintings to me, pointing out a large ornate scroll positioned prominently on the wall.

I shook my head. "It is very beautiful, but too expensive."

She instantly snatched a smaller framed picture from the wall and waved it. "This one is very good, very elegant, and quite affordable," she said in lovely accented English.

I caught a flash of blue and gold. "I'm sure, but there's no way I can get a framed picture back home without breaking it." I smiled to show there were no hard feelings and tried to edge away.

"Ah no, but look! We use only the finest unbreakable glass in our frames."

I caught Alan's eye as she rapped on the picture with her knuckles and then actually hurled it to the ground. He almost doubled over in silent laughter. Right then, I decided that I would buy whatever it was bouncing off the carpet, just so I could remember this moment.

The Cairo airport was a madhouse when we arrived for our flight to Aswan. Several tour buses pulled up to the curb at the same time and coughed up their occupants onto the pavement in front of the domestic terminal. Afraid of being swept away in the ebb and flow of humanity, we clutched our carry-ons and followed the bright pink Hello Kitty umbrella as if our lives depended on it.

Around us, people were speaking in every possible language. French seemed to be the most common after Arabic, but I heard snippets of German and Italian as well. Somehow, though, we fell into the correct line behind Anni and began the arduous passage through two separate security checks. Anni led the way, holding all our tickets in one hand, and no one asked for our identification at all. They screened our carry-ons very thoroughly, however, taking their time with each bag. As Kyla's bag went through, the bored security inspector perked up and made a gesture to two guards, who pulled her aside.

To my surprise, Alan immediately wheeled out of line and stood just behind Kyla, like a protective brother. Or so I hoped. I tried to hang back to wait for her, too, but Anni hurried over.

"Go and wait by the luggage and make sure your bag makes it onto the cart," she ordered.

Airports make me nervous anyway, but any hint that my bag might not be where it was supposed to be made my adrenalin surge. I rushed over to the cart and to my relief saw both my bag and Kyla's. A couple of porters began straining against the huge overflowing cart, pushing it away to be loaded onto the plane. I looked back and saw Kyla and Alan still talking with the airport security people. From this angle, it looked as though Alan was searching through Kyla's bag while she was busy arguing with the guards. Very odd, but maybe he was trying to prove there wasn't anything in there. More importantly, was he just being friendly with me in the papyrus shop, or had we actually had a moment? Maybe he was interested in Kyla after all. What puzzled me was why he seemed so interested in her bag.

Anni joined them and began sorting it all out. Frowning to myself, I joined the rest of the group and found myself beside Nimmi.

"I'll be surprised if we see any of our luggage again," she said. "You'd think security would be a little tighter here. Look at them, just taking all the bags in one great big pile."

"I'm sure they run them through a scanner," I said. "That's pretty much what they do at home."

Still, she did have a point. The bright red WorldPal baggage tags seemed to be giving our suitcases speedy and preferential treatment.

"Where's your lesser half?" Ben Carpenter cheerfully asked Nimmi. Lydia had apparently just finished a cigarette, and the two of them were rejoining the group. The faint smell of smoke hovered about them like an acrid perfume.

Nimmi rolled her eyes and gestured with her chin. "Look at him. Like a big kid."

We followed her gaze to a group of small shops, hardly more than stalls separated by racks of merchandise, lining a wall. To my eyes, each one was almost identical. Racks of scarves, cheap tote bags, t-shirts, and small souvenirs crammed into the space of a small closet. The only variation as far as I could tell was the volume and intensity of each respective shopkeeper. They called, shouted, flattered, and wheedled every passerby with incredible enthusiasm. Or, I should say, every non-Egyptian passerby. The Egyptians were able to walk by in relative peace. In front of one stall, we could see DJ haggling happily with a vendor for some trinket or other. Big and boisterous, he looked like he was having the time of his life, a huge smile flashing white in his dark face. I felt a little envious. Even here in the airport, I was too intimidated to try my hand at haggling.

Nimmi now looked around, then turned to Lydia. "Your niece? Where is she?"

"Sitting over there," answered Lydia, pointing. "She's better, but still pretty weak, poor thing. I was worried she'd be too dehydrated to travel, but Anni is going to arrange for her to go directly to the hotel when we get to Aswan. Anni's quite marvelous, isn't she?"

We all agreed that Anni was indeed marvelous. I glanced over to where the niece was sitting and saw a dark-haired girl wearing dark glasses slumped forward in one of the uncomfortable plastic airport seats, resting her forehead on one hand. I couldn't see her face, but she did indeed look miserable.

At last, Anni, Alan, and Kyla rejoined us, and Anni began counting to make sure we were all there.

"What happened?" I asked Kyla.

"They thought my curling iron was a pipe bomb or something," she said through clenched teeth. "I didn't think they were going to give it back. Luckily Alan stopped to help. They seemed to pay more attention to him." She gave him a flattering glance from under her long lashes, and he looked a little embarrassed.

Why anyone would bring a curling iron to Egypt was beyond me anyway, but I wisely didn't say anything.

Anni said, "Go and make sure your bag is on the cart." She hurried away to give the same instruction to the others.

Alan obeyed, giving me a quick glance that I couldn't read.

"He's a nice guy," I said.

She pursed her lips, not entirely happy. "Yeah, he is."

"You don't like nice guys?"

"I don't like them too nice." She grinned. "But at least he stuck around and protected me from the guards."

Alan turned, noticed us staring at him, and gave an uneasy grin. Probably wishful thinking that made it seem directed at me. He joined us, and Kyla immediately began thanking him for coming to her rescue. She shifted on one foot so that I was subtly on the outside of their intimate little circle. I had a sudden strong urge to pinch her, then felt a little shocked at myself.

"Where are they?" I heard Anni asking. She raised her voice. "Does anyone see Fiona and Flora?"

And sure enough, the ditz duo were missing again. Ben took Hello Kitty and began waving it rather wildly. DJ saw the motion, wrapped up his deal, and hurried back. Fiona and Flora did not appear.

Anni began handing out boarding passes, more concerned with the seat numbers than with the actual names printed on the passes.

"Hey, this isn't mine." Jerry Morrison looked down at his boarding pass, sounding irate.

"It doesn't matter," said Anni. "This way you can sit with your daughter."

He looked ready to argue, but Anni determinedly turned her back on him and continued handing out the passes.

I took the two passes she handed to me and gave one to Kyla. I looked at the card I was holding. "Apparently I am Mrs. Kim today," I said.

"I'm Mr. Gavaskar," said Kyla with a grin.

DJ loomed over her and laughed. "Take good care of my reputation," he boomed.

"Hey, what did you buy?" she asked him.

He held up a black statuette of Anubis, the jackal-headed god of the afterlife. "Ten pounds," he said enthusiastically. "We started at fifty."

We looked at him admiringly. Ten Egyptian pounds translated to roughly two dollars. I couldn't believe you could buy anything for that amount in any airport in the world, and the triumph of having bargained the price down from fifty was stunning.

He held out the little statue, and I took it eagerly. It was surprisingly heavy for its size, and I turned it over, looking at it from every angle. Real, authentic Egyptian crap. Probably made in China. A little chip on the bottom revealed white plaster under the black paint. Maybe two dollars was a fair price after all, but it didn't matter. I wanted one. I handed the statue back and reached in my purse to check the small wad of bills I carried in my wallet.

Kyla immediately held out her hand. "Gimme a one. Think I'll make a pit stop."

Reluctantly, I handed her the most tattered bill I had. "Don't spend it all in one place. And you owe me."

She took it gingerly between thumb and forefinger and headed in the direction of the ladies' room.

Foreign money never seems quite real anyway, and Egyptian currency was particularly difficult because apparently most of the bills had been printed during the reign of Ramses II. They were universally tattered, grimy, and faded. En masse they had a distinctive odor not unlike sweaty socks. Available in tiny denominations, they ranged from fifty piastres, which were worth about ten cents, up to fifty pounds, which were worth about ten dollars. The smaller the bill, the harder it was to obtain, too. Egyptians loved their one-pound notes, which were useful as baksheesh in places like the public restrooms. Almost everywhere, restrooms were guarded by grim attendants who doled out a few squares of toilet paper in exchange for baksheesh. The traditional sum was one pound, but when you have to go, you're not going to argue about getting change. Yesterday, I'd gladly handed over a ten-pound note, although considering the amount of toilet paper I'd received in return, I might as well have used the bill itself. At the hotel, I'd bought some postcards just so I could glean a few grimy one-pound notes in change. Somehow they seemed more valuable than the wad of tens I had crammed into my wallet.

Alan had circled back around after getting his ticket and now stood by my shoulder. Surely that was on purpose, I thought, pleased.

He glanced down at the bills in my hands. "Flashing your cash around, are you?"

"It's the only way to command real respect, and I'll thank you to show me the reverence that a couple hundred of these babies deserve," I answered.

"I would certainly have been more deferential if I had known you were loaded. Your highness," he added for good measure.

"That's much better." I grinned at him. "Hey, how much do you think I should pay for one of those cheesy gold pyramids?" I asked, nodding in the direction of the nearest booth.

He followed my gaze. "Ah, madam has exquisite taste. Would you like me to find out for you?"

"No, thank you. I'm just trying to get up the nerve to haggle, and I'd like to know what I should be shooting for. I'll do it another time." I put my wallet back in my purse and zipped it.

"You'll have plenty of chances if Aswan is anything like Cairo."

Kyla returned just as boarding for our flight was announced. Anni looked around frantically, then threw up her hands, which still held two boarding passes. Fiona and Flora were nowhere to be seen.

"Go get in line," she told us, then hurried off to speak to one of the officials behind a counter. A few minutes later we heard an announcement over the speakers requesting that they rejoin their party. Most of our group had already passed through the doors when they popped up from the direction of the restrooms. Fiona's jet black wisps were wilder than ever. In fact, if they hadn't had the sex appeal of runny cheese, I'd have guessed at an illicit liaison in the ladies' room.

"Damn, they made it," Kyla said under her breath.

"Were they in the bathroom the whole time?" I asked.

"Not while I was in there," she answered. "They probably got lost and took a crap in a broom closet."

Chapter 5

ISLANDS AND INTRIGUE

The flight to Aswan was uneventful. From the air, the Nile was a great green ribbon winding gracefully across the vast barren waste of the Sahara, and it was easy to see the vast power that water had in this desert country. In Cairo, the edges of the river's influence were blurred and obscured by human building, but away from the sprawling city, verdant life along the river banks stopped as if a great hand had drawn an uncrossable line in the sand. No wonder the ancient Egyptians had been so obsessed with death—it was visible on the horizon at every waking moment.

After leaving the airplane, we were met by a new bus that whisked us through the streets of Aswan for a quick overview. We stopped and saw the immense Aswan dam and were more impressed by the many guards carrying machine guns than by the giant slab of concrete that blocked the Nile. I found Lake Nasser impressive. A huge blue miracle in that dry land, although somehow sterile. No boats, no ramshackle piers selling ice and bait, not one fisherman in sight. Along the shores, a few scrubby plants grew in defiance of the desert, but beyond three or four feet, rock and sand held dominion.

We took a few perfunctory pictures and then thankfully hopped back on the bus, out of the wind and away from the machine guns. We zipped through the town, past the vast and fairly creepy cemetery, pausing for a few minutes at the Unfinished Obelisk, then on to our hotel, all at breakneck speed as if we were completing items on a checklist. Aswan High Dam, check. Unfinished Obelisk, check. Town market, check. It was a relief to stop and walk to the ferry that would carry us at its own slow pace to our hotel. Once there, however, we had only just enough time to check in and drop our carry-on bags in our rooms before rushing on to our next activity.

We had been promised a ride in a felucca, the traditional Egyptian boat with the huge triangular sail that seemed larger than the vessel itself. However, by the time we reached the docks, the khamsin wind had picked up again, tugging at our clothing and whipping a brownish haze of sand into the dry air. Little white-tipped waves scuttled across the surface of the water. From where we stood, we could see a lone felucca skimming rapidly over the surface of the Nile, its huge triangular sail leaning at an impossible angle. We looked at it doubtfully.

Anni was talking into her cell phone in rapid Arabic and now closed it with a snap. "It is too windy to take a felucca," she announced with regret. "We will have to travel to the gardens in a motor launch. I am very sorry, but as you can see, it would not be safe."

"Will we be getting a refund?" asked Jerry, thrusting out his jaw and stepping forward.

Anni smiled and patted his shoulder. "No, but you can have an extra dessert at dinner."

Jerry glowered, lips parting to start some kind argument.

From just behind him, Lydia said, "Sounds like someone needs a nap." Ben laughed. Jerry continued to glower, but made no further protest.

The motor launch was large, lined with wooden bench seats along the rails and covered with a striped blue-and-white canopy. Kyla and I boarded first and sat together in the middle of one side. As the others streamed on board, Alan followed Yvonne and Charlie. I looked away quickly, but not before noticing he was looking particularly fine in the afternoon sun. Kyla lifted her head and gave him an eager wave, which he acknowledged with a lift of his hand. But he stepped past her and sat beside me. I was sure it was out of politeness, moving to the rear of the boat to leave room for others, but I was pleased anyway.

He wore jeans and a white cotton shirt, sleeves rolled to his elbows, and I could see the sun-bleached hair on his tanned forearms. I was entirely too conscious that one of those arms rested on the railing behind my back and that a scant half inch of seat separated his thigh from mine.

So I babbled. I'm not even sure what nonsense spouted from my mouth. The sun was on my face, the wind in my hair, I was seated by a fabulous man, and I was in Egypt, floating on the Nile. And I was happy. Happy in a way I had not been for several years. I felt young and free and wonderful.

When we arrived at the island, Alan jumped up and helped position the gangplank from boat to shore. He then turned and took my hand to help me walk across. I felt his touch on my hand long after he released me. A special moment, it was ruined when he lingered to perform the same service for Kyla, and then Flora, and then every other woman on the tour. When he offered his hand to Ben, Ben just met his eye and said, "Watch it, mate," and both men laughed.

Kitchener's Island was a jewel, an emerald haven of life and beauty guarded from the looming dunes by the azure waters of the Nile. We climbed a steep hill from the landing and found ourselves in a miniature paradise. Hundreds of beautiful trees formed a canopy sheltering paths lined with flowering shrubs. Brilliant red hibiscus with blossoms as big as my head competed with miniature orange trumpets that gracefully climbed a trellis arching over the path. The powerful Egyptian sun filtered gently through a green filigree of leaves and branches. It was a gardener's triumph, a token finger raised defiantly in the face of the Sahara. For, of course, Kitchener's Island was a human creation just as much as any sphinx or pyramid. The land itself might be a natural formation, but all the plants had been collected from around the world by Lord Kitchener at the turn of the last century and brought to this place solely to satisfy the longings of a gardener far from home. That it had been protected and maintained during the intervening decades was a testimony to its beauty and scientific value.

A barefoot Egyptian boy waited at the top of the stair holding a packet of bookmarks made of papyrus and painted with colors that rivaled anything found in the garden. Out of long habit, we steeled ourselves to walk past without eye contact, but Anni unexpectedly stopped beside him and bought a set of bookmarks, then gestured to the rest of us.

"These are very nice and a good price. They make very nice small presents. Haki is asking only five pounds." Which was a dollar.

We obligingly crowded around the boy, who grinned hugely, teeth white against his dark skin. He quickly exchanged packs of bookmarks for pound notes, not stopping to count the bills, as if afraid his good fortune would vanish before he could finish. He need not have worried. A quick glance at his poor hands, twisted and maimed by either accident or nature, explained Anni's patronage, and we waited patiently for our turn. I bought five packs, figuring I could use them as rewards in the classroom or enclose them with my Christmas cards. He gave me an extraordinarily sweet smile and effusive thanks.

"*Shokrun, shokrun,* miss."

At the top of the hill, under trees so dense that the shade seemed as blue as the Nile, Anni gathered us together. I couldn't help looking about for Alan, but he was on the other side of our little circle. And he wasn't looking at me. In fact, he was scanning the scenery as though expecting to see something, or someone. Puzzled, I looked around too, but other than a few tourists, I could see nothing unexpected.

"At the far end of the island is a small marketplace," Anni said, pointing. "You cannot get lost here." She smiled to herself at that. It had to be nice for her to have us all in a contained space where she didn't need to watch us like toddlers. "We will meet there in one hour to look at the mausoleum of the Aga Khan and then return to the hotel. One hour!" she shouted at the disappearing backs of the Peterson boys.

The rest of us scattered too, almost before she stopped speaking. Kyla and I turned off the main path and headed straight for the water's edge. We didn't want to end up near anyone else and feel obligated to stick with them. The temperature was warm without being hot, the wind a mere breeze here in the shelter of the trees. I could see dozens of plants I didn't recognize at all. And we had a whole hour on our own in this beautiful place. I sighed contentedly, relaxed and happy.

Kyla's sigh coincided with mine, but the tone was somehow different. A little line appeared between her eyebrows and her lips were pressed together. You'd think that after all the years I'd known her that I could have read the warning signs better, but I was caught up in my own pleasure.

"A whole hour prancing around in the bushes, getting eaten alive by giant bugs," she said.

"Hey, stand over by that leaning palm tree. It's perfect—I can get your picture with the water and the dunes in the background."

Kyla loved having her picture taken, but even this lure wasn't enough to drag her out of whatever snit suit she'd decided to don. She just shook her head.

"Well, take mine then. It's too perfect to waste." I handed her the camera and went to lean against the tree.

She snapped the picture grudgingly and fast, without taking any time to line up the shot. Annoyed, I retrieved my camera and tried to view the picture, but the sun was too bright to see more than a figure by a tree. I'd just have to hope it was okay.

Kyla spotted a bench a few yards down the path and sat down, arms crossed over her chest. I followed slowly and stopped just out of reach.

"My super extrasensory perception is picking up a very faint signal. I seem to be getting something." I held a hand to my head as if concentrating very hard. "Yes, it's getting stronger. My powers induce me to believe that you might not be entirely happy."

I just think it's fortunate that people, and Kyla in particular, don't have the ability to shoot death rays from their eyes because I would have been melted into a little puddle at that moment.

"I'm thirsty. I want a beer," she announced, as though expecting me to conjure one from the air.

"You won't be able to get a beer here. You know the Egyptians don't serve alcohol any place except the hotels."

She clicked her tongue. "I can't believe we are stuck in this wilderness for a whole hour. There's nothing here but plants and dirt."

"What did you think a botanical garden was?" I asked.

"I feel like I'm just being herded around, like we're kids on a field trip or something."

"What did you think a tour was?"

She glared at me again. "Aren't these people driving you crazy?"

I thought about it. "Not really. This is a pretty good bunch overall. And we'd never be able to do everything we're doing without a tour guide. It's worth it."

"Ah, there you are!"

We both jumped. Out of the bushes stepped a very small Egyptian man, wearing khaki pants, a white cotton shirt open at the collar, and a relieved expression. "I have been looking for you everywhere. Come with me."

Kyla and I looked at each other. "I don't think so," we said in unison.

97

He looked taken aback. "But I have the items you wanted."

"We don't want anything," I said. I looked around uneasily. Although I could hear voices in the distance, at that moment I could see no one else along the path. The dense foliage made a very nice screen for a private meeting.

"No, no. There is a misunderstanding. I am Aladdin," he added, as if that explained all.

We just stared at him. I was hoping he would go away, or that someone else would come around the corner.

"Sisters? You are sisters? From Utah, yes? You must come with me. I am Aladdin," he repeated, and reached out as if he were going to take Kyla's arm.

With one swift movement, Kyla jumped to her feet and poked him in the chest. She was a tall girl, and her eyes looked down into his, shooting fire. "I don't care if you're Ali fucking Baba himself. We're not going anywhere with you, you got that? And if you don't leave us the hell alone, I'm going to start screaming, and then I'm going to beat the shit out of you. Do you understand that?" She was quivering with rage.

I rose also, not entirely sure whether I was presenting a united front with Kyla or whether I was getting ready to save this strange little man's life. Fortunately, Aladdin staggered back a few paces and held out his hands.

"Sorry. I am sorry, pretty ladies. I meant no offense." He backed away and then turned and ran. A wise man.

We watched him disappear around a corner. The world returned to normal. The sun was still shining on the water. The wind rustled in the branches overhead. I drew a deep breath of relief. "What in the world was that about?"

Kyla shot me a look that made me think Aladdin had the right idea.

I went on. "Did you hear him ask if we were from Utah? That's the second guy who's done that. Remember the freaky carpet guy in Cairo? He asked me about Utah too. Don't you think that's odd?"

She ran a scathing eye over my clothing. "Maybe he thought you were a Mormon."

I flushed. I was wearing my travel uniform. Jeans, oxford shirt with matching tee underneath, and sneakers. I looked fine. The fact that I wasn't wearing sky blue capris and suede flats did not mean I was a frump. It didn't.

"You know, if you're so interested in Alan Stratton, you only had to say," she went on.

My jaw must have dropped a little. "Because I talked to him on the boat? He was sitting next to me. Besides, I didn't realize you had called dibs. In fact, I seem to recall you saying something about the size of the stick up his ass."

"At least it's not as big as the one up yours."

Okay, that was a good one. Still, I couldn't let her distract me or make me laugh. That would send her over the edge, and besides I was getting really angry.

"Look, he's a nice guy, and I admit he's very attractive. But that's it. I'm not trying to steal him away from you. For one thing, I didn't know you wanted him and for another, that's really more your style. Not mine."

For a moment I thought she would explode, then she shut her mouth and almost visibly regained control.

"We could probably both use some alone time," she said.

Her tone was reasonable even if her teeth were clenched. "I'm going down to this market and see if I can find a cold Coke, since I can't get anything better. Why don't you enjoy nature for a while and I'll see you later."

She turned on her heel and stalked off without giving me a chance to answer.

This, too, was typical of her. She got into a mood and turned into Bitchzilla for a while, but sooner or later the evil spell wore off and she returned to her sarcastic, bossy, lovable self. It wasn't much fun for those of us who retained our human form full-time. And just when I thought I was used to her moods, she could still say something to infuriate me.

I started walking, mostly to have something to do. The path closest to the western shore provided a marvelous view of both water and sand. The far bank rose sharply from a scrubby line of trees in a forbidding bank of undulating dunes, giving way to the rocky outcropping that housed the Tombs of the Nobles. From this distance, the tombs, a series of small doorways carved right into the stone, looked more like a mysterious and primitive village than the resting place of the lords of Egypt. Steep rock staircases led from the doors right to river's edge. I started wandering slowly along the path, taking pictures of plants to my left and dunes to my right. I glanced at my watch occasionally. Sticking to a schedule was another of the small drawbacks that went with being part of a tour group.

A group of school children came running down the path, laughing and shouting. I smiled at them and turned down another path leading to the center of the island. I like kids in general, but I made it a policy to avoid roving feral packs of them.

As I reached the main path that ran down the center of the island, I saw Kyla talking with Alan. She was curling a strand of her dark hair around a finger and smiling that brilliant smile up into his face. I couldn't see his expression, but he wouldn't have been human if he hadn't been dazzled. In fact, the only surprising thing was the sharp pang of jealousy that stabbed through me. What did I care if Kyla flirted with some guy on our tour, a guy we would never see again after next Sunday? Yes, he was nice looking, but so what? I knew dozens of nice-looking guys. Well, half a dozen. Okay, three. And they were married. But, again, so what? I decided to slip down a side path before they could spot me, but I was too late.

"Jocelyn," called Alan and smiled, and I had no choice but to join them.

Kyla was shooting daggers at me to go away, but I ignored her and held up my camera. "Let me get your picture."

Alan smiled and stood straight, while she leaned into him in what I considered a most suggestive way. I snapped the picture.

"*We* were just heading toward the market to get something to drink," said Kyla.

"Yes, do you want to join us?" asked Alan.

I could see how enthusiastic Kyla was about that idea. I almost said yes just to annoy her, but decided there was no point. I had never been able to compete with her and any pathetic attempts on my part now would just embarrass me and amuse her. No . . . that wasn't fair. Kyla might be in full bitch mode at the moment, but she loved me and wouldn't have intentionally gone after someone that she knew I wanted, not again. I probably didn't want him anyway, I told myself sternly.

Realizing they were waiting for me to answer, I said quickly, "No, you all go ahead. I'm going to take some pictures on the Aswan side."

"We'll walk with you," said Alan pleasantly.

"No, really, that's okay," I said.

"But I want to go sit down," said Kyla at the same time.

"I'll catch up with you," I promised.

"No problem. This is on the way," he said. And the three of us walked on together.

Being a man, Alan was probably completely unaware that the warmth of the afternoon had just been replaced by a sub-arctic front. Kyla was refusing to look at me, her lips pressed into a thin little line. I wanted to kick her in the pants.

"Did Kyla tell you about our encounter with a guy named Aladdin?" I asked, desperate to say something.

"Aladdin?"

"Really. He said his name was Aladdin. He wanted to show us his wares. Very creepy."

I stopped to take a picture of the largest hibiscus I had ever seen. I loved plants, at least those cared for by others. I had a hard time keeping anything alive.

"What kind of wares?" asked Alan.

"I don't know. We didn't get that far. He wanted us to go with him, but Kyla convinced him otherwise. You were great, by the way," I added.

She was torn between annoyance and gratification. "Well, *someone* had to stand up to him."

Alan looked from Kyla to me, finally picking up on the undercurrents. "You were smart not to go with him, but he was probably just an overeager salesman."

I frowned. "Except he was really persistent. And he almost acted as though we should recognize his name."

"He probably thought that tourists like the name Aladdin," said Kyla impatiently. "What difference does it make, anyway?"

Alan looked like he was about to say something, but just then the group of boys playing in the grass kicked a ball too hard. It sailed past us and looked as though it was on its way to the Nile. Alan made a lunge for it, missed, and then ran after to save it from dropping off the steep bank.

Kyla took the opportunity to grab my arm.

"What is up with you?" she hissed in a low angry tone.

I eyed her narrowly. She wanted a fight, I just wasn't sure why. "What do you mean?"

"Alan. Do you have a problem with me talking to him?"

Wow. She used to be much more subtle when we were in high school and she'd been making the moves on Matt Fletcher even though she knew I had a huge crush on him. I'd cried into my pillow back then, but I was far too old for that now.

"Is that what you'd like? It's no fun if someone else doesn't want him?" I kept my tone low, but I didn't bother to hide my irritation.

She went white, then bright red. "At least I have a life. What do you have? Riding herd on a bunch of ungrateful delinquents all day and then spending the evening with a beer and a remote isn't much to be proud of."

"Better than vodka and a vibrator," I snapped.

We glared at each other like a couple of grizzlies getting ready to go at it over a cub. Or maybe like a sleek jungle leopard against a wildebeest. A peacock and a wet hen? A Doberman versus a dachshund? Anyway, all we needed was a fight ring and a bell to turn this into the ugliest showdown since Tyson gnawed off Holyfield's ear. Fortunately, Alan returned, tossing the ball back to the kids.

Kyla grabbed his arm. "Come on, Alan, let's go find a drink. Jocelyn, you can catch up later, right?"

Tactful she was not, but her methods were effective. Alan escorted her up the path at a very respectable clip, leaving me in the proverbial dust. He glanced at me over his shoulder, and I quickly turned to take a picture of something or other.

I managed to arrive in the little market on the southern end of the island right on time for our group meeting. Everyone else was already there, even Fiona and Flora. I joined Lydia, Dawn, and Nimmi at a low railing. They were looking down at a lower level where DJ was busy haggling with a woman over a brightly colored scarf. Even from this distance I could tell it was of exceptionally poor quality, but DJ was having so much fun. His hands waved enthusiastically as he talked, up by his ears one minute, down low the next. His audience was commenting loudly on his performance and giggling like kids.

I glanced back at the rest of the group. Kyla was sitting alone on a bench holding a plastic bottle of Coke, and Alan stood thirty feet away, talking with Ben and Lydia. I did not know quite what to make of that.

After a few minutes, Anni called us together and we followed Hello Kitty a very short distance to look at the Aga Khan mausoleum where it perched across the water on the western shore. By now, the sun was well on its way to the western horizon and the building was almost a silhouette. Although pretty in its way, and probably enormously expensive, the building was very new. I might have learned why this seemed to be such a tourist point of interest, but I caught sight of a man in white near the drinks booth and stepped away. It was Aladdin, looking pleased with himself.

I slipped away from the others and followed him a few paces, trying to look like I was just casually walking down the path. I probably didn't need to bother—he never looked back, and I didn't have to pretend long. He called a greeting to the man behind the counter of the cold drinks stand, and slipped inside the little booth. Just a hawker after all, I thought. I turned back and almost ran into Alan, who had come up behind me silently.

He looked at me with a strange expression. "Problem?"

I glanced past him to where Kyla was glaring. "No. Just wanted something to drink."

I turned back to the stall quickly and bought a Coke I did not want, glad that Aladdin was hidden from sight. I could feel Alan's eyes on me as I returned to the group.

By the time we got back to the hotel, I felt uncomfortable and discouraged. Kyla was frigidly polite, which on the whole was a good thing. She could have taken us right back to high school by giving me the silent treatment, a game she had mastered and practiced a lot. It was a game I didn't like much. My problem was that I was incapable of holding a grudge. One good night's sleep, and I was ready to be friends again. She, on the other hand, had once ignored me entirely for almost a month when I'd criticized the boyfriend du jour. She thawed toward me only after she learned through another friend that I'd been right and that he had been playing footsie with her archenemy, Sandra Kowalski. Since that day, we'd been best friends and hadn't had more than a moody spat or two or six hundred. Nothing serious though. Now we were seven thousand miles away from home and sharing a hotel room. We were going to have problems if she decided that I was untouchable.

Our hotel, the Elephantine Island Resort, was located on the high north end of Elephantine Island, which in turn lay in the middle of the Nile. The hotel itself looked like it had originally been designed as an air traffic control tower, but its rooms were clean and comfortable, if ordinary. I was starving and not very interested in talking, so while Kyla returned to the room, I sneaked down to the restaurant. Preparations for dinner were under way, but no one was paying me any attention, so I swiped a couple of rolls and a bottle of water, then slipped out the back and took the path leading down to a lower verandah. Two wrought iron benches rested under a clump of acacia trees, and I sank onto one. I could see Kitchener's Island with its lush foliage across a little strip of water and beyond that the rocky dunes that lined the banks of the Nile.

After a couple of minutes, I gave a little shiver. The winds were dying down at last and my little bench was sheltered, but the desert air cooled down fast. I wished for my sweater, but it was still packed neatly in my unopened suitcase, and there was no way I was returning to the room, at least not for a while. I looked out over the water. The felucca and the motor launches had vanished, as had the white-tipped waves. The

106

light changed slowly from the hard brilliance of day to a softer, ruddier glow. I began to relax. Blue shadows crept from under the trees and spilled into the water. The call to evening prayer floated across the water behind me from the Aswan bank, magnified by a loudspeaker. I listened, entranced.

"Mind if I join you?" a voice asked.

With a strangled squeak, I jumped about a foot and dropped my last roll.

"Sorry! I'm sorry. Didn't mean to startle you." Alan Stratton held up his hands, in which he held two glasses of red wine. He was grinning. "Here. I've brought a peace offering."

Mindful that Kyla had staked a claim, I gave him a smile that I hoped was pleasant and yet impersonal, the one I used with overly persistent PTA parents. The trick to getting rid of them was to appear to agree with everything they said, then sadly say the administration would not permit it, whatever it was. I wondered what the administration was going to have to refuse Alan this evening, and whether the administration was going to feel sorry. He looked exceptionally fine in the twilight, his hair still a little damp from his shower. He had changed for dinner and was wearing a dark blue knit shirt and khakis.

He sat down on the bench beside me and passed me a glass. He glanced down at the fallen roll. "Hungry?"

I looked at it sadly. "How did you know I was down here?" I asked. This bench was not visible from the patio above.

"Saw you walk past the bar."

Odd. I hadn't seen him in the bar, and I'd been on the lookout for people to avoid, not that he was one of those. I took a sip of wine and thought how romantic this could be if I were someone else.

"Here, I have something for you." He half rose and fished for something in his pocket. Sitting back down, he handed me a little gold pyramid exactly like the one I'd inquired about at the airport.

"Ooh," I said, very pleased. Turning it in the failing light, I could see it was even tackier up close than at a distance. "It's wonderful. Where did you get it?"

"Over on Kitchener's Island. You would have been impressed at my skillful haggling."

"I'm sure of that. How did it go?"

"I pointed. The seller said, 'For you, a mere thirty pounds.' I handed over the cash."

I burst out laughing. "I hate to break this to you, but that was not haggling."

He was grinning too. "I know. In fact, I'm pretty sure the guy was really disappointed. He was thinking he'd left money on the table."

"Well, I love it. Thank you very much."

"It's nothing," he answered.

We sat in silence, listening to the sound of the breeze in the acacia leaves. I sipped my wine and clutched my little pyramid like a talisman.

"I've always wanted to see Egypt," he said, gesturing at the Nile. "Ever since I was a kid. I was always particularly fascinated by the mummies."

"Well, naturally. The mummies, the grisly rituals, the dark tombs."

He smiled. "Did you like the mummy movies?"

"Loved them. Still do, actually. And it doesn't matter how old or cheesy they are. I think the thing I liked best about the old black and whites was that the mummy always moved so slowly. I always felt like I could have escaped from that kind of monster."

"Exactly. Unlike the heroine, who always seemed to fall down at exactly the wrong moment."

"Yes! Didn't you hate that? It was infuriating. An insult to women everywhere. My brothers made a lot out of that."

He looked a little surprised. "Your brothers?"

"Yeah, I have two. And miserable little pests they were, too. They went through a phase when they tried to tell me I couldn't play with them because I was a girl. At the time, I blamed those stupid movies where the girl was always such a wet blanket, but I finally figured out they were just little turds."

He laughed. "What did you do?"

"Oh, I used a combination of physical and mental violence, coupled with a total willingness to tattle at the drop of a hat. There are advantages to being the oldest."

"So the four of you are pretty close."

"Four? Oh, you mean Kyla. Yeah, we are. My brothers are both in California now, but I still talk to them every couple of weeks. And Kyla and I hang out all the time. Best friends, basically. Most of the time," I added thinking about the current situation, and deciding I really didn't want to talk about Kyla with him. "How about you? Any siblings?"

"Just one brother. In Dallas."

He took a sip of his wine and leaned back on the bench. I decided I liked the way his shirt was unbuttoned at the base of his throat, revealing just the right amount of chest hair. Realizing I was staring, I looked away hastily.

He shifted on the bench so he could look into my eyes, and I couldn't help but catch his eye again. Mesmerized, I continued looked back.

"So tell me about this Aladdin guy you met," he said.

Not what I was expecting. Where was the compliment about my beauty or wit? The gentle probing about my marital status? The comparison of my skin to rose petals? It took me a moment to process his words.

I said, "You pretty much heard it all. And you were right. Just a pushy salesman. I saw him later down at the market area, and he seemed to know one of the other vendors, so I'm sure that's all there was to it."

"Ah. Well, that's good." He considered for a moment. "Did he seem threatening when he approached you?"

"No, not really. Just insistent. Kyla was the one who seemed threatening. She sent him packing," I added, with a little laugh.

"She didn't want to talk about it with me. She kept changing the subject."

Well, of course. She wanted to flirt, and talking about pushy little salesmen was not conducive to romance. I wondered if he was really that oblivious to her motivations.

"You know," he said slowly. "Sometimes people lump siblings together. Judge all of them based on the actions of just one."

I nodded in agreement. I saw it all the time at school, and teachers were notoriously bad about it. In fact, I did it myself. I'd have a fantastic student one year and then get a sibling in class and expect the same stellar performance. Sometimes it

110

happened, sometimes it didn't. The same was true the other way, although I tended to feel sorry for the siblings of a trouble-maker and tried to give them the benefit of the doubt. But I definitely watched them more closely than the other students. It wasn't fair, but that was the way it was.

Alan looked out over the water. He seemed to be weighing his words. "Sometimes we get into something with a brother or sister, and then they go further than we intended. It can be hard to get back out."

"Did your brother get you into trouble, or was it the other way around?" I asked with a smile. I could envision him in the midst of any number of pranks, but I couldn't imagine any real trouble. He seemed like a decent guy.

He ignored this, and went on earnestly. "I just think you don't always have to finish everything you start. You know, if someone talks you into doing something and then things go bad, you could always back out. Just turn around and go home. Even if it seems too late, maybe it's not."

I blinked and let his words sink in, as if giving them a couple of seconds would make them more intelligible. It didn't. What the hell was he talking about? The twilight was turning the shadows purple all around us, and the last of the sunlight was deepening to crimson and violet on the western horizon. His eyes looked dark gray now as he watched my face, his eyebrows drawn together in a worried frown. He leaned forward, as if conveying something of great importance, but I could not figure out what it was. I thought back to the questions at the hotel, the odd way he'd stuck by Kyla and peered into her bag when they searched it at the airport, his interest in our encounter with Aladdin, and now this.

111

"Walk away from what?" I finally asked, as the silence between us lengthened.

He sat back abruptly on the seat, then gave a shrug and rose. "It's nothing." He looked grim, and yet somehow disappointed, as if I'd done something wrong.

"Tell me what you mean," I said. I could hear a pleading note in my own voice, and I didn't like it.

"Never mind. Come on, let's go back. It's about time for dinner."

And have Kyla blow a gasket if she saw us walking up together? "No, I don't think so. I'm going to sit here a few more minutes. You go ahead."

I watched him walk up the path until he was out of sight, but he never looked back.

Tuesday, Abu Simbel

Spend the morning at leisure in Aswan or join an optional excursion to Abu Simbel near the Sudanese border. Here you will see the magnificent sandstone temples of Ramses II and his beloved wife Nefertari, rescued first from the desert sands in the early nineteenth century, then again from the rising waters of Lake Nasser in the 1960s. In the afternoon, board your luxury cruise ship and begin your journey up the Nile, Egypt's mythic river of destiny.

—WorldPal pamphlet

Chapter 6

CHANGELINGS AND CHALLENGES

I awakened in the darkness to the sound of prayers broadcasting over the water. The red glow of the digital clock on the nightstand told me it was 4:30 a.m. On the other bed, I could hear Kyla breathing slowly, still in deep sleep. It would take a canon going off on the roof to wake her. I slipped out of bed and softly tugged the sliding glass door open and went out on the balcony, then immediately darted back to pull the bedspread off the bed. Wrapping it around my shoulders, I returned to the chilly darkness. The lights from the hotel reflected in yellow rippling streaks across the water. Under its still surface, the Nile was running swift and black and deep. I gave a little shiver, my feet freezing against the chill of the concrete. The eerie wailing of morning prayers, so alien to my western ears, made the little hairs stand up on the back of my neck. The morning chill finally drove me back to bed, but I lay awake for a long time after the haunting sound had ceased. I'd barely drifted off again when my alarm beeped, followed closely by the sound of the telephone with the wake-up call that Anni arranged every morning. Kyla and I dressed in groggy silence and staggered down to the hotel restaurant in search of coffee.

Breakfast was scheduled at the ungodly hour of six-thirty today because we were flying to Abu Simbel, site of the legendary temples of Ramses II. The hotel restaurant had just opened, an ordinary long room filled with large round tables, covered in white tablecloths, and already set with silverware and glasses. A long buffet was ready for us in the middle of the room, loaded with fruit, rolls, pastries, and a wide assortment of traditional American breakfast foods from sausages to Cheerios. Waiters in white coats carrying pitchers of coffee and glass carafes of juice waited for us to sit down.

Surprisingly, everyone but us seemed wide awake, and they were all chattering excitedly about the trip. I hesitated at the door, but Kyla headed straight across the room to join Keith and Dawn Kim and the Petersons, leaving me on my own. Still mad, apparently, although at least not openly hostile. I sat down at the next table beside Nimmi Gavaskar. An attentive waiter immediately filled my coffee cup, and I cradled it between both hands, enjoying the warmth and inhaling the rich fragrance. DJ returned from the buffet with a plate loaded with eggs, bacon, and sausages, and sat down on the other side of Nimmi. He was soon followed by the de Vances and less charmingly by the Morrisons. Looking at his plate, I felt my stomach rumble a little. I rose, deciding to fetch a couple of rolls, but somehow ended up with two croissants, half a dozen sausages, and a strip of crispy hot bacon. Buffets are my nemesis.

When I returned, the octogenarians Yvonne and Charlie were just announcing they were not accompanying the group to Abu Simbel.

"We're going to walk around the market, see a bit more of Aswan," said Yvonne, cracking open a hard-boiled egg with a spoon. Her bifocals made her faded brown eyes seem larger than they were.

The group gave a dismayed protest.

"Not going?" said DJ. "But you can't miss this!"

Kathy Morrison chimed in with her flat California voice. "He's right. It's one of the highlights of the tour. And you might never be this close again." She didn't actually add the words, "because you're so old you'll be dead before you could make it back," but she might as well have.

From her table, Kyla met my eyes with a delighted smirk, then remembered she was still mad at me and hurriedly looked away. I was pleased. She'd be speaking to me before lunch at this rate and maybe neither of us would have to apologize.

Yvonne and Charlie were not to be swayed. "It will be nice to be on our own," Yvonne said, stroking Charlie's arm slowly from wrist to shoulder. "After all, we are on our honeymoon."

That killed the protests dead, and with a little metaphoric shudder, the group dropped the subject.

After an uncomfortable pause, Nimmi turned to Lydia, who was just putting her plate down on the crisp white table cloth. "And your niece? How is she this morning?"

I'd forgotten all about the niece. Now that Nimmi brought her up, I realized I hadn't seen her since the airport in

Cairo. Anni must have performed some magic to whisk her away to the hotel while the rest of us bused around Aswan.

Lydia smiled. "She is much better this morning." She looked toward the doorway and made a little gesture. "Here she is now."

We all turned. An exceptionally thin girl entered the dining room through the wide glass doors and was walking toward our table. Her clothes looked far too large for her, as though she had lost a great deal of weight in a very short time. Her long straight hair hung loose around her face and the way she tipped her head had it swinging forward like curtains to hide her cheeks. Ben hopped up and pulled out a chair for her, while Lydia made quick introductions, and then leaped up to fill a plate for her. I smiled and said hello automatically, but I was shocked. Was this really the same vibrant young woman I'd noticed with Ben and Lydia at the airport?

As the others made small talk about our upcoming excursion, I covertly studied the niece. She was very close in age and coloring to the girl I'd seen that first day, but gone was the curling dark hair, the strong line of the jaw, the slightly crooked nose. Gone also was that subtle air of energy and enthusiasm that had been so obvious and attractive even across the crowded baggage claim. If I hadn't noticed her so particularly because of her resemblance to one of my students, I might have attributed her changed appearance to her illness. But this couldn't be the same girl. Could it? I did not know what to make of it. Why would Ben and Lydia be passing off an impostor as their niece?

Maybe the woman I'd seen in the Cairo airport had not been with Ben and Lydia at all. She could have been a fellow passenger with whom they'd struck up a conversation. But in that case, where had the niece been? Out of the corner of my eye, I noticed Ben watching me, a little line of anxiety between his eyebrows. He looked away the instant I turned toward him. Was it because I had mentioned that I'd seen the niece at the airport?

I rose and returned to the buffet for another slice of bacon that I didn't really want, just so I could get a good look at her on the way back without seeming too rude. The baggy clothing looked at least two sizes too big. She couldn't have lost that much weight in only two days. Was it possible the clothes weren't hers at all? I noted the way Ben hovered, arm protectively draped over the back of her chair, the way Lydia buttered toast for her and urged her to eat it. Standard treatment for an invalid, or something more? But what would be the point? Why arrive in Egypt with one girl and in less than two days trade her in for another? Friendly, funny Ben and Lydia were hardly likely candidates for sex slave traders. The best thing I could do would be to concentrate on enjoying my dream vacation and minding my own business.

The group met just outside the lobby after breakfast, where a team of white-jacketed bellhops were busy hauling our luggage from our rooms. To my surprise, the tour director, Mohammad, was waiting by the growing pile of bags. He had not come with us on the airplane, so what was he doing here? The houndstooth jacket was missing, and he looked larger than ever in a polo shirt and black pants. Not quite as tall as DJ, who towered over everyone else, Mohammad was even broader through the shoulders and chest, and without the jacket, I

119

could see that his stomach overhung his belt like that of a small-town Texas sheriff. Gone, too, was the relaxed, helpful attitude of a professional tour guide from the airport. Now, well, he wasn't quite tapping his foot, but he might as well have been. I wondered again about the phone call I'd overheard in the gardens of the Mena House. Could it have been Mohammad?

Anni rounded the corner from the hotel lobby and performed a perfect double take. Her eyebrows almost vanished under the folds of her red headscarf. Brushing off Charlie, who was trying to get directions to the town center, she hurried to Mohammad's side and began a rapid conversation in Arabic. The rest of us waited uneasily. Was he here because of Millie? Were the police going to show up? Were we still going to be able to go to Abu Simbel?

Eventually, they reached some agreement and Anni returned. She rejoined Charlie and Yvonne, produced a small map and quickly gave instructions. Yvonne nodded in understanding, although Charlie looked a little glassy-eyed and started asking questions. I suppressed a smile and hoped I'd be half as active and alert in fifty years.

Time was passing. We were already ten minutes past our appointed meeting time, and this time it mattered because we were catching a plane. Jerry Morrison looked at his watch and gave Anni a pointed stare. Even Ben and Lydia were shifting from one foot to another as Anni did her swift count. As usual, Flora and Fiona weren't there. Anni beckoned to a uniformed bellhop and gave him swift instructions in Arabic. He loped off in the direction of the elevators.

"Now you all have left your suitcases outside your doors?

Remember, we will not be returning here. Mohammad and our driver will take the luggage to the ship for us while we are away, and when we return we will go directly to the *Nile Lotus*. Do not leave anything behind. If you have personal belongings that you do not want to take to Abu Simbel, you can leave them right here, and Mohammad will watch them and ensure they make it onto the ship."

A little reluctantly, we left our carry-on bags in a little pile. "My computer is in that bag," said Jerry Morrison officiously to Mohammad. "It needs to be hand-carried at all times. No tossing or dropping. And it can't be left alone even for a minute."

"Of course, sir," said Mohammad. "I will handle it myself."

Jerry eyed him for a moment, then stalked away, only to return a second later and pull the bag out of Mohammad's hands. "Never mind. I'll carry it myself."

Lydia stepped past me, pulling a cigarette and her little ashes carrier out of her purse. "Probably doesn't want to risk losing his porn collection," she said in a stage whisper as she went by.

I suppressed a howl of laughter, mostly because I saw Jerry's head whip around, his expression irate. I looked around to see if Kyla had noticed, but she was standing alone, pointedly not looking in my direction. At the last minute, and somewhat to our collective disappointment, the bellhop returned with Flora and Fiona in tow.

At the airport, we went through the same chaotic check-in process as in Cairo, although because we had no luggage, the security checks took less time. The tiny airport seemed less strict, and only Flora was pulled aside to have her bag searched more carefully. The female security agent pulled an umbrella out of Flora's huge purse and looked at it in disbelief. The yearly rainfall in all of Egypt was basically zero. Flora tottered on through the metal detector and then wandered off toward the gates and had to be called back. The security agent put the bag back into her hands gently and looked as though she wanted to pat her on the head. Flora looked at her bag bemusedly as though she'd never seen it before. Eventually, Fiona caught up to her and led her away.

Anni handed out our boarding passes, as before trying to ensure couples or families sat together without any regard to the names on the tickets. When she called our names, Kyla took both passes from her. Then, before I knew what she was going to do, she descended on Alan.

"Here," she said, snapping his pass for herself and handing him ours. "You don't mind sitting next to what's her face on the way out, do you?"

She turned on her heel without giving him time to reply. I felt my face redden. Was she just that determined not to sit next to me, or did she think she was doing me a favor? Either way, we were going to have to have a little talk.

Alan made the best of it. "I'd be delighted," he called to her retreating back, then lowered his voice. "I hope you don't mind," he added.

"Not at all," I answered with what I hoped was a pleasant smile, even though I seemed to be unable to unclench my teeth.

We took our seats and waited through the safety lecture and then the recorded prayer in Arabic. As usual, I tried to guess what the singsong words meant. "Oh, Lord, please do not let us burst into a million flaming pieces. Do not let us crash in the desert and then be lost and die of thirst and heat in the sand. Do not let us resort to madness and cannibalism." Maybe I didn't like flying all that much after all.

To my surprise, Mohammad appeared at the last moment and swiftly took a seat near the front of the plane, as though hoping not to be noticed. If so, it was a vain hope. His huge shoulders overhung the back of his seat, and I could see his arm protruding into the aisle.

"Hey, what's he doing here?" asked Jerry Morrison. He was sitting behind me and he grabbed the back of my seat to pull himself up for a better view. My head jerked back, and I turned in protest, but he didn't notice. "He's supposed to be watching our luggage. It's a good thing I didn't let him keep my bag," he added, with a scathing look at Lydia.

"Oh, Daddy. It's all right. I'm sure he gave it all to the driver," said Kathy. Her tone was just as patronizing to her father as it was to the rest of us. I saw him give her a swift glare, but she was already leafing through her magazine and didn't notice.

No one else answered him. But he had a point. Why was Mohammad coming with us?

Chapter 7

MONUMENTS AND MURDER

I leaned back in my seat, hoping Alan and I weren't going to have any more cryptic conversations, but as it turned out, he seemed to have forgotten about his odd comments on Elephantine Island and instead chatted at length about the project that lifted the temples. I knew only the bare facts myself, and he was entertaining.

"When they built the Aswan Dam, the waters on this side started rising and they realized pretty quickly that they were going to lose Abu Simbel if they didn't do something. It was an extraordinary thing—no one knew how they could possibly move such an enormous structure, carved into the side of the cliff. But then one of the engineers got the brilliant idea to slice the carvings off the sides of the cliff and reassemble them in an artificial cave on top. They cut the statues, the carvings, the columns, everything into manageable pieces, carefully mapped and labeled everything, and then reassembled it all like a giant jigsaw puzzle. Honestly, that had to be almost harder than doing the original construction. And to top it off, the water was rising the whole time. They actually had to build a miniature dam around the monument to hold back the waters. Some of the pieces were even submerged entirely before they could get them out."

He could have been talking about earthworm excretion, and I would still have hung on his every word just to watch him talk: the way his eyes crinkled when he smiled, the way he moved his hands, the way his hair fell across his forehead. And he smelled good. By the time the plane landed, we had moved on to talking about other countries we had visited and traveling in general. I think it was the first flight in the history of flying that seemed far too short.

A coach waited to drive us up the steep hills from the airport to the temple. We did not see much of the town on our route. Only a few houses, a vast expanse of rock, and an empty sky. I thought of other deserts I'd visited. The Sonoran Desert in Arizona, dotted with saguaro cactus. The Chihuahuan Desert of West Texas with its prickly pear and yucca. Both seemed lush and tropical compared to this. A few straggly plants existed around some of the homes, but in the untended areas, white rock and dust stretched as far as the eye could see. I felt thirsty just looking at it.

The bus stopped in a gravel parking lot and we scrambled off. Our driver stood at the steps, offering his hand to the ladies, and just beyond him Alan waited for me, a smile on his face. My stomach did a little flip as I joined him. I could see Kyla ahead of us, walking beside Anni, who was holding Hello Kitty above her head. As usual, the path from the parking lot wound through a miniature marketplace. Eager vendors called to us and tried to interest us in packs of Abu Simbel postcards, miniature replicas of the monuments, and cheap t-shirts.

"Pretty lady! I have many things for a very pretty lady. Come with me!"

"Cheap souvenirs. The best prices! The best quality! Look! Look!"

By this time, we were almost immune to the colorful compliments and exuberant greetings, but I noticed that walking beside Alan provided a better buffer than when I was alone or with Kyla. The salesmen did not approach so closely or yell so loudly, and their comments were mostly directed at him. My chin just topped his shoulder, and I could glance across him into the stalls without worrying about making eye contact. I liked it.

Although haggling on my own seemed all but impossible in the face of the shouting, I was still determined to try it at least once. The little gold pyramid that Alan had given me was nestled safely in the bottom of my purse. Foolish to carry it around, but I liked having it with me and it weighed hardly anything. Oh well, maybe I would be able to find some little gifts in the alabaster and perfume shops that we were scheduled to visit later in the tour. Fortunately or unfortunately, there was no time to stop at a shop now, even if I could get up the nerve to try.

On the other end of the spectrum, DJ hurried forward to haggle at the nearest booth, but Anni grabbed his arm and propelled him onward.

"We will have time to shop after we go through the temples," she told him. Glancing back, she noticed Flora and Fiona had been cornered by three salesmen, and she hurried to rescue them.

We went through a modern building where Anni bought tickets for us. We had to open our purses for inspection and go though a metal detector before being allowed through to the other side. How sad that the world had come to this—a world where ordinary people thought nothing at all of the requirement for metal detectors and armed guards at a historical monument. The terrorists had a lot to answer for, I thought as I opened my purse for the guard's examination. I was glad I'd hidden Millie's bag at the bottom of my suitcase back at the hotel. I was still trying to figure out how to return the stolen items, although at this point it was going to be all but impossible.

Once out of the building, we could see nothing but a gravel path and a large domed mound. The white sun beat down on our heads and on the rock with a promise of coming heat, but right now the morning air was still cool and pleasant. After a few paces, our shoes were covered with white dust. I saw Kathy Morrison give a cry of annoyance as she wobbled down the path in her high-heeled sandals. Her red toenails were already obscured by grime. Even Kyla had worn more sensible shoes than those.

"You look pleased with yourself," said Alan under his breath, looking from Kathy to me, as though reading my thoughts.

"Because I'm a terrible person. You should take warning."

"I think I'll risk it."

Kathy fell behind as the rest of us followed Anni along the path. Three minutes later, we rounded a mound of rocks and stopped dead.

The great temple of Abu Simbel waited in the brilliant Egyptian sunlight. It had been old before the forces of Alexander the Great swept across Greece, before the Romans crossed the English Channel, before Christ walked the earth. Even knowing what to expect, I was unprepared for its sheer size and beauty. Three seated figures loomed sixty feet into the air, surrounded by scores of carvings and smaller statues, all guarding a dark and mysterious entrance. A fourth statue lay broken in half on the ground, recreated exactly as it had been found when the temple was rediscovered in 1813. All four statues had the same forbidding face, the face of the pharaoh. The dark doorway in the center looked small and mysterious, but it must have been twenty-five feet tall. Tourists walking through looked like colorful miniatures.

Every camera was out and clicking.

"Look at that," said Ben, and he gave a low whistle.

"Do you see the faces?" asked Lydia.

We might have been at a fireworks display. Everyone was pointing and asking each other if they could see the carving or the size or the broken figure. As though we could see anything else.

Behind us, Lake Nasser stretched to reach the horizon, a vast blue sea in the desert. Farther on, another temple waited, dwarfed by its neighbor. I scarcely took note of them. My whole attention was on the fabulous temple of Ramses II. How had people with little more than stone tools carved such enormous, breathtaking statues right into the side of a cliff? And how had they been moved, piece by piece, two millennium later? And more important, what kind of man thought it was a good idea to create four colossi in his own image? The sheer hubris of it was astounding to the western mind.

As we drew nearer to the monument, a photographer carrying a camera with a lens the size of a salami approached and spoke to Anni. She greeted him by name and told us that WorldPal had arranged for a group photo here.

"It's the only place on the tour that we do this. You of course do not have to purchase a picture, but they will be available before we are ready to leave."

No one protested, not even Jerry. Everyone was in a splendid mood and just being here seemed such an adventure. We lined up in three rows on the steps. Alan stood beside me and Kyla stood beside him, so it looked as though the three of us were together and happy. Fiona and Flora stood in the front row beside Kathy and Jerry, who kept trying to edge away from them. Kathy's nose wrinkled as though she smelled something bad, but she looked that way so frequently it might not have meant anything. The photographer snapped twice, and we were done.

On the outside, the temple walls and even the surrounding rocks of the cliff had been sliced away from the original cliff wall and then put back together with astonishing precision. The effect was perfect from a distance, but from a little bit closer, it had the feel of a mosaic.

Anni spoke as she guided us to the feet of the colossal statues. "This complex was built in the thirteenth century BC, not only to honor the gods, but to remind Nubia of the might and power of Egypt. However, by the nineteenth century AD, the temples were forgotten and completely covered by sand. Legend has it that a young boy playing with a ball kicked it too high and it flew up the rock face and became stuck. When he climbed up the sand dune to retrieve it, he saw that it was lodged behind a giant carved head. He later showed his discovery to the Swiss explorer J. L. Burckhardt. The boy's name was Abu Simbel, and the Europeans who followed to dig out the temples named the complex after him."

We looked up and tried to imagine the sand so deep that only the top of the pharoahs' heads protruded. Anni went on. "Ramses designed his temple so that twice a year, the sun would penetrate all the way to the back and illuminate the statues of Amun-Ra, Ra-Horakhty, and Ramses himself. The head of the god Ptah, ruler of the underworld, always remained in darkness, as is only right. Scientists believe that the day of the illumination is now one day later than it was originally, because the temple is now much higher on the cliff face."

I looked up into the haughty, sightless eyes of Ramses and wondered what he would have thought of the change. He had created his temple high on a cliff surrounded by desert and sun, the Nile nothing but a ribbon of blue and a distant voice swirling over cataracts far below. Now, with the vast blue expanse of Lake Nasser twinkling in the sun, only slightly less featureless than the pale sky above, I decided that maybe even Ramses would have valued water above his own glory. Then again, maybe not.

Walking closer, we could see the finer details, carvings of baboons and small people, captives and crocodiles. And even though the site had been moved, it still retained the otherworldly atmosphere of an ancient kingdom despite the multitude of camera-wielding tourists. Anni negotiated with the guards at the doors of the temple and after a short wait we followed Hello Kitty under the archway. Once inside the dimly lit interior, the wind ceased, which was a relief. Our eyes adjusted to the light and we were able to follow Anni as she quickly pointed out a few unique carvings. Technically, guides weren't supposed to go inside because it caused traffic jams in the confined space, but the real crowds had not arrived yet, and she was able to show us the highlights. The enormous supporting columns were thicker than tree trunks, carved and bearing the remnants of paint. The room must have been brilliant and amazing when new.

We left together and followed Anni toward the smaller temple, dedicated to the cow goddess Hathor and to the beloved wife of Ramses, Queen Nefertari. Two thirty-foot-tall statues of the queen were carved into the rock on either side of the doorway of the temple. Of course, for each statue of his wife, Ramses built two statues of himself, one on either side of hers, but at least her statues stood as tall as his.

As we walked over the flat between the two temples, the group fanned out a little. DJ and Keith swung wide to take a look at the lake. I overheard Keith saying something about fishing. Mohammad followed a few paces behind Flora and Fiona. It made an amusing picture. He was so large and they were so oblivious, zigzagging across the ground, bumping against each other, then self-correcting and steering away again. Mohammad looked like a sheepdog trying to herd two uncooperative ducks. He was sweating in the heat, and I could see the shine on his forehead and the wet patches under his arms. He was not enjoying himself. I wondered again why he had come.

Kathy Morrison was just pointing at the temple and turning to say something, probably completely fatuous, to her father, when she stumbled and fell. I'm sure her platform sandals had nothing to do with it, and I was able to suppress my concern and alarm remarkably well. In fact, I would have continued on to the temple without so much as breaking stride, but everyone else hurried to her side and clustered around. Alan gave me a look that almost made me laugh out loud, but he took my hand and we joined them. I didn't mind at all.

Kathy's face was already streaked with tears, and she was holding her ankle, lip quivering. Her father was trying to pull her up by her elbow, but she jerked away from him and waved him off. Dawn Kim knelt by her and firmly pulled her hands away, revealing an ankle that was already swelling. She clicked her tongue and lifted Kathy's leg, moving the foot back and forth, asking questions.

"A sprain," she announced. "You really should get some ice on it."

Anni looked around, her eyes pausing briefly on Alan before settling on her colleague. "Mohammad, you can take her to the first aid station?"

He looked over his shoulder as though she were addressing some other Mohammad. "Perhaps you should go. After all, a woman . . . going with another woman . . ." His voice trailed off.

Anni laughed. "But I cannot carry her. You and Jerry can take her, while I finish the tour."

For a moment, I thought he was going to refuse. His black eyes glittered with suppressed frustration, but then he seemed

132

to realize we were all staring at him and gave an ungracious shrug. He and Jerry each took an arm and hoisted her up between them. Fortunately for them, she didn't weigh any more than a wet cat, but I could hear her whiny voice complaining nonstop until they were out of earshot.

"Now what was that about?" Alan asked. He was also looking after the departing figures.

"Maybe he really wanted to see inside the temple," I answered.

But I didn't think so. Not wanting to be around someone like Kathy Morrison was easy to understand, but, after all, taking care of us was his job.

The second temple was much smaller, and after only a few minutes, Anni made a quick circuit, then left us with orders to meet in the marketplace restaurant in thirty minutes. Kyla slipped out a few seconds after Anni, and the others began trickling away. I was just starting to point out a brightly colored painting to Alan, when he gave my hand a squeeze and then dropped it.

"I'm heading out. I'll catch up with you back at the market."

He vanished into the bright light of the doorway without giving me a chance to reply. Suddenly, all the pleasure was sucked out of the day. Without Alan or Kyla to share the experience, it all seemed fairly flat. Worse, I could not help but suspect Alan had left to follow Kyla. Maybe that was just a coincidence. After all, he hadn't left with her. But I was pretty sure he had his eye on her. I just wasn't sure what that meant.

I waited in the cool dim interior of the temple, no longer really taking in the wonders around me. Realizing I was alone,

133

I walked back into the bright sunlight, trying to decide what to do. I could go back to the first temple, but everything was becoming very crowded, and I'd really seen it all. Without meaning to, I caught up with the Carpenters on their way back to the little market. Jane was silent and strained, but Ben and Lydia seemed happily content, and we all agreed that Abu Simbel was competely worth the journey and expense.

"It's hard to believe this was all built by hand. Stones carried hundreds of miles. Paints and workers dragged here from God knows where. I wonder why they did it," mused Lydia.

"Obsession with death, I expect. And self-obsession. They wanted to be sure they left their mark," said Ben.

"Not the pharaohs," she said. "The workers."

"Well, it was a job, wasn't it? They were probably glad of the work. This would be a hard country to scratch a living in. A cushy stone-hauling job, now that was probably a plum."

We laughed, trying to envision those times when stone-hauling might actually have been a great career.

Most of the group was already in the market when we arrived. Kyla lingered by a rack of postcards just a moment too long and was beseiged by two salesmen in white tunics. Farther down, I saw Flora and Fiona leaving another shop, clutching a small plastic bag. Just outside the open-air restaurant, DJ, Nimmi, and Anni were discussing the merits of our group photos with our photographer. Not that I was really looking, but Alan was nowhere to be seen.

"I see ice cream!" said Lydia, spotting a child with a cone. We snapped to attention like beagles spotting a hamster.

The restaurant was open on three sides, wooden columns supporting a flimsy roof designed to provide shade rather than protection from the elements. A counter ran along one side in front of refrigerated displays containing a variety of sodas, snacks, and ice creams. A couple of ceiling fans spun lazily from beams.

"Wonder if they have beer?" asked Ben. "Come on, Jane, Jocelyn. Let's get something cold to drink."

Jane, Lydia, and I went directly to a pretty corner of the room where chairs with brightly colored cushions clustered around a low table. We sank down gratefully, while Ben went to find drinks. Fascinating as monuments are, standing and walking unnaturally slowly are hard on the feet and back. Jane removed her sunglasses and settled back in her seat with a sigh. Although still wan, she seemed less nervous somehow, almost relaxed. Her aunt noticed too and patted her arm.

"I'm glad you decided to come," she said. Jane answered with a gentle smile.

"You know," I said as casually as possible, "I was at the airport when you were. I saw a girl standing by you who looked so much like one of my students. At the time I thought she was your daughter, but she must have been just someone you met on the plane?"

Lydia stiffened visibly. "I expect so. Are you sure it wasn't Jane?"

"No, I'm sure," I said. "Although she did resemble Jane quite a bit. She even had a sweater exactly like the one you are wearing now." I didn't know why I couldn't let it go. It wasn't as though I really thought that Ben and Lydia were doing anything illegal, and it certainly wasn't any of my business. It was just a puzzle, and I wanted to figure it out.

Jane threw an anxious glance at Lydia.

Ben returned with four Cokes, starting to complain about the lack of alcoholic beverages, when he noticed the look on his wife's face. With a swift glance at me, he set the drinks down with a little bang and turned on me, a cold anger in his eyes. Startled, I rose to my feet.

He had just opened his mouth to say something, when a scream rang out across the marketplace. It started low and then rose to a volume and pitch that made the hair stand up on the back of my neck. Ben waved at his wife, who put her arms around Jane's shoulders, and then he rushed outside.

I ran after him a second later, although if I'd followed my instincts I'd have curled in a fetal position behind a sofa and stayed there until someone blew the all clear.

The little market was total chaos. Tourists and vendors alike milled about trying to figure out what was happening. A second scream came from a little shop halfway down the row and we ran, arriving just behind Alan, who pushed past the circle of onlookers as if he owned the place. Where was Kyla? I looked around frantically for her, a panicked feeling in my stomach, but she appeared a few seconds later, running up from farther down the line of stalls. She had a packet of postcards in her hand. I heaved a sigh a relief, then turned to find out what was going on.

Alan returned from the interior of the shop, wading through the gathering crowd, his arm protectively around the shoulders of a woman who was sobbing hysterically. He said something to her, and she responded in rapid French. Seeing the blank, helpless look in his eye, I stepped forward.

"She says, 'He is dead, dead and covered in blood,'" I translated rapidly.

"You understand her? Here, take her to the restaurant and stay with her. I'll be right back." He pushed her at me and vanished again.

"Where are you going?" I called after him in outrage. The nerve of the man, giving me orders. I looked helplessly at the sobbing woman.

Kyla joined me. "Here, I'll take her. You follow Alan." She led the woman away without a word.

I wriggled my way through the crowd, no longer worried about being rude or accosted by vendors. I ducked under an elbow and then peered over the shoulders of two men. Sometimes being tall had its advantages.

In this case, advantage might not have been the right word. An Egyptian man lay on his face between two racks of souvenirs. A small trickle of blood marred the back of his neck and stained the collar of his galabia, although there was not enough to drip onto the ground. Had he been shot? No weapon was visible. It didn't seem possible that he could have died from such a small wound. Alan knelt on the dusty floor beside the body, looking grim. He checked for a pulse in the neck, then gently lifted the man's hands, examining the palms and fingertips. He said something in Arabic to one of the bystanders who knelt beside him. Arabic. Alan spoke Arabic? How did a guy from Dallas, a widower taking a trip he and his dead wife had planned, his first trip to Egypt, come to speak Arabic? He looked up and saw me and for a moment our eyes locked. For a split second, I saw my own doubt and suspicion mirrored back at me, but then he quickly rose to his feet. Looking around at the pathetic scene one last time, he then reached for my hand.

"Come on. We should get out of here," he said quietly in my ear.

I didn't argue.

We hurried back across the open market to the restaurant where Kyla waited with the sobbing French woman. I knelt beside her and spoke soothingly in French, asking her where her people were.

They had wanted to spend more time in the monuments, she said, and I translated quickly for Kyla and Alan. She herself had grown tired and decided to come back and spend some time in the little shops. She entered the most quiet shop where no one waited, and no one was calling and shouting. She thought the shop owner must have stepped out, and she was very glad to get to look at all the *petit* souvenirs without the attention of the *vendeur*. But then she kicked something with her foot and saw him lying on the floor. *Tant de sang.* All the blood. She burst into sobs again, then looking up she saw her husband and friends and ran to join them.

"Where did you learn your French?" asked Alan casually.

"Her mother is French," said Kyla, when I did not reply immediately. "She's completely fluent, lucky thing. Italian, too. She practically grew up in Italy. Her father was in the diplomatic corps."

"And you also?" asked Alan.

"Not a word," she answered with a grin. "I took Spanish in high school, for all the good that's done me. I've already forgotten most of it."

Alan was shaking his head as if puzzled. "You really aren't sisters, are you?"

"What have we been saying? Of course we're not sisters. If we were sisters, we'd hardly be going around saying we're cousins, now would we? Our fathers are brothers. And we don't even look alike," she added for good measure.

"And how about you?" I asked quietly. I held his eye for a moment. "A financial analyst from Dallas? You sure know your Arabic. And your pulse points."

He flushed a little. Kyla looked from me to him and back again. "What are you talking about?"

"I know a little Arabic," he admitted. "I took some college courses, thinking it would help me land a job. It might have sounded like I know the language, but I really know very little, and I've been assured my accent is atrocious."

"What were you saying, then?" I asked, not quite believing him.

He hesitated. "Just asking if anyone had seen someone leaving the shop," he said. But too late and too little. He really was a terrible liar. But if he was hiding something, I could not imagine what it was.

"And did they?" asked Kyla.

"No," he answered shortly. "No one saw anything."

Exactly like the events at the pyramids when Millie had been killed. A dead body on the ground, but no witnesses, even though the place was crowded. No outcry, no screams, not even much blood, never mind what the French woman said. Just a silent death. Only this time, instead of one of a tour group of foreigners, the victim was an Egyptian native. A simple shopkeeper, here in the sunny marketplace of Abu Simbel. None of it made any sense.

139

"We should ask Flora and Fiona," I said, suddenly remembering. "They were in that shop about ten or fifteen minutes earlier."

"How do you know?"

"I saw them coming out. You might have seen them, Kyla. They were coming out while you were stopping at the postcard shop."

She shrugged. "I didn't see them, but it doesn't matter anyway. They could have stepped on the dead guy and not have noticed."

Mohammad appeared, moving fast. "Everyone, let us meet at once back at the bus! Tell the others. We don't want to get stopped here and miss our flight."

Anni hurried up behind him. "Mohammad is right. Here, Alan. You take Hello Kitty and start for the parking lot." And she thrust the pink umbrella into Alan's hands and hurried away to gather the rest of the group. For a moment, I thought he would protest, but he seemed to think better of it.

We sprang into action. The commotion had drawn everyone together into the center of the market. It was a simple matter to wave Hello Kitty frantically at our fellow passengers and then dash back to the buses. Alan led the way quickly, the feeling of urgency affecting the group. Perhaps we would not have reacted so rapidly had the memory of waiting for hours at the pyramids not been relatively fresh in our memories. Even Flora and Fiona fell into line and for once weren't the last on the bus. It was Jane's reaction that shocked me. I thought she was going to faint. In fact, if Ben hadn't put his arm around her, I think she would have melted to the ground.

Terror poured from her like water from a fire hose. Ben and Lydia half dragged, half carried her to the bus.

Anni urged the driver to start the engine and we were halfway down the hill and on our way to the airport before we saw the first police car. We tensed up as they drove past, but then gave a collective sigh when they didn't turn around and come after us. We couldn't have been more relieved had we been guilty of the crime ourselves.

"Thank goodness we got out of there," said Nimmi.

"And thank goodness it had nothing to do with us this time," said DJ.

I felt a little sick inside. DJ hadn't seen the dead man, didn't know the death was a duplicate of Millie's. Whatever had happened, it most certainly had something to do with us. I just wasn't sure how to find out what it was.

Chapter 8

SHIPS AND SHOPLIFTING

The rest of our tour was to be spent aboard a cruise ship, traveling north on the Nile toward Luxor. On the flight back to Aswan, Kyla sat next to me, our quarrel forgotten. The shock of the death had knocked the sense back into both of us. Alan ended up sitting several rows behind me where I couldn't see him. I wasn't sure whether I was pleased or not. I had about a million questions for him, but since none of them were remotely polite, I wasn't sure I would have the nerve to ask them anyway. Questions like, who are you really? Are you a policeman? A spy? Or are you a murderer? No, none of those would have been appropriate for a plane flight.

Back in Aswan, a bus waited to take us to the docks where four large cruise ships floated on the dark waters of the Nile. The four ships might have been built to the same pattern. Tied together side by side like four horses pulling the same chariot, they occupied only a single mooring in the small harbor, and passengers had to walk through one to get to the next. The captains were clever enough to have them lined up in order of departure, and so when we arrived back at Aswan, we passed through the lobbies of three of the floating hotels before we stepped aboard the *Nile Lotus*.

I'd never been on a cruise ship before and had to make an effort to keep my jaw up. Chandeliers, curving staircases, marble floors. The tantalizing odor of lunch and the sound of flatware on china drifted through open doors, reminding us how hungry we were, and spurring us from one ship to the next. Our ship, when we reached it, seemed to be in the middle of the pack in terms of luxury and right at the top in terms of brightness and pleasant atmosphere.

Kyla put her hands on her hips. "Well, this looks like it might be acceptable."

I grinned at her. "Your majesty is pleased?"

"I'll let you know when we see our room. Depends on how much bilge water is on the floor."

"And I was assured there was a two-rat limit for every room."

"Well, okay then."

Our hand luggage waited in a pile beside the front desk and we gathered our belongings while Anni doled out the keys to our rooms. We could hear shouts outside. Then the ship gave an almost imperceptible shiver and, slowly, like a glossy crocodile sliding down a riverbank, glided out onto the Nile.

Despite earlier events, I couldn't help giving a shiver of my own. To be floating on the Nile was a dream so deep that I'd never really thought I'd ever see it happen. For a moment, I felt disconnected, as though I were on a movie set and nothing around me was quite real. The noise of the groups scrambling for luggage, calling to each other, asking questions—mostly about keys and lunch—seemed insignificant as I stared out the huge windows of the lobby and the ship slipped through the sapphire water.

"Hey, I got our keys. Come on, let's dump our stuff and head for the dining room. I'm starving," said Kyla, breaking the spell.

Our cabins were on the second floor, up the great curving flight of stairs, and Kyla and I looked at each other before we opened the door.

"If we have bunk beds, I call the top," she said with a grin.

"If we have hammocks, I call the one without the rats."

But when we opened the door we were very pleased to find what could pass as a very decent, if small, hotel room in any city. If the bathroom hadn't been raised about six inches higher than the rest of the room with a door that closed like a porthole, and if the banks of the Nile weren't streaming by outside the huge picture window, we could have fooled ourselves into thinking we were in France.

Kyla threw herself onto the closest bed. "What a morning," she said.

"Get up," I said, tossing my bag onto the far bed. I knew that she'd let me have the bed nearest the window as another peace offering. "Lunch calls."

She bounced back up immediately. "Say no more." She vanished into the tiny bathroom, and I sat down to wait for her.

"What do you think about that guy being dead?" she called through the door.

I knew I should be used to her habit of talking while on the toilet, but I wasn't.

"I think he was murdered," I called. "And I think it has something to do with our group."

"What?" she shouted. Because of course by this time she was washing her hands and couldn't hear the conversation she'd started.

I didn't bother to repeat myself until she reappeared. There should be rules about talking on the toilet. In fact, there probably were. I was pretty sure Miss Manners would have something to say about it.

"Murder's a pretty strong word. But it does seem to be too much of a coincidence," she admitted, as she stepped out.

"Millie was killed exactly the same way. You remember, Alan told us she'd been stabbed in the back of the neck. We just didn't see it on her because she was lying on her back. This guy was on his face."

"That must have been pretty awful."

"Well, yeah. What with being dead and all."

"No, I mean for you. More awful for him, of course," she admitted. "But still not much fun to see."

"The really weird thing was Alan," I blurted out. I hated the feeling of mistrust that I couldn't put aside. "He was checking the body and asking questions."

"Pretty sexy, huh?"

"No!"

She raised her eyebrows.

"No!" I insisted. "Checking dead bodies is not sexy."

"Methinks thou doth protest too much," she misquoted gleefully.

"Are we in high school here? Focus!"

She opened her bag, pulled out her makeup kit, and

emptied the contents onto the vanity. "Look, maybe he's just a take-charge kind of guy," she said, applying lipstick. "He just likes to know what's going on. You can't honestly think he's involved in any way."

I didn't reply. That was just what I was beginning to think. "We don't really know anything about him," I said slowly.

"We know lots of things. He's from Dallas, he's a financial analyst, his wife's dead, and he's got a nice ass."

"Okay, we know that last one," I admitted. "We've seen that for ourselves. But we don't really know that other stuff. If you think about it, we don't know anything about anyone here, except what they tell us."

"What do you mean?"

"Look. I've told everyone here that I'm a high school teacher, God help me. It happens to be true. But I could just as easily have said I was an artist or a programmer or a financial analyst. You'd know I was lying, but no one else here would. They have to take what I said on faith. It's the same with everyone else. Anyone could be lying."

She frowned. "But why would they?"

"Well, normal people wouldn't, because they don't have anything to hide and because keeping up a lie is a lot of work. But if you were planning to kill someone, you'd probably want to use an alias," I pointed out.

"So what, you think Alan is serial killer?" She rolled her eyes.

"No. Of course not. Not exactly, anyway. It's just . . ." my voice trailed off. I wasn't sure what I meant.

She put her hands on her hips. "Now you're just being ridiculous. No one would come on a tour to commit multiple

146

murders. That doesn't even make Hollywood sense. You have to do better than that."

"I can't," I said. "You're right, it doesn't make sense. But you have to admit something really odd is going on. And I want to know what it is."

Later that afternoon, however, I wasn't thinking about murder. The next evening's entertainment was to be a costume party, and Anni was pushing hard for all of us to come to the party in full Egyptian dress. After lunch, she suggested we meet her in the ship's gift shop, where we would be able to purchase one of the inexpensive Egyptian tunics called galabias as well as jewelry and other accessories, all about as authentic as the plaster statues in the street stalls. We knew it was a chance for her to get us to buy something from someone who was almost certainly a friend. We didn't care. I, for one, was dying to acquire a few Egyptian things, and she had promised to assist with the bargaining.

Located on the third floor beside the door that led to the sunning deck, the gift shop was brightly lit, and stuffed to bursting with gold jewelry, small trinkets, plastic pyramids, and carved wooden boxes. Silk scarves in every imaginable color hung from pegs, and several silver racks sagged with the weight of dozens of multicolored galabias of the sort that probably had real Egyptians laughing themselves sick. It didn't matter in the slightest. Half our little group filled the shop, while the other half waited in the hall for a chance to squeeze inside. The only people I didn't see were Jerry and Kathy, who were probably down in their rooms tending to her ankle. I couldn't actually imagine Jerry participating in a costume party anyway.

The shopkeeper was a rotund middle-aged Egyptian with the patience of Job and a perfect grasp of English. Unlike his counterparts in the markets beside the monuments, he was obviously used to American and European tourists and stood back and let us look to our hearts' content. He brought out gold pieces from under the counter for Nimmi and Lydia to admire. Seeing DJ rifling through a rack of clothing, he hurried from behind the counter, produced a magnificent black galabia with flowing headdress, and helped DJ try it on. With his dark skin and protruding belly, DJ looked like a desert sheik. Laughing helplessly, Nimmi searched out a bright red galabia and paired it with a belly dancer's jingling belt. DJ began haggling right away.

Kyla found a flowing golden galabia that looked more like a pretty dress than a tunic. She slipped it on over her clothes and looked in the full-length mirror. The color brought out the golden highlights in her hair and the pale tan of her skin.

"That's perfect on you," I said honestly, if a little enviously. "Now you just need some gold jewelry."

"Can I see that ankh?" she asked the shopkeeper, pointing in one of the display cabinets.

I wandered away to search through the racks. Nothing was going to compare with the golden outfit, so I started looking at the darker colors. I wondered how many of my choices in life were based on trying not to compete with my cousin. I pushed the garments along their racks and stopped at a deep blue. I considered. The fabric wasn't the same quality as Kyla's gold, but it wasn't as expensive either. It was marked one hundred Egyptian pounds and a quick calculation made that about $20. I pulled it from the rack. Anni joined me.

"Ah, that is very nice," she said. "And here, look at this."

She pulled a matching scarf from a hook on the wall and wrapped it around my head. Little fake gold coins dangled from the edges and framed my face. She pulled me in front of a mirror. I thought I looked very exotic and mysterious. Then I blinked, and I looked like a not-so-young tourist playing dress-up with a cheap scarf. I squinted my eyes, trying to get the initial illusion back, then decided it didn't matter.

"I'll take it," I said, starting for the counter.

Anni looked at me pityingly. "No, no. You never say that. Here, watch me."

She took my things to the cash register and made a little gesture to the shopkeeper.

"Ah, excuse me," he said to Nimmi, who was now admiring several pieces of gold jewelry. She gave him a smile of assent, and he turned back to Anni, leaning over the counter with a spark of enthusiasm in his eyes.

"Ah, Mr. Elgabri, I would like to introduce to you Miss Jocelyn Shore, from America. She is a very special person, and part of this very big group who will be buying many, many fine things from your shop."

I listened, admiring Anni's skill as she very politely pointed out to him that I deserved only the best prices, and moved smoothly into telling him that the things I had chosen, although very beautiful, were really not worth the amounts on the price tags. He was smiling and agreeing how special I was, but pointing out that I had excellent taste and had obviously chosen some of the finest items that he carried. I grinned helplessly, face very red, knowing I would never, ever have the courage to say any of those things. In fact, it would be worth extra not to have to haggle for what I wanted.

Out of the corner of my eye, I noticed Nimmi was still fingering the pieces of jewelry in the small black velvet tray sitting before her on the counter. Briefly, she laid an elegant little hand over a ring, and when she lifted it, the ring had vanished.

Shocked, I completely lost the thread of conversation between Anni and Mr. Elgabri. This was the sort of thing I had come to expect when I took my students on a field trip. So many of them were under enormous pressure from their friends, and of course a significant percentage were amoral little bastards who shouldn't be allowed out of their cages. But this was a new one. Could a woman like Nimmi, obviously wealthy, obviously socially elite, steal from a shopkeeper who probably earned less in a week than what she spent in a day? I didn't think so. Not today.

She made a show of pushing back the tray and started away from the counter.

"Great ring," I said to her. "That will look terrific on you, Nimmi. May I see it?"

She flushed, a subtle red color creeping up her neck and tinting her cheeks. Anni and the shopkeeper stopped in midsentence to stare. For one instant, I knew she was considering denying that she had a ring, but the pressure of three pairs of eyes was too much, particularly when Mr. Elgabri looked down at the jewelry tray.

Shooting me an ugly look, she held out the ring, and I took it, holding it to the light and admiring it. It wasn't too bad. A broad gold band shaped into the Eye of Horus, the ancient symbol of protection.

I smiled as I handed it back. "Really lovely and so unusual. You'll enjoy that forever."

With a huge smile, the shopkeeper turned to her and asked if she were ready to check out. Trapped like a rat, I thought. She looked around frantically, but her husband had made his purchases and was no longer in the shop. In fact, I suspected that she'd waited for him to leave before she tried her sleight of hand. With a rigid smile, she opened her purse and pulled out her wallet.

"Oh, no. I don't have nearly enough cash," she said.

I hoped she didn't have acting aspirations. Usually when you saw someone give a performance that bad, they were moments away from being eaten by a mutant rubber shark. "I don't suppose you take credit cards."

She would have been right in most places, but this was a Swiss-run tourist boat. "Of course we do," said the shopkeeper, holding his hand out. And she had no choice but to hand over her card.

I turned back to Anni and asked for a demonstration of how to tie my scarf, mostly to avoid any more evil glances. Nimmi might suspect, but she could never be sure that I had done it on purpose. She completed her purchase and stormed out, her face still brick red.

With a big smile, the shopkeeper met Anni's eye, then said to me, "For a lovely lady, the price is eighty pounds. And you will be so kind as to accept the scarf as my gift. It suits you perfectly."

Anni patted my shoulder lightly. "You will not get a better deal than that. And you didn't need my help after all."

* * *

After shopping, Kyla decided that a nap in our cabin would be just the right thing, but I was feeling oddly restless. I handed her my purchases to put away, then climbed the stairs leading to the sundeck of the *Nile Lotus*. I blinked in the brilliant sunshine, then gave a little shiver. Here on the river, with the March breeze streaming across the bow, the temperature was cool to the point of being chilly.

The sundeck was huge, stretching almost the full length of the ship, and lined with deck chairs gleaming green and white in the sun. In the center, a very large white canopy covered a bar and about twenty lounge chairs, providing a generous patch of shade for anyone who couldn't take any more sun. No one was taking advantage of it. I could see a few diehard sunbathers draped over the green-and-white-striped chairs along the rails, white flesh blinding in the light, but several others were huddled in their towels.

I walked toward the bow of the ship. A tiny swimming pool in one corner looked like a miniature oasis, complete with turquoise water and sand-colored decking, but no one had dipped so much as a toe in it all afternoon. In two or three more weeks when the temperature climbed, I was sure it would be packed with laughing tourists.

I glanced over the railing. The water swirled far below, deep blue churning to frothy green along the white sides of our ship. The eastern bank seemed nearer than it was, a strip of halfhearted dusty green holding back a sweep of sand and rock. Along a narrow dirt path running beside the river, a man in a gray galabia rode a tiny donkey, his feet almost dragging on the ground. He clutched a short switch in one hand and tapped the donkey's behind every few seconds, but the skinny boy trotting after them on foot had no trouble keeping up. The *Nile Lotus* churned on, leaving man, boy, and donkey behind.

I had just decided to return to my cabin, when I saw a scrawny arm waving frantically at me from the after deck. Charlie de Vance grinned at me and then called, "Just bring us a couple of those towels, would you, honey?"

I smiled back and scooped up four of the soft, fluffy white towels stacked beside the bar and took them to where he and Yvonne were sitting like two plucked chickens on lounge chairs in the back corner of the deck. Unbelievably, both were wearing bathing suits, which, though modest by modern standards, still revealed far too much saggy, spotted skin. A pink flush indicative of early sunburn tinted Charlie's chest above an expanse of sparse white hair, and goose bumps covered his scrawny thighs. Yvonne's fingers had turned an odd bluish color. They took the towels I offered gratefully.

"Who would've thought it would be so nippy?" asked Charlie, pulling one towel around his shoulders like a shawl and spreading another over his legs. "All you ever read about is the desert heat."

"It's winter, if you think about it," I answered. "Spring won't be here for another week and a half. Still part of the 'season' for the archaeologists."

"Well it was hot enough by the pyramids."

Yvonne patted his arm. "More sheltered there, with all that stone absorbing the heat and blocking the wind. Remember how cool it was at Saqqara."

I started edging away, not wanting to get trapped into an interminable discussion about the weather. Charlie noticed and patted the chair next to him. "Pull up a pew, missy. We haven't had a chance to talk with you properly this whole trip."

Short of hurtling myself over the side, which suddenly didn't seem like such a bad idea, I was trapped. Charlie drew a deep breath in preparation for his first question.

"So you two are here on your honeymoon?" I asked quickly. The important thing at this point was to maintain control of the conversation.

Charlie grinned proudly and patted Yvonne's hand. "We sure are."

"How did you meet?"

"Our fiftieth class reunion," answered Yvonne with a fond smile. "We've actually known each other most of our lives. We were high school sweethearts."

I was touched. "So you met after all those years apart? And it was love at first sight?"

"Exactly." They looked into each other's eyes. "Yvonne's husband had passed away two years before. And when I saw her again after all that time, it was like I was right back in high school. Head over heels in love. Prettiest little thing I ever saw. Of course, getting rid of my wife wasn't all that easy."

If I'd been drinking milk, it would have spewed out of my nose. "What?"

"Oh, yes. Sue Anne didn't understand at all."

"Well, she had a point, Charlie," said Yvonne. "I mean, you two had been married forty years."

"And that was enough! Forty years of my life I gave that woman. And then when I saw you, I knew I finally had a chance at happiness."

I goggled at them, mouth hanging open. I couldn't help it.

Yvonne went on. "It was the same for me. I took one look at Charlie and knew I had to have him. I felt bad about being a home wrecker, but at our age, you have to either shit or get off the pot. If you'll pardon the expression," she added with an apologetic glance at me.

The sunbathers by the pool finally gave up, tossed their towels on their chairs, and hurried inside. I watched them enviously.

"So what happened to your wife?" I asked. My voice squeaked a little.

"Oh, she came out of it smelling like a rose. I think the only things I walked away with were my clothes, my clubs, and my stamp collection. Not that that isn't worth a pretty penny. Sue Anne never understood stamps," he added with a touch of bitterness. "No, she got the house and my Social Security checks, and I got Yvonne. When you think of it, I'm a kept man now."

He leaned over to nuzzle Yvonne, who nuzzled back. I looked away quickly.

"I've got plenty for the both of us," said Yvonne with quiet satisfaction. "I was a criminal defense lawyer for twenty years, before I moved into corporate takeovers. You know," she added to Charlie, "if your kids would start speaking to you again, I think we'd be completely happy."

Appalled, I decided it was time to change the subject. "Criminal law? You must have run into your share of interesting cases."

"Oh my, yes. So many horrible people, most of them. But they paid through the nose for my assistance. I was quite good, you know," she added.

I considered and then decided there was no harm in asking. "What do you think about the two murders that we've had?"

Charlie looked blank. "Two?" he asked, puzzled.

Yvonne gave me a sharp glance. "I've been wondering about that myself. Dawn told me about the shopkeeper at Abu Simbel when you all got back. Too much of a coincidence, is that what you are thinking?"

I nodded.

"I tell you what I've noticed. Not everyone on this trip is exactly what they say they are. Take Jerry Morrison. He says he's a real estate attorney out in California, and maybe he is, but he is mighty nervous about something that's going on back there. I thought he was going to have apoplexy when he found out there was no Internet available on the ship. And talk to his daughter. She says he pulled this trip out of thin air only a week ago and insisted she come with him. Sounds like someone needed to get himself out of Dodge in a hurry."

"All the way to Egypt?"

She shrugged. "Not a bad place to hide. It's not easy to get around in this country if you're not on a tour. And the tour itself provides plenty of protection. Armed guard on the bus, people around all the time. Plus, I'm pretty sure this was one of the places his daughter really wanted to see. And he needed a pretty big carrot to get her to miss a week of classes. She mentioned it wasn't even her spring break."

So she had. But Jerry on the lam from shady connections back home? Although pleasant to contemplate, it seemed pretty farfetched to me. Moreover, I couldn't see any connection with the murders.

"You're thinking that doesn't have anything to do with anything." Yvonne smiled at me. "Probably doesn't, but you never know. You never know what small thing might turn out to be important. I spent my career making connections among seemingly unrelated things. You can't believe some of the information I gathered when I was working with my criminals . . . I mean, clients. Background stuff, details that didn't have much to do with the case at hand, but which turned out to give me an edge when I was building the defense. You have to pay attention to the things that don't make sense."

Which meant I should be on high alert right now. Nevertheless, I excused myself and escaped below as quickly as I could.

Wednesday, Edfu

Wake to find your ship has arrived on the shores of the ancient city of Edfu. After a leisurely breakfast, board a horse-drawn carriage for the drive through town to the Temple of Horus, where a magnificent black stone statue of the falcon god guards the gates. Built during the reign of Cleopatra only 2,000 years ago, the temple is young by Egyptian standards and in almost perfect condition. Return to your ship to continue your cruise down the Nile. Spend the afternoon on the sundeck, sipping drinks and watching white-clad farmers working their fields as they have done for millennia.

—WorldPal pamphlet

Chapter 9

HAWKERS AND HORSES

During the night while we slept, the *Nile Lotus* churned its way downstream sixty-five miles to the desert town of Edfu. Our wake-up call split the air and our eardrums at some ungodly hour, and Kyla and I dressed wordlessly and staggered down two flights of stairs to the dining room, looking and feeling a lot like zombies, only less alive. Three cups of coffee at breakfast revived us to an extent, enough anyway for Kyla to glare at me over the steam and say, "I'm never going on a tour again. Never."

"Fine."

"Really," she said. "Never."

"Sure, that's fine," I answered.

"No, I really mean it. No one should have to wake up this early on vacation."

"You're absolutely right," I answered.

She glared at me, annoyed. My third cup of coffee was kicking in, and I was starting to feel better. I eyed the buffet with growing interest, watching a cook in a crisp white jacket expertly flip an omelet from a skillet onto a plate and hand it to a woman with a smile.

"You don't care."

"Nope. Want an omelet?"

She followed my gaze. "Sure, what the hell. Bring me a bagel, too."

The rest of the group appeared in twos and threes in varying states of alertness. Anni arrived looking refreshed and happy. I was pretty sure I wasn't going to win my bet with Kyla. If Anni hadn't had a nervous breakdown or an explosion by this time, after two plane rides and two murders, she wasn't going to have any trouble with the next few days. I had a good feeling. Nothing else could possibly go wrong and, besides that, nothing that had gone wrong over the past few days was any of my business. I would turn Millie's bag over to Anni on our last day, and she could dole out the stolen items as she saw fit. And I would concentrate on relaxing and enjoying the rest of the trip.

We met in the lobby a half hour later. The early morning air was clear and surprisingly cool as we disembarked. The ship moored at a dock right beside the shore, and we had only to walk across a short gangway to reach the bank. The smell of horse sweat and stale urine wafted to us on the light breeze, strong and acrid in the crisp, bright air. At least twenty black carriages waited patiently along the landing, some with awnings, some open to the sky, all pulled by small dusty horses wearing blinders.

"Jesus H. Christ on a popsicle stick," swore Jerry, taking

one brief whiff and slapping a hand over his nose and mouth. "What a freaking shithole."

Yvonne de Vance pursed her lips and gave him a cold stare from haughty eyes. Lydia Carpenter stepped around him as though avoiding a particularly foul dog deposit on the sidewalk. He noticed and gave her a mocking smile. I looked around. Ben and Lydia were here, once again flanking their niece Jane like bodyguards. I did not know what to make of it at all, but I gave a mental shrug and told myself it was none of my business. Which only had the effect of making it even more interesting. Maybe I could get Kyla to chat with Ben and Lydia later, since they had been avoiding my gaze since Abu Simbel.

I looked at the horses carefully—I'd read many travelers' tales on the tourist Web sites bemoaning the treatment of the Edfu carriage horses. To my relief, the animals, although scrawny and ungroomed, did not appear to be either starving or mistreated. Anni arrived, spoke to the lead driver, and then herded us into an orderly line.

"Do not tip your driver until you get back here," she warned. "He will wait for you while we tour the temple. And remember, the fee has already been paid. If you do wish to tip, you can give him two pounds. If he takes your picture, you can add a little more, but do not give more than five pounds. The drivers compare tips with each other and brag if they get a large tip. This causes some of them to start demanding money of their passengers." She clicked her tongue disapprovingly. "They are becoming very rude, and they sometimes frighten the tourists."

It sounded exactly as though she was describing the bears at Yosemite. Don't feed the animals, they might bite. And conversely, she made us sound like a nervous herd of cattle on the plains, looking for an excuse to stampede.

When our turn came, Kyla and I hopped into a dilapidated black carriage pulled by an unenthusiastic white nag, which left Alan paired with Jerry Morrison. According to Jerry, Kathy's ankle had swollen up like a balloon, and she hadn't even made it down to breakfast. Jerry appeared alone, looking a little lost as he realized that the rest of us were looking away just like kids avoiding the teacher's eye in the hopes of not being selected for a question. He had not made himself pleasant to a single person on the tour—and didn't look as though he was going to start now. I could see the two men eyeing each other with dislike as we drove away.

Our driver cheerfully pointed out the sights on the short drive through town and up the hill to the temple. We had to lean forward to see because the carriage had a protective awning, complete with a red fringe. The tune of "Surrey with a Fringe on Top" kept running through my head in a most aggravating way. And why should I suffer alone?

I hummed a few bars under my breath. Kyla whipped around on me like a Doberman on a housebreaker.

"Oh, no. No, no, no. Tell me you did not do that," she moaned.

I hummed a little more, just to ensure she wouldn't be able to get it out of her head, and then leaned back, content.

Edfu as a town teetered on a very fine edge between prosperity and devastation. Most of the tiny shops that we slowly clip-clopped past were humble indeed, and the atmosphere in general was run-down and somewhat desperate. Still, men were out and about, sitting and smoking in small cafés or talking with animated hand gestures and laughing, and the shops were open, which was a good sign. The recent decrease in tourism had hit towns like Edfu very hard, but they were surviving in spite of it all. And then too, the morning was beautiful, and we were in the mood to be pleased with everything.

"You never see any women sitting and eating in the cafés," said Kyla thoughtfully.

"Probably because that's where the men are."

"So are they not allowed, or are they just smart?"

We giggled.

Our driver parked the carriage in a long row of covered stalls, which reminded me of a SONIC drive-in, minus the teenage girls on Rollerblades swooping by with trays of tater tots and limeades. Although cool right now, later in the season the heat would be unbearable on the asphalt, and it was comforting to know that horses and drivers had shade at least. Our driver hopped down with the agility of a boy and offered a hand to assist us from the carriage, his smile revealing several missing teeth. We joined the others around Hello Kitty, and walked past the inevitable line of stalls to the temple.

One of the more enterprising young entrepreneurs jumped out in front of Kyla and me.

"Hello, pretty ladies!"

Kyla ignored him and kept her eyes straight ahead, while I tried to look away. He waved his hands as though checking to see if we were blind. I couldn't help grinning, which was a huge mistake.

Encouraged and elated, he began walking backward in front of us, slowing us down, but not enough to get by. The rest of the group streamed past us heartlessly.

"I have many fine things in my shop, beautiful things for beautiful ladies," he announced.

"We can't stop now," I said. "We have to stay with our group."

"No, no, it will not take any time at all. You can easily meet up with your group," he said persuasively, stumbling a little as he continued backward.

"No, we can't," said Kyla shortly.

He got another idea. "On your way back, then. On your way back, you will stop in my shop. I will make you a very good bargain. A beautiful bargain for a beautiful lady."

Kyla just snorted, an unladylike sound reminiscent of a camel. I would have to find out how she did that.

"At least tell me your name. Tell me your name, pretty lady."

With an evil sidelong glance at me, she answered, "Jocelyn," and pushed past him with a burst of speed.

I scurried to catch up, cheeks red, listening to his shouts of "Jocelyn, Jocelyn, come back!"

"Good one," I admitted to her, as she burst out laughing.

It is a sad truth that repetition dulls appreciation. What had been mesmerizing at Giza, fascinating at Aswan, and interesting at Abu Simbel had finally become monotonous at Edfu. The huge walls, covered by magnificent carvings that we had never seen before, seemed disconcertingly familiar. The height and the massive weight of the rocks were old hat. Entering a courtyard, we did perk up a bit at the black stone statue of Horus, the falcon god, wearing the crown of Egypt. Not large by Egyptian standards, it stood only six or eight feet tall, but we had seen nothing like it before, and it presented a good photo opportunity. We took turns standing in front of it, obligingly handing cameras back and forth to get pictures.

Alan joined us, speaking to me for the first time since Abu Simbel. "Here, give me your cameras and I'll take the two of you," he offered.

Well, it wasn't romantic, but at least it was something. And we didn't have many pictures with the two of us, so we handed over the cameras and posed. After making the obligatory rabbit ears behind my head and posing for two snaps, Kyla bounced forward and claimed the cameras.

"Now you stand there with Jocelyn," she ordered.

Alan obligingly traded places with her. Kyla took a step back as if she was having trouble getting us both in the picture. "Move a little closer together," she called.

We each took a step at the same time and bumped together. Alan laughed and threw his arm around my shoulders, and Kyla snapped the picture. For one second I leaned my head against his shoulder. And then I caught myself and stepped away smoothly with a smile and a word of thanks. Was it my imagination or did he seem just a little disappointed? I knew I was. I could still feel the pressure of his arm on mine.

He looked as though he were about to say something, when Charlie de Vance made a kind of hooting noise like an owl caught in a blender. "Yoohoo! Mr. Stratton. Alan! You remember how to work our camera. Would you mind?"

Alan gave me an amused glance under his lashes and then turned with a smile to help.

Kyla and I walked on. When we were a few paces away, I turned on Kyla indignantly. "What was that about? Making me take pictures with him?" I asked under my breath.

"Oh come on, you have the hots for him so bad. You needed a souvenir of the hot guy who got away."

"What makes you think he's going to get away?" I asked indignantly. "And anyway, I do not have the hots for him. I told you before, I don't trust him. I think he's up to something."

She rolled her eyes. "Yes, of course. He's some crazed psycho killer. Well, here's photographic evidence."

She pointed her little Canon over my shoulder and snapped.

I turned my head and saw Alan bending over to retrieve Yvonne's bag for her.

Kyla grinned. "Now you have a picture of his heinie, too. We have him coming and going." She giggled to herself on and off for the next five minutes. She has a truly unfortunate habit of cracking herself up.

I didn't think Alan could have seen her snap the picture of his backside, but he did not rejoin us. Oddly, he trailed after Ben, Lydia, and Jane almost the whole time, sometimes chatting with them, sometimes just loitering nearby. He couldn't be interested in Jane, I told myself. She's way too young for him and so scrawny. I considered her, following listlessly behind her aunt and uncle, dark glasses hiding the even darker circles under her eyes, and I thought again of the vivacious, laughing girl I'd seen with the Carpenters in the airport. And this girl's terror at Abu Simbel. Surely that had

168

been excessive, even for a nervous invalid, if that was what she was. I did not know what to make of it.

I caught up with Dawn and Keith Kim along the high wall where Anni was pointing out the carvings of crocodiles.

"Before the Aswan dam was built, many crocodiles lived along the banks of the Nile, all the way to Cairo and beyond to Alexandria. But after the dam was finished, they vanished too. We hardly ever see them anymore."

"I bet nobody misses them," I said, by way of a conversation starter.

Keith looked at me earnestly. "You don't understand how devastating the dam has been on the environment here. The crocodiles aren't the only creatures affected. Without the annual floods, the farmland is not renewed every year. Farmers are resorting to using chemical fertilizers, which have been killing wildlife and plants. Even the papyrus reeds are dying out. And people have been able to build much nearer to the banks of the Nile, which causes more pollution than ever to reach the river water."

I was already regretting that I'd said anything. "I'm sure you're right," I agreed quickly.

Dawn gave Keith a half-amused, half-exasperated look. "She doesn't want to talk about the environment, Keith. No one wants to talk about the environment."

He frowned at her, opening his mouth to protest how shortsighted or selfish that was, but Dawn cut him off and turned to me.

"I wanted to ask you about yesterday," she said. "You actually went into that shop, didn't you?"

Her almond-shaped eyes gleamed with curiosity under

skillfully applied shadow and liner. She really was a very beautiful woman.

"Yes, I did," I admitted. "It was horrible. That man was just lying on his face on the floor."

"Was there blood?"

"Dawn!" protested Keith.

Dawn looked annoyed. "Oh like you don't want to know. I'm sorry that that poor man is dead. So tragic. Blah, blah. But damn it, it's interesting. Why shouldn't I ask?"

I tried not to laugh. I knew I liked Dawn.

"Ask away," I said. "I don't know much anyway. But the thing that hit me most was how similar it was to what happened to Millie. Pretty strange coincidence."

"What do you mean?" ask Keith, but Dawn was nodding.

"Exactly. Two people killed. Makes you think."

"Don't be ridiculous," Keith protested. "There's no connection at all between the two . . . events. One was an American tourist, in Giza, hundreds of miles away. The other was a simple shopkeeper. Completely different," Keith added stoutly.

"Both stabbed in the back of the neck," I pointed out. "Neither one of you noticed anything unusual in the market before it happened, did you?"

Keith sputtered. "Look. This is our first vacation together. Whatever is going on, it doesn't have anything to do with us."

Dawn gave him a look, then turned back to me as if he hadn't spoken. "We didn't notice anything, or at least I didn't. The shopkeepers are so aggressive and in your face, I can't even see what they're selling, much less pay attention to anything else going on. You know what it's like when you go into one of those shops."

I didn't, but I nodded anyway, not wanting to admit I'd never had the nerve to do more than lower my eyes and rush by, ignoring the calls and offers of the hawkers.

"Oh, you and your conspiracy theories," said Keith indulgently. "Look, just because someone totally unrelated to our group died someplace we just happened to be, doesn't mean there is something going on. I still don't think Millie Owens's death was anything more than a really sad accident. You read about people breaking their necks all the time in strange ways."

"But she didn't break her neck," Dawn protested. "Alan said she was stabbed."

"Oh, Alan," Keith's voice was laden with scorn. "What does he know about it? I'll tell you what. Nothing. He just wants to dash around looking important and listening to himself talk."

"That's not true, my love. Alan is a very smart man. Very educated."

"Hmph," he snorted. "I don't know why he's talking to you about it anyway. It's none of his business. He's just a busybody. Worse than Millie . . . God rest her soul," he added quickly, suddenly aware he'd spoken ill of the dead. "Alan's been asking questions all over the place, stirring everyone up. I tell you what, I saw Fiona and Flora go into that shop about ten minutes before that French woman started screaming, but I wasn't going to tell him. He'd just hound them to death, poor senile old things."

"Do you think they're senile?" I asked, trying to steer the

conversation away from Alan, of whom Keith was obviously jealous. I wondered if Dawn had made some admiring comment about him.

"Of course they're senile," Dawn said, apparently glad to find something on which she could agree with her husband. "Classic dementia. Look how they're always confused and always late. They never seem to know what's going on. How they were able to make arrangements for this trip is beyond me. I suspect a young relative handled everything for them. I know Fiona has a son—we were talking about him at dinner. I wish I could give him a piece of my mind. Those two should not be on the loose in a foreign country. What if they wandered off?"

Probably exactly what the son was longing to find out, I thought cynically. And with the possible exception of Dawn Kim, I think we were all right with him on that.

"They seem to be handling it, overall," I said weakly.

"Exactly what I tell her," said Keith. "Senile or not, they are doing fine and you should leave them alone."

"I was a nurse for fifteen years," she explained to me. "And I can tell you they're not fine. Have you smelled them? Urine! On Flora, at least."

I had gone to considerable trouble not to get within smelling distance of either one of them, and now I was going to redouble my efforts.

"That's terrible," I said truthfully.

"Something needs to be done about it." She looked from her husband to me as if expecting us to march off and take action. I made my escape quickly.

* * *

On the walk back to the carriages, I steeled myself and decided enough was enough. I couldn't possibly leave Egypt without trying to haggle for something in a shop. I had a large, smelly wad of Egyptian pounds in my purse, and I was determined to spend it on something. Accordingly, I slowed down. The boy who had walked backward for us was nowhere to be seen. I was a little disappointed, because I thought that kind of initiative should be rewarded, but I tried to decide from a distance which little stall looked the most promising. As far as I could tell, they were all identical, with racks of postcards and brightly colored dresses swaying in the gentle, cool breeze.

"What are you doing?" Kyla asked, slowing with me.

"I want to buy something."

"You're kidding. What could you possibly want here?"

"Nothing. I just want to try it."

"You should wait and let DJ help you. They'll eat you alive."

I grinned. "I know. I'll make some guy extremely happy and come away with a total piece of crap. I just want to try."

She rolled her eyes. "I can't bear to witness the carnage. I'll meet you back at the parking lot. Remember we only have fifteen minutes."

"Plenty of time for me to get ripped off," I said, as we started toward the shops.

We were immediately besieged.

"Hey, pretty lady! What's your name? You are very beautiful. What's your name?"

The hawkers were relentless. "Pretty ladies, you sisters!" called one. "Pretty sisters. I would pay five hundred camels just to gaze on your beauty. No, one thousand camels!"

Kyla stiffened, threw me a malevolent glance, and dashed away, although I wasn't sure whether it was the reference to sisters or camels that ticked her off the most. Either way, this guy had won me over. I moved toward his stall.

However, just then another shopkeeper, a young man with a missing front tooth, jumped out and waved frantically at me. "No, no! That's the wrong place. You should come in here. Pretty lady from Utah. In here!"

I hesitated. Utah again. What the hell was it with Egyptians and Utah? I shook my head and gestured to indicate that I was going with the guy who thought I was worth five hundred camels. However, to my surprise, camel boy had lost his smile and was backing away from me into his stall. He waved his hand as though to shoo me away. The man with the tooth, or rather, without the tooth, beckoned me again. I took a hesitant step into his stall, quickly glancing around at the racks of t-shirts, the scarves, the revolving stands of postcards. Surely there was something in here that I could haggle for.

But before I could choose something, three large men wearing white galabia appeared from the back and surrounded me, blocking my way out. I froze in alarm. The way they were standing effectively hid me from anyone passing the shop front. A fourth man pulled a rack of men's shirts into a new position and blocked any chance I had to escape. I tried to keep my face calm, heart pounding in my chest. This could not be happening.

The oldest man present, dark hair greasy and graying, stepped forward and thrust something under my nose. "Here it is," he said.

I tore my eyes away from his face and glanced down into his hand. A gleam of gold shown through his fingers, and he opened his palm to reveal the most exquisite necklace I had ever seen. Lapis lazuli and brilliant red carnelian glowed against the gleam of gold metal work. He scooped up the pendant so that it draped heavily across both his hands, a stunning piece and obviously genuine. Even the clasp at the back was ornate and fine. Without thinking, I put out a finger to touch it and he snatched it back, holding it in his fist, high near his ear.

"The price has gone up," he said unpleasantly.

I bet it had. Nothing else in here was half as good. I'd seen necklaces like this in the window of a fine jewelry store in Cairo, and the original or something very much like it in the Egyptian Museum.

"Okay, well thank you for letting me see it," I said, trying to keep my voice calm.

I looked around again for a way out but I was still blocked. I chose the smallest of the four, a younger man whose eyes were on a level with my own, and gave him my best teacher stare. "Please move, I want to get by."

He actually shifted half a step before a sharp command from Mr. Greasy with the necklace brought him back into position. I didn't take my eyes off the young man's face.

"I want to leave," I said forcefully and walked right into him.

Give him credit, he wasn't made to be a bully or a thug. He couldn't scramble away from me fast enough, and I was almost out of the store before the man with the necklace caught up to me and grabbed my shoulder and spun me around. He thrust the necklace into my face, his fingers pressing painfully into my arm.

"You will give me fifty thousand pounds more. We have heard about what happened, and the deal has changed."

"I don't have fifty thousand pounds, and let go of my arm or I'll scream." Inside, I was already screaming, but I kept my voice steady.

He released me instantly, but thrust his face into mine. His breath smelled of tobacco and garlic.

"Maybe your sister has it then," he said with an ugly look. "Mahmoud can go to bring her here. Then we can negotiate."

Terror for Kyla raced through me like an electric shock. "No!" I almost shouted the word. "I don't want your fucking necklace, and I'm leaving! Now!" I spoke as forcefully as I could, surprised and a little proud my voice did not squeak. I had never been so frightened.

He reached out a hand, and I filled my lungs in preparation for the scream of my life. But at that moment, a fifth man burst from behind the curtain in the back. "Enough!" he shouted.

He thrust himself in the middle of the group, a small old man with a forceful personality. He tore the necklace away from Mr. Greasy's grasp and pushed it into my hands. "Here. Take it and go. The deal stands. I am sorry you were troubled."

And before I knew it, I was back on the asphalt with the Egyptian sun streaming down over my shoulders clutching a very beautiful and obviously expensive necklace for which I'd paid not a pound. Behind me I could hear voices shouting at each other in Arabic. I thrust it into my purse and rushed back to the waiting carriages, half walking, half trotting as fast as I could. I kept expecting to hear shouts and running feet behind me. Shaking, I made it to the parking lot, spotted the white horse, and broke into a run.

Kyla was already waiting near our carriage, and the rest of the group who had been standing in a little knot in the parking lot began moving to locate their own carriages. Seeing the activity, our drivers, who were laughing and chatting with each other in the shade of an empty stall, hurried back.

"What happened to you?" she asked with a sharp glance. "Why are you running? You're not late. And whoa—you look green." She eyed me with the beginnings of concern.

"Haggling is much worse than I thought," I said. I tried to make it sound light, but my voice trembled a little.

"My God, what happened? Are you all right?"

"I'm fine. And I'll tell you later. Or I'll try. I'm not really sure what happened."

Kyla started to grill me, but just then Anni walked by, counting under her breath. Her headscarf today was a deep blue, framing her face and making her large eyes seem darker than ever.

"Where are Fiona and Flora?" she asked me. "You're the last one back. Did you see them in any of the shops?"

"No, but I didn't really look." I decided not to admit they could have been lying on the pavement on fire, and I wouldn't have seen them on my dash out of that shop.

She sighed. "Well, the rest of you start back to the ship. I will try to find them. Remember what I said about tipping."

* * *

In our cabin before lunch, I flopped down on the bed and told Kyla how the men had surrounded me and demanded fifty thousand pounds before just handing me a necklace. I still felt a little sick inside when I thought of how frightened I'd been.

She looked at me skeptically. "Those guys are pretty aggressive. It's too bad there were so many of them, but are you sure they asked for fifty thousand pounds? Are you sure it wasn't fifty? There's nothing in any of those shops worth fifty thousand."

Instead of arguing, I pulled the necklace from my purse and handed it to her. Her eyes widened.

"Dear God, this is gorgeous. No way did they just give it to you." She carried it to the window spread out over both hands and turned it in the sunlight. It was so beautiful it almost glowed.

"They did, though," I answered, closing my eyes. "But not before scaring the living daylights out of me."

"But it looks real, not like most of that cheap crap in those stalls. It has to be worth a fortune."

"Maybe it's just a really good fake."

"Even so, it has to be worth a lot more than nothing. I mean, it's absolutely fantastic." She held it up to the light from the window, admiring it.

"I can't explain it. I don't even know what happened. Maybe the head guy was sorry his thugs had scared me and just gave it to me by way of apology," I speculated doubtfully. "You know, so I wouldn't cause a big fuss with the tour company or the police. I imagine they'd get into a lot of trouble if anyone found out they'd been scaring the tourists."

"Well, that's true at least. They'd probably get closed

down altogether. Still, you'd think they would have given you some postcards or a plastic pyramid or something and not this pretty little thing. Can I borrow it?"

"No!" I snapped. "I'm going to wear it with my galabia tomorrow night."

"Ooh, that will look fabulous."

Chapter 10

LOUNGES AND LIZARDS

Dinner that night was another all-you-can-eat buffet featur-
ing a giant roast, some unidentified fish, and heaping caul-
drons of spaghetti. Definitely something for everyone. Even
though I was trying to eat moderately, I still ended up with
far too much on my plate. Everyone was present except Kathy,
who was still playing the invalid card and eating in her room,
and Alan. I was more disappointed by his absence than I
wanted to admit.

After dinner, Kyla and I decided to join the group for
drinks in the ship's lounge. Anni had promised some form of
entertainment, and since the ship was chugging along in the
middle of the Nile, we did not have many other options. I
wore my black skirt with the white shirt tonight. Kyla, however, chose a hot pink silky top with a low neckline over black
and pink flowered capri pants and matching pink flats. She'd
pulled her hair up in a French twist, and little strands escaped
and curled about her face artistically. At this point in the trip,

I'd almost given up being jealous and was now trying to figure out how she had managed to fit so many outfits in her suitcase. I ran a brush through my hair, applied a pink lipstick, and decided that would just have to do.

The ship's lounge was located on the same main level as the lobby, a large room, spanning almost a third of the length of the ship. A ten-by-ten-foot square of wood parquet, floating like an island in an ocean of blue carpet, formed a small dance floor in the middle of the room. At the far end, toward the ship's bow, stood a bar manned by two crewmen in white jackets, who were busily handing out weak drinks to a small line of tourists. All around the edges of the room, attractive chairs and sofas were arranged in large horseshoes so tour groups could sit together comfortably. The design was an odd marriage of luxury hotel and airport boarding area.

And the place was packed. All of the horseshoes were occupied, mostly with strangers traveling with other tour groups. It took me a minute to spot our little group sitting on the right near the dance floor. I was actually pleased to see them, familiar faces who would welcome me and obligingly scoot down to make room on the couch. I started for them, but Kyla had other plans.

"Bar," she said, steering me forward. I waved at Nimmi as we shot past.

When we reached the front of the line, I waited while Kyla requested a cosmopolitan and then provided the bartender step-by-step instructions to make what was probably the strongest drink he had ever seen. The splash of cranberry juice that she requested was barely enough to turn the vodka pink. She took a sip.

"Perfect. Or almost. The vodka's not really cold enough, but it will do. Want one?"

"No, thanks. I want to remain conscious. Heineken, please." I had seen the small green bottles on a shelf behind the bar, and I didn't have to worry about tainted ice when drinking bottled beer.

"Make it two," said a voice behind me, and I gave a little jump.

Alan Stratton had walked up behind us while we were watching the drink being made. He gave me a smile. Well, he probably gave us both a smile, but I pretended it was for me. At least I was included somehow. There was just something about the man. Whenever he stood within twenty feet of me, I was unable to remember my suspicions about him and could only stare at him dumbly with my tongue hanging out. Or worse, make inane conversation. I did it now.

"How did you like Edfu?" I asked, taking a sip of my beer.

"Very impressive," he answered. He reached past me to accept the beer from the bartender. "I have to admit I know almost nothing about it. Never heard of it before this trip."

"Me, too! I'm going to have a lot of research to do when I get back."

Kyla snorted into her cosmo. "Research. Dear God, you are such a nerd."

I flushed a little, then shrugged. Of course she was right.

Alan just laughed. "Glad I'm not the only one. I want to find out more, too."

"You know, to my shame, I think the most fascinating part was the carriage ride through town. The slow pace, seeing the people at their everyday activities, hearing the hooves on the cobbles. It gave a taste of what it must have been like back in the twenties when Howard Carter and the rest were seeing all these ruins for the first time."

"That's exactly it!" answered Alan. "The ride going up to the temple—you're right, it really seemed straight out of another era. I wonder if that could be done at other locations."

Kyla looked at the two of us. "Probably, but why the hell would you want to? The tour is short enough as it is. Why waste time being hauled around by some poor horse?"

He looked a little deflated. "I suppose you're right."

"No she's not," I said. "I think it would be great. Have a sort of Howard Carter tour. Get some of those old 1920s Bentleys or whatever kind of cool cars they had back then at some of the sites and use camels or horses at others. The transportation could be as much a part of the experience as the actual monuments."

Drinks in hand, we strolled back to where the group was sitting. An instrumental version of "Friends in Low Places" provided a surreal soundtrack for the scene. Alan and I glanced at each other.

"Who knew Garth Brooks was big in Egypt?" he asked with a grin.

"Who knew Garth Brooks had already been turned into elevator music?"

"Who knew the two of you were so boring that this is your idea of conversation?" said Kyla, looking around. "Come on, where's the entertainment?"

"Right here." Anni walked up behind Kyla while her back was turned. She thrust a potato and a handful of rope at me and then another at Alan. "I have trouble with knots. Could you tie the rope to the potatoes? Everyone," she lifted her voice and beckoned to the group, "come along. We're going to play a little game."

Within a few moments, the entire group stood in two teams around the tiny dance floor. Alan and I each held a rope at waist level and attempted to swing a potato between our legs to whack other potatoes across the floor. If and when the potato crossed the line, we were to hand the rope off to a teammate and continue the relay. It was harder than it looked, because potatoes don't roll in a straight line, nor is it easy to aim one hanging on a rope, particularly when it has to go between your legs. We were laughing before we started.

One last blow and my potato finally rolled across the line, beating Alan's by several feet. I handed the rope to Chris Peterson, who was almost hopping up and down with excitement, and went to look for my Heineken. The bottle was warm, so I returned to the bar for another. Looking back, I saw Chris's potato swing far too high and catch DJ in what politeness would call the upper thigh. He doubled over, only to be met with screams of laughter from his own side and yells to Chris to keep going from the other. I giggled and leaned against the bar to watch, pleased that such a simple child's game could work so well with a relatively sophisticated group of world travelers.

To my annoyance, Jerry Morrison stalked over and demanded a scotch and soda. He was dressed in Ralph Lauren khakis and a pressed white shirt, open at the collar to reveal a thick gold chain nestled like a snake in the forest of hair at his throat. Tonight, his hair was slicked back from his forehead, revealing just a touch of gray at the temples. He acknowledged my presence with a frown, his sharp little eyes taking in my beer and boobs at the same time.

"Stupid game."

"Oh, I don't know. It's pretty fun if you give it a try." I tried to maintain a pleasant expression and started edging away.

"You'd think for as much as this trip cost, they'd provide some real entertainment. Oh, come on!" this to the bartender. "Put some scotch in it! Here, give me that." He snatched the bottle from the startled man's hands, sloshed some soda from the glass into the sink and poured scotch until the glass overflowed.

"Pathetic," he muttered, wiping at the wet glass with a handful of napkins and taking a big gulp.

He caught me staring. "I know. You think I'm an asshole. I don't care."

I lifted my eyebrows in a judgmental, steely sort of expression that usually caused the teenage recipients to stop whatever they were doing and slink off. Jerry just grinned and took another swig.

"Did you know I'm a lawyer? In LA. Made full partner at thirty. Now I own my own firm. Clients coming out the wazoo, just lining up to consult me, and I charge 'em five hundred bucks an hour."

"Nice," I said, because he expected it. I was trying to envision clients coming out his wazoo. Not a good image, no matter what a wazoo was.

"You and your sister are nice-looking women," he said, pursing his lips as he tracked Kyla, who was now swinging the potato and laughing. "And that one really knows how to shake it. You should take some lessons from her."

My jaw dropped just a little, but I recovered quickly. "How many of those have you had?" I asked before I could stop myself.

He gave a shout of laughter. "Finally! Damn, it's hard to get a rise out of you. You've got that ice princess thing down pat. Can never tell what you're thinking."

I stared, not sure whether to laugh or stalk off. Or hit him.

"See? Even now, you probably want to hit me, but you're just staring like a fish. You ever think about going into law? You'd be great at negotiations. Or poker."

I took a deep breath, then a drink of my beer. "Is this what you do? Prod people to see their reactions?"

"It amuses me," he admitted. "And God knows I need some of that on this snooze cruise."

I thought about what Yvonne had said about him and decided there was no harm in doing a little prodding of my own. "Why did you come on this tour, anyway?" I asked. "You don't seem like a tour kind of guy." I carefully kept my tone neutral.

"What kind of guy do I seem like?" he said in a pseudo sexy voice, leaning toward me. Then, catching my look, he threw up his hands, slopping scotch onto my shoes. "Okay, okay. Don't slap me."

He took another sip. The Rolex on his wrist gleamed in the light. "No, this really isn't my thing. Egypt. Tours. Smelly old ladies. Jeez, what a nightmare."

"So?"

He narrowed his beady little eyes. "Can you keep a secret?"

"Probably not."

He grinned appreciatively. "There's a load of crap. Bet you

186

could keep a secret better than most people. But you're too smart to make a blind promise. I like that."

He looked around, as if noticing for the first time the steady stream of passengers lining up at the bar just behind us. He took my arm just behind the elbow, a macho gesture I particularly hate, and led me several paces away. I jerked my arm away, but it didn't seem to bother him.

"This might surprise you, but I'm divorced," he said with a little ironic gleam in his eye.

"No!" I replied, suddenly amused. I still distrusted him, of course, but apparently there was quite a bit more to Jerry than I'd originally thought. I hadn't anticipated the sense of humor for one thing.

"Twice. And willing to go for number three. Just say the word." He leered at me suggestively.

"My God, you're an ass!" I blurted out.

He seemed almost pleased. "I know! And I hear that more often than you might think. Anyway, I've done something that, in retrospect, perhaps wasn't the smartest thing I've ever done, so I decided this trip might help."

"You're running from the mob?"

"What? No! I'm a divorce lawyer, for Christ's sake. I don't launder money or organize hits or whatever. Jesus!"

I gave an apologetic shrug.

"No, the stupid thing I did was turn in Kathy's mother for tax evasion," he said glumly.

"What?"

"Yeah, I know. Not too bright. She's going to find out it was me, and even if she doesn't, she'll know it was me anyway.

187

I've got some contacts, and I found out the shit was going to hit the fan this week, so I decided that leaving the country would be a good idea."

"You don't think Kathy's going to be furious when she finds out? You think this trip will make up for it?" I asked.

"Oh, she'll be pissed all right. I can hear the ranting now. 'I'll never forgive you, Daddy. I'm never going to speak to you again, Daddy,'" he squeaked in a surprisingly accurate falsetto, then returned to his normal tone. "I should be so lucky. She'll be talking again as soon as she needs some money. I'm loaded. And she still has another year of college and then law school to get through. So I have a little leverage," he added cynically.

"Then why the trip?"

He sighed. "Postponing the inevitable mostly. Plus, it might get me some points with her. It's something she always wanted to do. See Egypt, I mean. This second-rate excursion was the only one I could find that started at the right time." He drained the rest of his scotch. "I don't exactly connect with her in daily life, if you know what I mean. And it does have the advantage of having us out of communication with the rest of the world. Very unlikely that she'll make the effort it would take to call home."

"But you were upset when you found out we didn't have Internet access." I didn't tell him how I knew it.

He didn't seem to notice. "Yeah, but that's because I'm watching my stocks. I've got a few tricky investments going. I've got a broker who has his instructions, but you don't get to where I am by trusting people." He looked across the room to where Lydia and Ben were now swinging potatoes and laughing.

"Look at those idiots. Smoking all the time. Don't even care that it's killing them and stinking up everything around them. And you know what? Every time I get a whiff, it just about kills me I want one so bad. Even after ten years."

"Why are you telling me this?" I finally asked.

He shrugged. "I figured you thought I was an asshole."

I considered. "And so you thought that telling me you hate tours and the people who take tours and that you're only here to bribe your daughter not to hate you because you ratted her mother out to the IRS for petty revenge would change my mind on that?"

"Exactly. Well, and to point out it was my patriotic duty to turn her in. I had to."

I started laughing. Across the room, the potato game was coming to an end and our group was splitting up, some leaving to go their rooms, a few returning to the bar or to our seats in the horseshoe. A disk jockey arrived and began setting up in the jumble of electronics behind the bar.

Jerry held up his empty glass. "Look at that. There must be a hole in the bottom of my glass. And in yours too." He took my empty bottle from my hand. "Can I buy you another?"

"They're free," I pointed out dryly. "But sure." And was rewarded with an unexpectedly sweet smile. Too bad he was so slimy that he practically left a shiny trail behind him.

He returned with the drinks just as the music was starting up. Handing me my beer, he said, "I don't dance. In case you were wanting to."

"Nope. Besides, you're old enough to be my father," I responded. "I wouldn't want you to break a hip."

"Ow! That was cold. And untrue. Very untrue. Maybe I will dance. Do you want to dance?"

"No, thank you. I don't dance with geezers."

Half-amused, half-annoyed, he was just opening his mouth to protest when Charlie de Vance tottered over. He was looking particularly snappy in red suspenders and a matching red bow tie.

"Dance, missy? My wife lets me loose on the single ladies before she'll dance with me, and I can't pass up a chance like that, now can I?"

"Yes, I'd love to," I said instantly. I turned to Jerry. "Here, hold my beer, will you? And don't spit in it."

Charlie looked a little shocked and kept glancing back at Jerry as he led me to the floor. "You don't think he would really spit in it, do you?"

"I'm sure he wouldn't," I reassured him. "But I'd just told him I didn't dance with older men." He looked at me enquiringly, and I added, "I didn't say anything about older gentlemen."

He laughed at that. "You're a smart one."

We began swaying back and forth to the music. He held me very stiffly and correctly at arm's length, and I saw Yvonne wink at me as we slowly crept by.

"Now be honest, Charlie," I said. "Did you want to dance or were you performing a social rescue?"

He grinned sheepishly up at me. "Bit of both maybe. But it's no chore on my part."

As the song ended, he led me to where Yvonne waited, and I sat beside her.

"I'll get your drink back, shall I?" asked Charlie, and slipped away.

Yvonne patted my hand. "Dreadful interference on my part. But I couldn't imagine anyone wanting to talk to that man for as long as you did. Besides he had the look of someone on the verge of drunkenness. I definitely noticed him swaying."

"It was very nice of you. And Charlie."

"Yes, Charlie's very special." Her expression softened a moment, but then she tapped my arm smartly. "So, did you find out anything of interest?" she said with a gleam in her eye.

I suddenly had the feeling that, without knowing it, I'd become her own personal private detective. Or her pawn. I wasn't sure I liked how easily she had manipulated me, but I had to give her credit for intelligence and determination.

"I know what he told me," I said slowly. "It sounded true, but that doesn't make it true."

She nodded. "Good. The minute you realize that anyone could be lying, you have an edge."

"He said this trip is a bribe to his daughter to make up for something unpleasant he did or is doing to her mother."

"And you believed him?"

"I did. It was pretty unflattering to himself. He had no reason to lie about it. It doesn't mean it's his only reason for being here, but it rang true."

"Well, we'll keep him in mind, but I think we can safely move him to the back burner." She clicked her tongue. "And he was my best suspect, too. It's always easy to believe the worst about the unpleasant ones, isn't it? So, we move on. What about your Mr. Stratton?"

"Alan?" I asked uneasily. Her question made me realize how much I didn't want to suspect him.

Her expression told me she knew what I was thinking. So much for the fabled ice princess look that Jerry seemed to think I had. "There's certainly more to him than meets the eye. A single man, alone on a trip like this, especially at his age. Have you noticed how he manages to talk with everyone and yet not really join any group?"

I had noticed, but I hadn't thought much about it. Even now I could see him in conversation with DJ and Nimmi. DJ was leaning forward eagerly, moving his hands as he talked. Beside him, Nimmi sat upright, fastidious and delicate, like a little cat next to a Saint Bernard.

We sat in silence for a moment.

"I wish I knew what was going on," I said finally. "But I don't know what I can do about it."

She gave the smallest of shrugs. "Murder is the business of every human being. We all can and should do whatever is possible. For you and me, that might be just the smallest task of keeping our ears open." She smiled and patted my hand. "Find out what you can, but don't let it spoil your trip. And now, I see Charlie coming this way. I'd prefer not to speak about this in front of him. It upsets him."

"Of course. He's a very thoughtful man."

"Do you know, I've been in love with him since high school?"

"You missed a lot of time together."

"Not wasted time, though. We each had lovely lives. And I doubt we would have been good for each other any earlier. I was too driven. But it's very good to be together at the end."

Charlie returned with the drinks, glancing over his shoulder to where Jerry was trying to talk to Kyla. She looked like she was smelling something bad. Charlie said, "I got you a fresh beer. No sense in taking chances."

Thursday, Valley of the Kings

Travel through the desert wasteland to the Valley of the Kings, final resting place of the pharaohs of Egypt. Here you will walk the dry white hills and descend deep into the mysteries hidden for countless ages beneath the desert floor. Visit the famous tomb of the boy king Tutankhamen and see the final resting place of Thutmose III. Then on to the Valley of the Queens where the royal wives and children were buried. After lunch, visit the world famous alabaster shop and finish your day at Deir el-Bahari, the enduring temple of Queen Hatshepsut, the only queen to claim the title of pharaoh in Egypt's long history.

—WorldPal pamphlet

Chapter 11

TOMBS AND TROUBLES

I stopped at the front desk the first thing in the morning. We were now docked at Luxor, our final destination. A few people loitered in the lobby, waiting for the bell that signaled breakfast. Fiona and Flora stood nearby, peering through the doorway into the next cruise liner and whispering together. I took a quick peek between their fuzzy little heads to see what was so interesting, but didn't notice anything except another gold and crystal lobby. The *Nile Lotus* was the closest tour boat to the shore, indication that we weren't going anywhere that day.

I turned to the desk clerk.

"Good morning, madam," she said in perfect English. "May I help you?"

"Yes, the safe in my room isn't working. It isn't staying closed, and I'd like to leave some things in it."

"I am so sorry, madam. We will repair it as soon as possible. What is your room number, please?"

"211. Is there any way it could be fixed before eight-thirty? That's when we're leaving."

"I will ask, but our handyman does not come on duty until that time. I am very sorry."

I nodded. The breakfast bell rang and people began streaming down the steps. Kyla appeared, wearing white linen pants with a lime sleeveless shell and matching lime flats. White linen. Pressed. She'd sent a sack of things to the ship's laundry service the day we arrived on board, but I hadn't seen what was in it. Her hair was pulled into an elegant twist, fastened with a silver filigreed clasp. I glanced down at my jeans, sneakers, and oversized oxford shirt. Another day of Beauty and the Frump. Pointless to get angry.

She joined me. "Can they fix it?"

"Unlikely. She said they'd try, but I don't think there will be time before we leave."

"Well, be sure to take your passport with you. And the plane tickets. Oh, and that necklace. I don't care what you say, I know that thing is worth a fortune. And what about your iPod?"

"Yes, Mom," I said sarcastically, pausing to let Fiona and Flora precede us down the steps. Never get between two old ladies and their chow was my motto. Besides, this way if they fell, they wouldn't take me down with them.

At breakfast time, the dining room was brighter and less formal. The buffet was set up at one side of the room, loaded with an amazing variety of fruits, cereals, rolls, and pastries. Steaming silver serving dishes contained eggs, sausages, bacon, and oatmeal. Once again, a chef stood behind a set of gas burners, ready to cook an omelet to order. Several people waited in line in front of giant silver urns of coffee and hot water, looking sleepy. The room was filled with the sound of voices and the clinking of flatware on china.

I started to limit myself to a couple of crusty rolls, then changed my mind and loaded up with a little bit of everything. Screw my weight, I thought, I'm on vacation. I balanced a glass of juice on one unoccupied inch of space on the rim of my plate and joined the group at one of our three tables. DJ, Nimmi, Keith, and Dawn were already well into breakfast and greeted us enthusiastically. Ben and Lydia were finished and still sipping coffee. To my surprise, their niece, Jane, was present, listlessly picking apart a roll. She looked miserable.

Kyla took the seat beside me and set her plate down. It contained a single croissant and piece of pineapple. I took a sip of my juice and then started in on my cheese and bacon omelet. It was marvelous. Kyla cast a disapproving eye over my breakfast, half disdainful, half jealous. I needed a distraction before she could start in on its nutritional value.

"Are you going to come with us today?" I asked brightly, turning to Jane, who was sitting to my right.

Instead of answering, Jane shot a nervous look at Lydia, who pursed her lips thoughtfully.

"You know, there's no reason you shouldn't. It might do you good to get off the ship," Lydia said.

Was it my imagination, or did Jane give a little shiver? It might just have been the illness, but she looked almost frightened. Why should she be scared to get on a tour bus, escorted by a tour guide, tour group, and armed guard, to visit the Valley of the Kings, one of the most public and busy tourist destinations in the world?

"I just don't feel up to it," she said finally. "I think I'll just stay here and read. I can go on the deck and get some fresh air if I feel like it later."

"It's a shame that you've missed so much of the trip," said Nimmi sympathetically. "Perhaps you should let DJ take a look at you. He is a very good doctor. Very good. And he would not mind at all."

Nimmi was busy cutting up several sausages as she spoke, and it looked as though she had already put away a pile of scrambled eggs and a cup of oatmeal. How in the world did she stay so tiny? Just then, DJ reached his fork and speared three or four pieces from her plate and popped them into his mouth. Ah.

"Yes, I would be happy to review your medicines. What are they giving you? Antibiotics? Those might be making you feel bad, you know," he said.

"That's very nice of you," said Jane, "but really, I'm fine. Just a little weak still. I'm sure I'll be able to go out tomorrow. The doctors said to expect I'd be tired."

"Ah, well, then, I'm sure you are right. But let me know if you start to feel worse. I am glad to help. Very glad."

"You know, you absolutely have to come back some other time to see everything you've missed," said Keith. "Nothing in the world compares to Egypt. Nothing. In fact, this is my third visit, and second time to take this same tour."

Everyone turned to him in surprise. Other than his brief impassioned outburst at the Temple of Horus, it was the first time Keith had volunteered anything more than a quiet good morning. And he'd been to Egypt three times? Very interesting, although I was wondering why anyone would do the same tour more than once. Surely there were other things to do in Egypt.

As if reading my thoughts, he said, "You see something new every visit. I had a different guide last time, and let me tell you, Anni is better by far. Much more knowledgeable, and better organized. Last time we had a British man named Raymond. I'm pretty sure he was reciting from a guidebook half the time, and just making up things the rest." He shook his head. "Friendly, though. And he did know where all the bars were." He smiled at the memory.

Dawn lifted one perfectly waxed eyebrow above icy eyes. "Yes, do tell us more about your honeymoon with your first wife. I'm sure we're all fascinated."

Keith froze and then went beet red. For a moment, an awful silence descended on the table, and then DJ exploded into a loud guffaw and slapped Keith on the back.

"Oh man, you have done it now. Run. Run while you can," he shouted. Heads at other tables turned in our direction.

We all howled with laughter, even Dawn, although I wasn't convinced she was as amused as the rest of us. And it was a good cue to leave to get ready for the day. But I couldn't help glancing back at the table where Jane still sat with Ben and Lydia. Their heads were together and they were talking earnestly. And they were not smiling.

To my surprise, the repairman was in our room when we popped up after breakfast. He was just closing the door to the closet.

"Ah, good morning," he said cheerfully. "I have just fixed the safe. It was only the backup battery. Sometimes they go out."

"Fabulous," said Kyla.

"Thank you very much," I added.

We hastily filled the tiny space with our passports and valuables—including the necklace—and then ran back to join the group in the lobby. For once, everyone appeared more or less on time, even Flora and Fiona.

The drive to the Valley of the Kings took less than an hour. On the way, we saw the house that Howard Carter built during the years that he was excavating the tomb of King Tut, a sand-colored building on a hill, its domes and arched windows making it look very exotic. A couple of stunted trees stood near the walls, monuments to someone's stubborn efforts with a watering can. No other vegetation could be seen anywhere in the relentless barrenness. I knew the British used to, and in fact still did, abandon Egypt in the summer months when the desert heat became unbearable. Even now, in late March, the temperatures were already rising and reflecting off the rock. Someone local must be keeping the trees alive.

I was almost beside myself with excitement as the white hills rose up on either side of us until they became low cliffs. Holes and doors dotted the chalky white rock, evidence of unlikely habitation in that parched land. Were they storage caves or dwellings, I wondered, nose pressed almost onto the glass of my window. Inside the bus, a faint air-conditioned breeze streamed over us, laden with the smell of upholstery and rubber and bus. Our insulated little world, traveling in our tourist bubble to the unimaginable past of pharaohs and mummies and death.

Or not. The bubble part was real enough, but the Valley of the Kings was firmly anchored in the twenty-first century.

A huge parking lot, already half filled with tour buses, guarded the entrance of the valley; it was followed closely by a large modern visitor center, complete with queues of fat, sunburned German tourists and the usual phalanx of vendors with their depressingly vast and cheap assortment of crap. The same crap we'd seen at every single monument we'd visited. If it weren't impossible, I'd have bet the same twenty or thirty vendors were tearing down their stalls each day and scampering ahead of our bus to set up again at our next stop.

We disembarked and formed our own queue behind Hello Kitty, winding our way nonstop through the center. The walls were lined with timelines and photographs of archaeological digs. Charlie tried to pause to read about what we were to see, but the rest of us pressed forward, eager to see the tombs for ourselves. I did notice with some malevolent pleasure that Kathy had bright red shoulders under her most unsuitable tank top. She must have been sunning herself on the top deck of the *Nile Lotus* yesterday afternoon for hours to have obtained that particular shade of scarlet.

On the other side of the center, we boarded tiny trams, the kind you see at very small carnivals. Puffing, they hauled us up a fairly steep narrow road to the mouth of the high valley that held the tombs of the pharaohs. Ahead, a naturally pyramid-shaped mountain rose into the deep blue sky, and all around cliffs shot up out of the white dusty ground, becoming steeper and higher the farther we went.

We hopped off and Anni handed out colorful tickets good for three tombs.

"Only three?" asked Jerry Morrison in disbelief.

"We don't have time for more than that," said Anni with

a smile. "Remember, we go from here to lunch and then to the alabaster factory. Now, if you all will follow me, I will show you which are the most interesting tombs, and then we will meet back here to take the tram to the buses. Everyone look at your watches. Two hours. Meet here at noon. All right?"

Jerry and his daughter instantly veered off to the left, scorning to stay with a tour group. Kathy was still limping just a little.

"Good riddance," muttered Ben. "Maybe they'll fall in a pit."

"Ben!" said Lydia, automatically reproving.

The rest of us obediently followed as Anni pointed out the most famous tombs. KV 17, the tomb of Seti I, who built the great temple at Abydos. KV 11, Ramses III, Egypt's last great pharaoh. And of course, KV 62—Tutankhamen, the boy king whose tomb was the archaeological find of the century and the inspiration for dozens of movies about curses and mummies.

"I know you will all want to see this tomb, but it is really not very impressive. There is nothing left inside. It is very small and empty," said Anni, without much hope.

I wondered if she really thought she could persuade us. We would all wait however long it took to see the most famous tomb in the world. No matter how unimpressive or disappointing, we had not come all this way to walk past the location of Howard Carter's triumph, the place where hidden treasure beyond our imaginings had been discovered, and where a mummy's curse had its beginnings. Almost in unison, our entire group stampeded down the dusty path to the entrance to Tut's tomb.

Twenty minutes later, we were back on the path. "We should have listened to her," said Kyla. "Pretty lame."

"No it wasn't!" I protested. "It was fabulous. Anyway, we had to see for ourselves. And it was pretty cool anyway. So small, so secret. It's what kept it safe all these centuries."

She did not look convinced.

"Now where to?"

I consulted a pamphlet I'd picked up in the visitor center. "Seti I. This way."

We passed a couple of openings and joined a line of tourists who were inching forward toward a rectangular opening in the side of the white rock.

Kyla clicked her tongue impatiently. "Why this one? There are a couple over there without the tourist hordes."

"There's a reason for that. This is the longest tomb in the valley and has the most and best paintings. Besides, it's Seti I." I grinned.

"How do you know this shit? And who the hell is Seti?"

"You know, the pharaoh from *The Mummy*. The guy who got stabbed? The fat dude who had his concubine painted so no one could touch her?"

She gave me a pitying look. "You are so pathetic. I would honestly be ashamed if I knew what you were talking about."

"So you do remember."

A group of Germans lined up behind us, and behind them Alan Stratton stepped quietly into line. As usual, he was alone, although I'd seen him talking with DJ and Nimmi earlier. I turned back, quickly enough to alert Kyla.

She leaned out of line, saw Alan, and waved. "Come up

here with us," she shouted, earning disapproving glares from a dozen Germans.

"Thanks, I'm good here," he declined.

She turned back with a little pout. "You know, sometimes I think that man is completely antisocial. Or gay. Do you think he's gay?"

I did not. "Maybe he just didn't want to cut into the line."

"We could go back and join him," she suggested, but I grabbed her arm.

"No! Just leave it alone. He's a big boy. He can stand in line by himself."

"Do you think he's following us around?" she asked thoughtfully.

I looked at her in exasperation. "Is it hard carrying around that big an ego? I mean, do you have trouble getting through doors or does it fold up for traveling?"

She just grinned. "I have a healthy amount of self-respect and I'm not ashamed of it. But I didn't actually mean that for a change. I meant, literally, do you think he's following us around. He's sort of . . . there, every time we turn around."

"All of us are there, every time we turn around. We're on a fucking tour, for God's sake."

She raised her eyebrows. "What kind of language is that in a cemetery? Anyway, you're so busy trying not to have the hots for him that you're not paying attention. Look around. No one else from the group is in line here. They probably figured out shorter lines were better."

"Fiona and Flora are up there ahead of the Japanese." I pointed to a pair of garish floral polyester shirts. "Besides, this tomb will be worth it," I promised, although I had no idea whether it would be or not.

"That's not the point. We have to stand in line for some creepy hole in the ground. It might as well be this one. What *is* the point is that ever since Millie got murdered, neither of us can swing a dead cat without hitting Alan Stratton. Which would be okay, except I don't think he's interested in hitting on me. Us, I mean," she added hastily.

I had a hard time choosing which statement to be most outraged over. "Creepy hole in the ground?" But was she right about Alan? Ordinarily, I'd have to say Kyla's instincts were spot on when it came to men. I thought about the few moments we'd shared on Elephantine Island and my little gold pyramid. Had the small spark I'd felt then been only on my side? Probably.

The line inched forward until we could see the entrance, a rough rectangle cut almost horizontally into the gentle slope of the hill. A steep stairway descended into blackness and I felt a shiver of excitement. I wished I could push all these pesky Germans aside and rush down the steps.

However, we eventually reached the doorway, and once inside, our eyes adjusted to the dim lighting. The stairway transitioned from modern concrete to ancient stone, cut and smoothed by hand and now a little worn, not by sandaled feet, but by the Nikes of countless tourists. A steep corridor followed the steps, walls lined with paintings of red-and-black vultures holding large feathers in their claws beneath cartouches and glyphs that offered protections and instructions for the dead. The cryptic and beautiful symbols had existed in darkness for over three thousand years until the early 1800s, when an Italian archeologist named Giovanni Belzoni made a discovery that was as famous in its time as the discovery of the tomb of Tutankhamen would be a century later. Of course, archaeology wasn't quite as sophisticated back then, and many of the friezes had been damaged by water and smoke. Some were even cut off the walls and sent to museums across Europe. Nevertheless, what remained was breathtakingly beautiful.

The tomb grew hotter and stuffier the farther we went. Did the fierce Egyptian sun make its presence felt even through yards of limestone and sand, or was it the body heat and breath of countless tourists that gave the air the humid, unpleasant feel of a cheap sauna? We moved on. I wished my memory were better. I'd studied what I was going to see, but now, confronted by the fading paintings, I could no longer remember which was the Book of the Dead, the Book of Gates, or the Litany of Ra.

At the bottom of another short flight of stairs, we passed through an archway and unexpectedly found ourselves stepping onto a wooden bridge. The floor fell away into darkness on either side. I balked and clutched my purse. Saying I did not like heights was sort of like saying mice did not like snakes.

Kyla moved forward without me, then turned back. She took one look at my face and rolled her eyes. "Oh, get a grip," she said. "It's only about fifteen feet high."

I gingerly took a step forward and peered over the edge. She was right. Fifteen or twenty feet to the bare stone below, although that was bad enough. The bridge was a wooden plank walkway lined with a flimsy railing atop matchstick posts that were supported by a couple of very thin cables. A murmur from the people behind me shamed me into taking a hesitant step forward. The bridge seemed sturdy enough. At least it didn't move. I stayed right in the middle, sweaty hands fastened on my bag.

"I wonder what this room was for," said Kyla, leaning over the railing with careless ease.

"They call it the well chamber." I was pleased that my voice sounded only slightly squeaky.

"Dear God, did you memorize the guidebook? Besides, it doesn't look like there was ever any water here."

I made the mistake of glancing down again to see and felt almost sick. I quickly focused on the back of Kyla's shirt and took a deep shaky breath. I heard her snort.

"You're doing fine," she said, encouraging, if somewhat patronizingly.

We were just passing the midpoint of the bridge, my eyes already focused on the far side, when the lights went out. I froze with terror. Someone, I hope not me, gave a little scream, and everyone else began talking at once. I couldn't remember how far the edges were. At first, everything seemed pitch black, the kind of black you see only in caves when the guide turns off the lights and tells you to try to see your own hand in front of your face. I shut my eyes and couldn't tell the difference. Gradually, however, I could make out the dimmest of dim lights behind us, streaming down from a higher corridor. People were passing the word back, and soon we heard shouting in Arabic. I could feel my heart hammering in my chest.

"Well, this is fun," said Kyla. She sounded more annoyed than anxious.

People were starting to shift and move around. Probably no one was thrilled to be stuck on the bridge, suspended over a dark chasm. A couple of people moved past me back toward the light, and I was forced to inch a little closer to the rail to let them pass. Just then, someone pushed me hard.

"Hey!" I gasped as I fell back against the rail. It was more solid than it looked, thank goodness. Besides the fear of falling, my main emotion was outrage that anyone would be rude enough to shove.

But I knew I was in trouble when that same someone grabbed my purse and almost yanked it off my arm. I was able to clutch it to me just in time, mostly because my arm was threaded through the strap. I jerked back hard. A second later, I heard an odd ripping sound and felt a small sharp pain along my forearm. My purse instantly felt empty, and I heard the sound of small objects falling to the stone. I let go of the bag and struck out as hard as I could. My fist caught someone with a glancing blow. It was promptly returned and with far better aim. A sharp punch connected solidly with my stomach. I staggered back against the rail again, gasping for breath.

"Jocelyn!" I heard Kyla shouting a few paces away.

The attacker kicked my feet out from under me, and I spun and fell hard. The cables that made up the lower part of the railing bowed alarmingly, and my feet slid off the bridge. I screamed. In the utter darkness, I clutched at the cables, all my attention focused on not sliding under the wire into the dark pit below. My attacker kicked again, narrowly missing my face.

Kyla began shouting for help. People behind us milled about in the darkness as the tourists farther down the passage decided to panic and run up toward the light. On the plus side, the flood of people pushing past swept away my attacker. On the minus, they jostled me even farther toward the drop. My feet dangled helplessly in thin air, and I struggled to pull myself up, clawing at the planks. Someone stepped on my hand, and I almost went over the side, but I managed to grab at a cable. I screamed again.

The lights came on, revealing pandemonium. A stream of legs and sneakers passed before my eyes as people charged toward the exit. No one noticed me. I struggled to get my knee back over the edge. The cable was cutting into my palms. I didn't think I could hold on another moment.

And then Alan appeared. With one smooth motion, he grabbed me by the arms and hoisted me back to safety.

I clung to him. He folded me in his arms and held me tightly while I trembled. The rest of the people behind us streamed past, until the two of us were left alone in the middle of the bridge.

"Are you all right? What happened?" he demanded, tipping his head to peer into my face.

"Someone stole my purse and then tried to push me off the bridge," I managed. I was trying hard not to burst into tears. "And they hit me," I added, lip quivering.

A muscle in his jaw tightened. "Who did? How many were there?"

I wanted to say five or six. A dozen. All heavyweight wrestlers.

"Just one," I admitted. "I think. I couldn't see anything."

I heard footsteps and turned my head to see Kyla hurrying back down the steps. She looked pale even in the dim light.

"They pushed me right up the stairs," she said indignantly. "I had to run with them or they would have trampled me." She scanned the two of us up and down. "Are you all right? One of you is bleeding," she announced.

Startled, I looked down. Sure enough, there was blood on Alan's nice white shirt. Had he scraped his hands when he pulled me up? I reached for his hand and then saw my sleeve. Neatly slit from elbow to wrist, it was stained bright red. I pulled the fabric aside and saw a hairline slice across my skin. I hadn't even felt it, but now it began to hurt at once.

"A knife did that. Or a box cutter," said Alan grimly, holding my arm and examining the wound. "And razor sharp. They must have tried to cut your purse. Thank God it's not deep. But we need to get you to a doctor."

"But my stuff," I protested. "Look!"

The contents of my purse lay scattered down in the bottom of the well chamber. Alan leaned over the rail and I resisted the urge to pull him back. We could see my bag lying crumpled on the stone below, surrounded by scattered small items. My wallet lay a couple of feet away, unopened. But everything was well beyond our reach from the bridge.

Alan looked grim. "I know it was dark, but did you notice anything at all? Could you tell what he was wearing? Was he tall or short? Did he say anything?"

I thought hard. "He didn't say anything, and I couldn't see him. But I don't think he was very big," I said at last. "I tried to hit him, and I'm pretty sure I caught his shoulder. He just didn't seem very solid. But it happened so fast. I'm just really not sure."

He pulled me close again, his arm wrapped around me protectively. To my dismay, I felt a big tear well up and trickle down my cheek, followed closely by another. I pulled away abruptly, turning so he wouldn't see. I pulled up the bottom of my shirt so I could wipe my eyes. He pulled me back gently and pressed my head to his chest. He smelled so good. I couldn't help myself, I started bawling.

The Egyptian authorities arrived at last. Alan took charge, pointing first to my arm, then to my scattered belongings fifteen feet below. He started explaining, first in English, then in broken Arabic. Before long, he and the three Egyptians were talking at the same time, gesticulating wildly.

Kyla tried to lead me away. "Let Alan handle it," she said. "Let's go find you a Band-Aid. A big one."

Alan looked over his shoulder. "Wait just a minute and I'll go with you."

"Well, at least let's go sit down on the steps," Kyla urged.

I knew she was right, but I felt unaccountably stubborn. "But I haven't seen the burial chamber yet."

Her jaw dropped a little. "You've got to be kidding me."

"No, I'm not," I said. "Look, once we leave, you know they won't let us back in. Let's just dash down there while nobody's looking."

It was true. None of the men were paying any attention to us at all. And we were so close. "You're insane," she hissed under her breath, but she followed me to the other side of the bridge.

We hurried through two more chambers, down a short flight of stairs, and at last came to the burial chamber with its arched ceiling, painted midnight blue and decorated with hundreds of characters in white. A miniature zoo of hippos, lions, crocodiles, and oxen mingled with people. All stood in profile, some fully human and some with the heads of animals. Stars

213

and glyphs dotted the grid etched on the surface, full of unde-cipherable meaning. I'd never seen anything so beautiful.

The walls were just as fabulous, painted from floor to ceiling in reds, golds, tans, and blues. A beautiful woman floated on a boat with two trees and two attendants. Guard-ing all, the goddess Isis spread her great wings protectively near the ceiling. The striking colors glowed like jewels on dark velvet. I could not take it all in. It would be impossible to see and appreciate everything in a month, much less a few stolen moments.

"Well," said Kyla finally. "All right. You were right. There, I said it. It was worth the wait. And very clever of you, I might add, getting rid of all the other tourists, so we could have a private viewing."

I grinned. My arm was stinging, but it had almost stopped bleeding and I didn't care. She was right. It was worth it all. We moved together into one of the little side chambers where one wall was decorated with a figure of an enormous cow sur-rounded by tiny people.

"The Book of the Heavenly Cow," I announced.

"You're kidding, right? A holy cow?"

We laughed together, and I scrubbed my cheeks to wipe away any remains of tears. Sounds echoed down from above, thumps and clanks, voices, sometimes in a low murmur, some-times raised as though shouting orders. The air was still stuffy and humid, even without the crowd. Now that I was over the first shock, my mind was racing, and I didn't like my own thoughts.

"You know," I said slowly, "whoever tried to take my purse had to be someone who was fairly close to us in the line."

"Well, duh. Oh, I see. You mean one of the tourists? Or maybe a thief disguised as a tourist?"

"Maybe. Probably. But what if it was one of us? What if it was Alan?" My voice broke as I said it. I didn't want that to be true.

Kyla looked at me, appalled. "But he was helping you. He pulled you up. And you said yourself the person was short."

"Yeah, I know. But that was just an impression. It was so dark, I just can't be sure. And Kyla, who else could it be? It had to be someone fairly close in line. A common thief couldn't have been hiding on that bridge. And that someone picked me. Out of all the people on the bridge, they picked me."

"I'm sure it was just random. You were there, you had a purse. It could have been any other woman just as easily."

"Maybe. But I bet I'm the only one in the entire valley who owns an extremely beautiful, very mysterious Egyptian necklace."

Her eyes widened. "Your necklace! Did they steal your necklace?"

"No! I'm not retarded," I snorted. "I wasn't carrying it in my purse—I left it in the safe. You saw me put it in," I reminded her.

She breathed a sigh of relief. "Then what did they take?"

We looked at each other. "I guess we'll see when the Egyptians gather everything up. But it looked like the wallet was down there in the well, and that was the only thing that had anything valuable, if you call about one hundred dollars worth of Egyptian pounds valuable."

"Well, it might be valuable to someone. I mean, the thief

can't have meant to drop it over the edge. He probably didn't expect you to fight back."

We stood in silence for a few minutes and then slowly moved back into the main chamber with its arched ceiling. My arm was aching now for real.

"It's ridiculous to suspect Alan," said Kyla finally. "I don't believe it."

"I don't want to believe it either," I agreed. But the doubt lingered. "Let's go back. They must be done by now."

We were just starting up the low steps in the next chamber when we heard footsteps drawing closer, and Alan appeared, looking harried. He stared at us in disbelief.

"We thought you'd gone up to the surface. Everyone has been looking for you."

I searched his face, but all I saw was concern and maybe a little exasperation.

Kyla gave him a brilliant smile. "You told us to wait for you. You didn't expect us to just stand there doing nothing."

"And I had to see it," I added apologetically.

He glanced around at the brilliant paintings and just shook his head. "Come on."

And that was pretty much the end of our visit to the Valley of the Kings. Once on the surface, I was dragged to a very nice first-aid building where they sprayed some stinging disinfectant on my arm and then wrapped it up like a mummy. Kyla disappeared while I was getting patched up, but returned after a few minutes bearing a t-shirt covered with hieroglyphics. "Twenty pounds," she said triumphantly. "I haggled."

I was just putting it on and trying to straighten my hair,

when Anni brought in a distraught Fiona, followed closely by Flora.

Anni rattled off something in Arabic, and the nurse put a protective arm around Fiona's shoulders and led her to a chair. To my surprise, Fiona had blood on one sleeve.

Anni closed her eyes briefly, and then joined Kyla and me. "How are you doing? I hope your arm does not hurt too much."

"No, it was just a scratch," I reassured her, then looked over at the sisters. "What happened to them?"

"Fiona fell on some stairs and scraped up her hands."

"Probably in that stampede," said Kyla. "I almost fell myself."

"Probably. But she fell again on the way here. I am worried about the two of them." She bit her lip and lowered her voice. "I am not sure they are really well enough to have made a trip like this one."

She wasn't going to get any argument from any of us on that one.

At that moment, Flora looked over at me like a little owlet, all eyes and glasses. Her mouth formed a perfect circle as she gazed at my bandaged arm.

"Aren't you on our tour, dear?" she asked. "What happened to your poor arm?"

I did not quite know how to respond to this. Too many details would either frighten or confuse her. After a pause, I just said, "I got pushed and fell when the lights went out in the tomb."

She drew in a quick breath. "That's what happened to Foney, too. My sister," she added by way of explanation. "We're traveling together. On a boat."

217

"Us, too," I said, nodding. Poor old thing. We'd been to-gether for a week, and she didn't even recognize me. I hoped that Fiona wasn't as bad off and was looking after her.

She smiled vaguely at me and wandered back over to her sister. An Egyptian official entered the room with a se-curity guard and joined us. He carried a paper bag and held it out to me.

"We have retrieved your belongings. Would you be so good as to examine them and let us know if anything is miss-ing?" he asked in flawless English. His accent was British.

I took the bag and emptied it on the examining table be-hind me. My purse was there, sliced right through the side. I looked at the thick leather and felt a chill. That could so easily have been my arm. I picked up the wallet and opened it. Cash, my health card, and my driver's license were still there. Lip balm, tissues, tickets for the tomb entrance, tic tacs, it was all there. I looked up, puzzled.

"I think that everything is here."

The official relaxed and smiled. "Very good. And your injury?"

"It's nothing," I answered firmly. The last thing I wanted was to get caught up in some huge investigation. I just wanted to get on with the tour. Fortunately, that seemed to be what everyone wanted.

"I want to assure you that we will pursue this matter most diligently. And more security guards will be posted. This is not something usual here. In fact, it has never happened before."

"I'm sure that's true," I reassured him. "Can we go?"

He looked so relieved that I wasn't going to make a fuss that I thought he was going to hug me. Fortunately he restrained himself. "Of course. I wish you a wonderful trip through our country. I hope this has not tainted your experience."

"Not at all."

On the way out of the valley, we stopped at an alabaster factory, or what Anni referred to as a factory. In fact, it was a small one-story building made of cinder blocks. Covering one wall, a garish painting of questionable artistic merit depicted a plane and several oddly proportioned people.

"The painting indicates the owner is very devout and has made the trip to Mecca," said Anni as the bus rolled to a stop. "Moreover, it indicates his success in the community because he was able to make the trip by airplane."

A few paces from the bus, several men sat on cinder blocks in the dust. They talked and laughed with each other until we drew near, then fell silent, eyes lowered. The owner came out and greeted us, gave a brief history of alabaster, and then had one of the men hold up a half-completed piece destined to become a vase. The yellow dusty lump of rock was not what I expected at all.

"This is hand-carved alabaster," the owner said, holding it up so that the light filtered through the stone. "You see how fine and translucent it is. The unevenness of the surface is how you can tell it was made by hand. This," he said, holding up another vase, of similar size, "was made by a machine. Both are very beautiful," he added quickly, "but very different."

We looked at the two vases. I could tell the hand-carved piece was supposed to be more highly prized, more authentic, but for once in my life I wasn't drawn to the most expensive item in the shop. The machine-made vase was smooth and polished, the grain of the stone visible, the translucent quality far stronger. I was so disappointed in myself. It was like seeing an authentic Picasso next to a Monet print and secretly preferring the print.

Inside, the shop was bright and airy, walls lined with shelves holding every possible form in alabaster. Carvings of Egyptian cats, of Anubis, of the Eye of Horus. Small pyramids, large pyramids, and dozens of canopic jars topped with scarab beetles or falcon heads. The Peterson boys were frozen in front of one item, pointing and giggling until their mother actually slapped the backs of both red heads and shooed them away. Curious, I went to look. A huge alabaster phallus lay on a wooden stand. Ben Carpenter caught sight of it and rushed over to get Lydia. They both burst into giggles.

Jerry Morrison ambled over, curious. Taking one look at it, he caught my eye and said, "Yeah. That's about the right size."

I snorted, and Lydia shot him a look of deep loathing, but Ben gave a grin. "I don't know, mate. Australians are a good deal larger than that little thing."

"It's big enough to knock both of you upside the head. Men!" Lydia said, appealing to me.

"I know."

I joined Kyla, who was looking at some small bowls. She glanced up at me. "These would be perfect for ice cream. I wonder if you can put them in the dishwasher."

"I doubt it. They're really soft stone."

"Well, I'm going to ask that guy over there." She gestured to one of the salesmen.

"Somehow, he doesn't look like the kind of guy that runs his alabaster through the rinse cycle."

220

She looked at him, a young man who seemed a little over-whelmed by all of us swarming around the floor. He had one hand near his nose as if he was thinking about going for the gold. "Hmm, you might be right. I'll ask Anni."

DJ called to Nimmi in a loud voice from across the room and pointed out a set of four large canopic jars. She joined him and looked down at the little collection doubtfully.

"But they are perfect. Look how large they are," he was saying.

I frowned. "Look, there he goes again. He's going to buy those."

Kyla glanced over at him. "What is he going to do with all that junk? And those jars are just morbid. I know they haven't actually been used, but they still creep me out."

"I guess you could put anything in them. Flour, sugar. They'd be heavy as hell, though."

She set the bowl down with a bang. "That's it! That's what he's doing."

I looked at her blankly. "Buying kitchen storage?"

"No, idiot!" She took my arm and pulled me into a corner. Lowering her voice, she said, "He's going to try to smuggle something out. He's buying all that crap to hide the one or two real thingies that he's smuggling."

"That's ridiculous."

"Is it? Think about it. He gets up to customs with a whole carry-on full of cheap souvenirs. The customs guy is going to take a quick look, check out one or two crappy plaster statues and a plastic pyramid, and pass him through without a second glance."

I tried to find a flaw in her logic, but couldn't. "Okay.

221

That's actually a brilliant thought. It would work perfectly as long as he didn't seem nervous, or do something to make them take a closer look."

"Exactly!"

"Except for one thing. Where is he supposed to get the authentic stuff?"

"Oh." She pursed her lips together. "I see what you mean. Wait. Mohammad!"

"Mohammad?"

"Sure. He's been awfully suspicious lately. Coming with us when he wasn't supposed to. That weird phone call you heard. And he's always coming and going without a word. I mean, for example, where is he now?"

We both looked around. Sure enough, Mohammad was nowhere to be seen.

"He might just be out at the bus or talking with those stone carvers out front," I suggested. "And I'm not even positive that was him on the phone back in Cairo."

"I bet it was. And maybe he's out there now receiving stolen property. Maybe real canopic jars. He'll pass them over to DJ later. DJ will have a receipt showing he bought canopic jars. Who would be able to tell?"

"What are you whispering about?" asked a voice.

Kyla gave a little squeak, and we both jumped. Alan had somehow appeared out of nowhere. I looked down at his feet. He was wearing tan Docksiders, perfect for sneaking around.

He raised his eyebrows. "My God, you two look guilty. What are you up to?"

"Not creeping around, listening to other people's conversations," said Kyla, a little tartly. Handsome guy or no, she didn't like being made to look foolish.

"I didn't hear what you were talking about, although now I'm curious," he answered. Seeing our expressions, he threw up his hands. "Don't worry, I'm not asking!" He turned to me. "So, are you buying anything?"

I shook my head. "I don't think so. We decided nothing is dishwasher safe, and I already have a giant alabaster dung beetle."

"I guessed as much," he answered with a grin.

A loud crash made us jump. We turned to see Fiona and Flora standing over the remains of a very large alabaster horse. Its body was snapped right off its legs, and the head rested several feet away. Chris Peterson stooped to pick up the little head, then with a quick glance to see if anyone was watching, slipped it into his pocket. The little turd. But if they swept the pieces into a trash can instead of collecting them for repair, I probably wouldn't say anything to his mom.

Flora bent over to pick up one broken foreleg and burst into tears. Fiona stood by, patting her shoulder and looking frightened.

"It was an accident, really, it was an accident. She didn't mean it," she was saying over and over, just like a school kid fearing parental retribution. The oldest man present, whom I assumed was the owner, stepped over and gently ushered them to a couple of chairs behind a counter in the back. He gestured and a young woman hurried over with glasses of water.

I turned back to Alan, but he had moved away and was now leaning over the counter talking to the boy who stood behind it. The boy was nodding his head, gesturing at the ditz duo, then leaning in to listen to Alan. What in the world was that all about? And by the time he turned back to me, our time in the shop was up. It occurred to me that Mohammad wasn't the only one who came and went and had mysterious conversations.

My arm was hurting a little and I felt oddly drained by the time we got back to the *Nile Lotus*. Kyla and I returned to our room, threw ourselves down on our beds, and heaved great sighs, almost in unison. Then we laughed.

"Party tonight, sleep in tomorrow. No getting up early for bus rides and crypts, right?" asked Kyla. "I mean, don't get me wrong, this has been a blast. But I never want to see the inside of another bus as long as I live."

"Yes, tomorrow is a day 'at leisure,' unless you want to get up early with the gang and go on the hot-air balloon ride."

"Which I don't."

"No," I said. "All I want is a nap."

Chapter 12

NECKLACES AND KNOCKOUTS

We both slept for a while and awoke feeling much better. A hot shower worked wonders, too, and except for getting my bandage soggy, I felt much better. Dinner was uneventful, and afterward we returned to the room to dress for the galabia party. I took the necklace out of the room safe and put it around my neck.

"That looks beautiful," said Kyla admiringly.

And it did. The deep blue of the galabia set off the gold and lapis perfectly. The red carnelian pieces gleamed like drops of blood. I shook my hair from its usual ponytail and pinned it up into a French twist, then went to work with Kyla's eyeliner pencil to outline my eyes in what I hoped was the Egyptian way. I stared at myself doubtfully in the mirror.

"What do you think?" I asked her. "Egyptian royalty or cheap hooker?"

Kyla came up behind me, fastening an earring. "You look fantastic," she said earnestly. "You should wear your hair like that all the time. Alan won't be able to take his eyes off of you."

I protested a little, but not too much. After all, I wanted to believe her. About the beautiful part anyway. And, okay, about the Alan part too. I still wasn't sure I trusted him, but having him worship my beauty would be acceptable. Probably Kyla was right and I was just imagining things about him. He was just a take-charge kind of guy, and there weren't any ulterior motives or clandestine activities going on. The few odd things that had occurred, well, it was a foreign country and there were such things as coincidences. And after all, here we were, on a cruise ship on the Nile. With a single, attractive, mysterious man and a party on the deck under the moonlight. If I couldn't stir up a little romance tonight, I might as well pack it in forever.

The sundeck of the *Nile Lotus* was full that evening. Sometime during the day, the crew had moved all the sunning chairs against the railings and set up a small dance platform beside the bar in the center. Strings of white lights hung along the rails and around the bar, giving everything a festive look. Passengers streamed up from below, talking and laughing. Every member of our group wore a new colorful galabia, except Jerry, who wore pressed khakis and a sour expression.

"I overheard Anni talking to that other guide in the corner. They have some sort of contest between the group leaders to see how many of their passengers they can get to participate," Lydia said as she joined us.

"Do you think they have a bet?" asked Kyla.

"I hope so. I'm pretty sure Anni has won hands down. I

don't know how she does it—she can get us all to do just about anything she wants. I would have bet money myself that you'd never get Ben into a dress, but there he is." She was grinning with delight.

Ben toddled over, holding two martinis and looking sheepish. The galabias did look a bit like dresses, now that I thought about it. The other men wore their pants under the garment, but Ben's white legs protruded under the hem like hairy little sticks for about six inches before vanishing into white socks and tennis shoes.

"You're looking quite dashing tonight, my love," Lydia told him fondly. Only the accent made it possible to say something so outrageous. I smiled at the two of them.

"Where's Jane tonight?" I asked, looking around.

Ben and Lydia looked at each other. "She's not feeling well again. We tried to encourage her to come up for a breath of air, but she preferred to stay below. This trip has been a bit of a washout for her, I'm afraid."

Before the silence could become uncomfortable, Kyla broke the spell. "Those look good," she said, eyeing the martinis. "I'm going to go get one. What do you want, Joss?"

"Bloody Mary if they've got tomato juice. Wine if they don't."

"They do." Ben turned to me as Kyla left. "I saw the bartender mixing one a minute ago." Then his eyes widened. "Smashing necklace, Jocelyn."

Lydia turned to look and her eyebrows rose almost to her hairline. "Well, well. That is a beautiful piece. May I?"

I nodded and she leaned in very close, lifting it to get a better look. She straightened and gave me an appraising look.

"That is exactly what I've been looking for myself. If you don't mind, can you tell me where you got it?"

"Edfu. And it's kind of a funny story." I gave her a shortened version, but even that was strange enough.

"Bizarre," she said when I'd finished. "They just handed it to you and shooed you out?"

"Basically. I guess because they'd scared me."

"Well, you're very lucky. It's lovely."

The atmosphere had changed subtly. The evening was still beautiful and clear. The breeze still blew gently. Lydia and Ben still sipped their drinks and smiled, but something was different. It crossed my mind that perhaps they didn't believe me. I couldn't really blame them. I almost didn't believe it myself.

"Let's go find a seat near the band," said Ben, and they left.

I decided not to tell that story again.

I found Kyla, and we sat near the railing. Far below in the inky blackness of the Nile, we could see the golden lights of our ship reflecting on the still surface of the water. Now that we were away from Edfu, there were very few lights on the shore and it was impossible to tell where the water ended and the land began.

A band of Nubian drummers came running up the stairs from below, beating their drums as they came. The tour directors rose and began prodding their charges, and in a remarkably short time a conga line had formed. Kyla hopped up instantly and joined in. I sat, sipping my Bloody Mary. More alcohol was required before I'd feel up to dancing on deck, I thought.

I saw Alan before he saw me. Coming up from the stairs,

he stood and watched the line of dancers winding erratically around the deck, led by a drummer whose smile gleamed white in his dark face. For a moment, he just stood, a dim form on the sidelines, and then he saw me and made a beeline to my side. I felt my heart beat a little faster.

"Come on," he shouted above the din and reached out a hand.

Before I knew it, we had grabbed onto the tail end of the line. I held on to an elderly man I hadn't seen before and Alan grasped my waist. His hands were very warm through my blue galabia. I started laughing with pure pleasure.

The conga ended a couple of minutes later, but the Nubians played for about thirty more minutes. Then we played a few cruise games that everyone enjoyed immensely but would later claim were silly. Left on my own, I would have watched from the sidelines, but Alan and Kyla between them made that impossible. We swung potatoes on strings, did the hokey pokey, and made fools of ourselves for longer than I would have thought possible. DJ was in his element, throwing his head back and laughing his big laugh. Nimmi had either forgiven me for thwarting her shoplifting attempt in the gift shop or decided I hadn't known what I had done because she joined us, talking and laughing. She admired my necklace and waved DJ over.

"Look! Do you see this? This is exactly what I want." She shouted over the music.

He looked dutifully and gave a great big smile. "When we find another, you shall have it. I will make a wonderful bargain for you."

It was ridiculous to suspect such a loud, happy, and

basically nice man could be a smuggler. I felt a little ashamed of myself for even thinking such things. Eventually, the games ended and a disk jockey arrived and began playing softer music that had been popular once and now was heard primarily on elevators and oldies stations. Anni and the other tour guides said their good nights and went below, as did about half of the passengers. The rest of us ordered more drinks and flopped onto the lounge chairs. It felt wonderful lying there looking up at the stars, the air cool on our hot faces. The lights of the ship were no competition against the diamond-hard brilliance of the stars. A few couples danced on the makeshift dance floor.

I finished my drink and looked about for a place to set my glass. Alan took it from me and set it on a table. He held out a hand.

"Will you dance with me?" he asked.

I took his hand and followed him to the dance floor. As I walked past, Kyla gave me a grin and a thumbs up. I hoped Alan hadn't noticed, but that seemed unlikely unless he had been suddenly stricken blind. Fortunately it was too dark for him to be able to see how red my face was.

He took me in his arms, and we began swaying back and forth to the music. He smelled nice, like soap and new clothes and man. I relaxed against him and breathed him in. He moved his hand gently over my back and looked down into my face.

"Tell me about your necklace," he said.

Not the most romantic conversation starter, but it would have to do. I went over the story of my necklace for a third time.

"That is very strange." He leaned away from me so he

could get a better look, although how much he could see in the moonlight was anyone's guess. "It's obviously valuable."

"I know. I mean, even if the stones and gold aren't real, it's still worth something. And they just handed it to me."

"Do you think that those men mistook you for someone else?"

I considered, then shrugged. "That seems the most likely thing, but who in the world did they mistake me for? If they had made a deal with someone, wouldn't they know what that person looked like?"

"You look a lot like your sister."

"Cousin," I said automatically. "But it's not like Kyla was supposed to be picking up a necklace."

"Are you sure?"

I looked up at him, puzzled. "What do you mean?"

"Maybe she was the one who was supposed to go into that stall. It's not the first time on this trip something strange has happened to you. Think about the guy on Kitchener's Island who wanted to show you something. Or the guy in the carpet shop. And now this. Is it possible that she was supposed to pick something up from those people? But you being around messed up the exchange?"

"That's completely ridiculous." I stopped dancing. "You can't seriously think that Kyla has some sort of clandestine deal going on with illegal contacts in Egypt. She's a programmer, for God's sakes. She's never even been to Egypt."

"Are you sure about that? And these days, deals don't have to be arranged in person. Does her company have international offices?"

"No!" I snapped. "Well, yes, probably. But so what? What company doesn't? That doesn't mean anything."

"You don't find it odd that everywhere we've gone on this trip something strange has happened to you? Someone has asked you to go somewhere with him or given you a necklace or attacked you in a tomb?"

"Of course I find it odd. Almost as odd as I find you and all your questions." A cold and unexpected anger was rising inside of me. "Who are you? You're no financial analyst from Dallas. Asking questions, speaking Arabic. Are you FBI? Or CIA? Or just a cute policeman with nothing better to do than flirt when you don't mean it so you can ask your stupid questions?"

I pushed away from him and actually stamped my foot. "You just stay away from me. And from Kyla," I added. "We don't have anything to do with any of this. You're the one mistaking us for someone else."

I stormed off before he could see that my eyes were filling with very inconvenient tears.

I thought briefly about returning to my seat by Kyla, but I was so angry that I was shaking. I decided to return to my cabin. The night was over for me. I could have wept with frustration and disappointment. I stumbled down the half flight of steps that led to the gift shop, and paused briefly to wipe my eyes. As I lifted my head, I saw the flash of an unexpected movement in the shadows and then something hit me very hard.

I must have dropped like a proverbial stone. I don't remember falling, I don't remember blacking out, I don't even remember being frightened. There wasn't enough time. One minute I saw a movement out of the corner of my eye, and the next I was lying on the carpet looking up into Alan's face. Kyla was behind him, shouting for a doctor in a loud high voice. I blinked and tried to raise my head, which was a mistake. Searing pain shot through my temples. I felt nauseated. Other people were arriving and talking at the same time. I was so confused.

"A passenger has been attacked," I heard Alan say to someone. "We need a doctor and you need to search the ship at once."

Someone had been attacked? I wondered who it was. Mostly I wondered why I was lying on the floor in the hallway.

Kyla now knelt beside me and took my hand. Even in my current state, I couldn't help but notice how white she looked and that she was trying not to cry. Very puzzling. I sort of drifted off again. When I opened my eyes next, DJ was shining a little penlight into my face in a most annoying way. I flinched away.

"Stop," I protested and sat up.

Surprise and relief showed on everyone's faces. DJ gave a huge smile. "Ah, this is a very good sign. Her pulse is strong and her eyes are focusing properly. I do not think she has a concussion. Nevertheless, she should be kept awake for the next two hours. Someone should stay with her."

"I'll stay with her," said Kyla, her voice quavering a bit.

"Did she see who it was?" asked Ben from somewhere behind Alan.

"Should we get her to a hospital?" asked someone else.

"I'm fine," I said, with the same instinct that makes people deny they were asleep when they've very obviously just been awakened. I didn't really know if I was fine or not, but I did know I wanted everyone to stop talking about me as if I weren't sitting right there. I put my hand to my head and to my surprise felt wetness there. I looked down and saw blood.

"What the hell? Did I fall down the steps?"

Alan looked grim. "Someone hit you. And your necklace is missing."

I clapped my hand to my throat. Sure enough, my beautiful, mysterious necklace had vanished.

Friday, Queens and Karnak

Spend the morning in Deir el-Bahari, the monumental temple of Queen Hatshepsut, Egypt's only female pharaoh. Stop for pictures at the two Colossi of Memnon, which guard the way to the Valleys of the Kings and Queens. Experience a grand finale to your sightseeing in the Nile Valley with the stunning monuments of Karnak, the greatest city of ancient Egypt. As you stroll among the pillars of the colossal Temple of Amon-Ra and along the Avenue of the Sphinxes, you will believe you have journeyed back in time.

—WorldPal pamphlet

Chapter 13

HEADACHES AND HATSHEPSUT

The rest of that evening and much of the next morning was a bit of a blur. The ship's crew saw to it that another doctor was brought on board at the crack of dawn, ostensibly to check me out but in reality to wake me up and make sure I wasn't going to sue.

Kyla, for once dressed in jeans and a t-shirt, followed the doctor out and returned a few minutes later with a tray stacked with rolls, fruit, coffee, and juice. I looked at her gratefully.

"Wow, room service. I might need to get hit on the head more often."

She snorted. "There are easier ways to get breakfast in bed. For example, making a phone call."

"Yes, but then I would have had to give a tip. This is loads better."

"Seriously, how do you feel?"

I stopped chewing for a second to consider, then answered

with my mouth full. "Headachy, but pretty good. So what's going on down there?"

"You're the talk of the town. The prevailing theory is that some thief must have sneaked on board earlier in the day and been waiting for a chance to steal something valuable. And then apparently slipped overboard and swam away, because no one has been found and the guards in the lobby are positive no one left the ship."

"That's ridiculous. They check for boarding passes every time we sneeze. There's no way a stranger could get on board."

She agreed. "It had to be a crew member or a passenger. You really didn't see a thing?"

I shook my head and was immediately sorry. "Not really. I think whoever it was must have been waiting in the shadows behind the gift shop, which would at least rule out Alan."

"Alan? You're kidding, right? He was completely freaking out."

"Who found me?" I asked her.

"Well, he did. He sounded the alarm and started ordering everyone around. He got the crew to call a doctor and search the ship, and he refused to leave your side. He was . . ." she paused, searching for the word. "He was distraught. I think he really likes you."

I wanted to believe her. "He was the first on the scene. Maybe he was the cause of the scene. What better way to clear himself of suspicion than to sound the alarm. He could have had the necklace in his pocket."

"You're insane. He's a nice guy. And I'm telling you, he was panicked."

"Maybe he hit me harder than he intended. Okay, okay."

I held up my hands as she started protesting. "Maybe I'm just being paranoid. He might not have stolen my necklace, but there is something very odd about that man."

I thought about mentioning Alan's suspicions of her, but then decided against it. For one thing, she might not be as amused as I was, and for another I just didn't have the energy to tease her.

I got up slowly and dressed. My headache settled into a dull heaviness, and mostly I mourned my missing necklace. As much as I'd adored it before, now that it was gone, it was ten times more desirable. I felt as aggrieved as if I'd spent every cent I had on it and not as though it had been handed to me in a trinket shop in an Egyptian bazaar.

Kyla hovered at my elbow as I made my way down the flight of stairs to the ship's lobby. My head gave a little throb with every step, but I decided it wasn't too bad overall. Half our group was already present, and the other half was slowly streaming in.

"I can't believe you're up already," said DJ heartily and much too loudly. I winced a little. "Your head must be as hard as a rock."

"You can't possibly be going on the tour this morning," said Nimmi, critically running her eyes over my pale face. "You don't look at all well."

Just what a girl loves to hear. I always wondered why people think it's okay to tell someone they look like crap. If they were feeling bad, it certainly did not make them feel better. And if they were feeling fine, what a slap. I suppose it was a backhanded way of expressing concern.

"Of course I'm going," I said firmly.

Flora and Fiona toddled in together. Flora's shirt was on inside out.

"How are you feeling today, sweetie?" asked Fiona.

"Fine, thank you," I answered as cheerfully as possible.

"I'm so glad to hear it. Dreadful thing. Just dreadful."

They wandered off toward the ladies' room, and I overheard Flora asking, "Has she been ill?"

Kyla caught my gaze and rolled her eyes. I suppressed a giggle.

Our last full day for sightseeing had come at last. Somehow it seemed like a very long time since we had stepped off the plane in Cairo, excited and happy. Tomorrow we would pack up and fly back to Cairo, then spend an afternoon in the bazaar before catching our flight back to the States. Today, however, was the true grand finale. Deir el-Bahari and Karnak. The words themselves echoed in the mind like a single violin string plucked in an empty hall.

We walked up the steep ramp from the dock to the street above and climbed on board our bus. As always, Achmed waited for us beside the open door, eager to offer a smile or a steadying hand. The group, or most of us anyway, displayed various stages of travel fatigue. Kyla still looked perfect. The ship's laundry must have starched even her jeans, and she looked as fresh and crisp as the day we'd started. I'd yet to see her wear the same outfit twice. On the other hand, my jeans were on their third wearing and my t-shirt had the deep wrinkles that only come from days of being rolled and squashed in the bottom of a suitcase. I wore my light blue windbreaker more to hide the state of my shirt than to ward off the chill of the morning air. I just hoped the wrinkles in my shirt would shake out before the heat of the day made me take the jacket off.

I was pleased to note that I wasn't the only one. Flora and Fiona hardly counted, since they'd looked bad the first day and had gone downhill since, but Tom Peterson had a small stain on his shirt, and Susan looked just as rumpled as I did. Yvonne de Vance looked fine in her expensive Chico's travel collection with its dark colors and unsquashable synthetic fabrics, but Charlie looked as though he'd pulled his clothes from the bottom of a damp laundry basket. I relaxed.

A little to my surprise, Alan claimed the seat directly in front of me and Kyla. He had not been present in the lobby, and he looked as though he had not slept well. His eyes were red and he was paler than usual. I wondered if I looked as bad and decided that he wouldn't appreciate any remarks on it.

Kyla took one look at him and said, "God, you look like crap. What did you do last night?"

He stared at her coldly. "A touch of the Mummy's Revenge, if you must know."

She wrinkled her straight little nose. "Say no more. Please. God, I hope it's not contagious."

"Your compassion does you credit," he said with an ironic glance at me. I looked away. Let him try his damn jokes on someone he didn't suspect of smuggling and murder. And someone who didn't suspect him of the same thing. Something about that thought made me pause. There was a flaw in my reasoning, but with my head aching, I couldn't quite work out what it was.

Like the ancient Egyptians, we crossed the Nile from

east to west, a deeply symbolic journey. Of course, they had ferried across in tiny rocking boats, constantly on the lookout for crocodiles and floating hazards instead of riding in a massive luxury coach over an asphalt bridge. Nevertheless, I could feel the power of the journey. Crossing the Nile to the west, toward the setting sun, was a journey toward death and the afterlife, the reason they built almost all their massive necropolises, tombs, and temples on the western shore. The eastern side was for living.

This morning, however, the sun was hovering low over the eastern horizon, casting a rosy bronze glow on the smooth surface of the water. In the deep blue of the western sky, three rainbow-hued hot-air balloons hung in the still air like beads on a necklace.

We passed a few tiny houses made of mud bricks and straw. Several had small donkeys standing sleepily in pens or tethered by a rope to an acacia tree. The scene had not changed for a thousand years.

"Look, there are children playing by that ruined little house," said Kathy Morrison.

We all turned to look. Anni smiled and took the microphone. "Those houses are not ruins. They are occupied family dwellings."

"But there's no roof," said Lydia Carpenter. And indeed, from the raised bed of the road, we could clearly see the naked tops of the walls.

"Egyptians build their homes as they can afford the materials. I have been told many times by my clients how strange this seems to visitors from other countries, but you must remember that this is the desert. It does not rain here, nor does it snow. A roof is not required. Those taking the balloon ride sometimes pass over these houses and can see families inside sleeping."

The bus pulled into a small parking lot, and we caught a glimpse of the fabled Colossi of Memnon, two enormous statues guarding the entrance to the mortuary temple of Amenhotep III. We disembarked, most of us moving fairly slowly, the exception being Chris and David Peterson, who ran ahead, took a single look at the massive statues before us, and darted off, apparently to look for rocks to chuck at each other. I longed for that kind of energy. Every step I took sent a dull ache through my head.

The colossi looked like they had been smashed to the ground by a giant child and then put back together like Humpty Dumpty. Which is basically what had happened. An earthquake in the second century AD had destroyed much of the temple complex, and the river and stone-pilfering pharaohs had done the rest. Now, all that remained were the broken seventy-five-foot seated giants, reassembled by modern hands and standing silent guard over a barren sweep of rubble.

I walked slowly away from the group to get a better view. To my surprise, Alan joined me. I didn't move. It would have taken too much energy to walk away from him. We stood looking at the giants. Or I looked at them. He seemed to be concentrating on me. I don't know why that made me just a bit happy. There was just something about the man. I tried reminding myself that he had very likely been the attacker who knocked me over the head. Maybe my necklace was in his pocket right now.

"How are you feeling this morning?" he asked.

"Fine. Maybe a little headachy."

"I think they might have looked better left unrestored," he said. "Like the broken colossus at Abu Simbel."

I made an effort to be polite. "Maybe. I admit I would like to have heard the ruins moaning when the wind passed over them, the way they used to. That must have been extremely creepy. But you wouldn't be able to tell just how huge they were. Even patched together, they are pretty impressive."

"'Look on my Works, ye Mighty, and despair,'" he quoted.

"Ozymandias, King of Kings," I supplied, surprised.

He turned to me suddenly and took my hands in his. "Jocelyn, listen. I . . . I need to tell you something. And to apologize."

His hands were large and warm. I looked down at them, making no move to withdraw my own. He was close enough that I could smell the scent of his soap on his skin and feel the heat from his body. I lifted my eyes to his, questioning.

"I'm . . . damn it. This is harder than I thought." He took a deep breath and started again. "Look, I'm not exactly who I said I was."

I yanked my hands away. "Well, duh. You sneak around, you talk to the police, you speak Arabic. Is your real name even Alan?"

"Yes! Yes it is," he gasped.

"Are you married?" This was important.

"No! I've never been married."

"No dead wife who planned this trip?"

He had the grace to look ashamed. "No. That was just to explain being alone."

244

"Financial analyst?"

"Not really. I sometimes balance my checkbook," he added hopefully.

I ignored this. "Was anything you've told me true?"

He opened his mouth, and then hesitated. Across the parking lot, Anni was waving the Hello Kitty umbrella and the rest of the group was slowly moving toward the bus. Mohammad stood alone at the edge of the parking lot. He appeared to be staring straight at Alan and me, and for some reason that made me uneasy.

"There's not really time now. Can we talk later?"

It was my turn to hesitate. I finally said, "What is the point? You've done nothing but lie to me, and after tomorrow I'll never see you again, so what difference does it make?" I could feel the bitter disappointment of that statement filling my mouth like vinegar. I swallowed it down. "And whatever it is you have to say, tell me why I should believe you now."

He looked stricken, but he didn't answer. I turned and joined the others. A part of me hoped he would follow, that he would stop me and beg me to listen, but he just stood there, and when he finally got on the bus, he sat in a different seat.

We stopped next at Deir el-Bahari, the great temple built by Queen Hatshepsut. Carved directly into the face of the mountain, the temple looked as though it had been created from a single great block of white stone. Three separate levels of courtyards, protected by striking columns, were connected by a massive ramped stairway that gently climbed from the valley floor. Compared to the other mortuary complexes we had seen so far, this one looked more like a queen's court instead of a temple dedicated to death.

The parking lot was already crowded with tourists, and we could see a school bus unloading a large group of children. The most interesting field trip I ever took as a child was to the capital building in Austin. These children casually dropped by the greatest monuments in the world. I wondered if they fully appreciated it. Watching two boys scuffle with each other, I decided probably not.

Anni kept us on the bus for several minutes, providing a brief, insightful history into the reign of Egypt's only female pharaoh and describing what we would see. I didn't hear a word. I was busy concentrating on not turning around to see what Alan was doing, while also trying to figure out why Mohammad had left the bus and was standing outside talking on his cell phone. He paced up and down making sharp little gestures with his free hand and occasionally glancing up at the bus windows. I wasn't sure if he could see us or not through the tinted glass, but it made me want to duck down.

Kyla, who never even pretended to listen to Anni's lectures, noticed too. "I wonder what he's up to?" she mused. "I don't even know why he's on this trip. He never does anything useful."

"I think Anni must have told him to ride herd on Fiona and Flora," I answered in a low tone. "He's been following them around lately."

"Hmmph," she made an unladylike sound through her nose. "Well, if he can keep them to the schedule, more power to him. But I still think he's got something going on the side. I mean look at him. Stomping around, all upset."

Anni finally opened the doors and led us out.

"Hat-Ship-Suit!" she shouted after the Peterson boys as they bounced down the steps like super balls. "You pronounce it Hat-Ship-Suit! Not Happen-shit! Wait!" But they ignored her and raced ahead.

The Egyptians had cleverly placed barriers in strategic locations to ensure that everyone arriving from the parking lot had to pass a long row of stalls. With the exception of DJ, who hurried forward and began haggling for all he was worth, we no longer lingered to look or even bothered to be polite in our refusals. One persistent young man pushed a handful of wooden beads under Kyla's nose and a fistful of postcards into mine.

"Get out of my way or I will fucking kill you," Kyla snapped.

Whether he spoke English or not, her meaning translated remarkably well, and he dropped back with a little squeak.

I nodded to her appreciatively. "Very nice."

She flashed me a brief smile, then quickly turned steely eyes on the next vendor, who melted away. "Remember how concerned we were to blend in and be respectful of a different culture?"

"You mean three or four days ago? Yes, I remember. But man, they beat it out of you quick."

"They'd do so much better if they got out of our faces. I'd like to have thirty seconds to look without getting hammered by offers, although DJ doesn't seem to mind." She glanced over her shoulder at him. "If he's not smuggling stuff, then what the hell is he doing? Buying all that crap is odd."

"At this point, I'd think it odd if he didn't buy something," I answered.

"So what did Alan say to you back at the colossal thing-ies?" she asked, giving me a sidelong glance.

"Colossi of Memnon," I corrected automatically. I thought about it, then shrugged. "He admitted he's been lying about almost everything. Nothing we didn't already know."

"Did he say why?"

"He didn't have time. And I told him I didn't care anyway. I mean, what difference does it make?" Even I could hear the pain in my voice. It was too much to hope she hadn't noticed.

"I think it matters," she said carefully. "I was there when he found you on the stairs, you know. I've never seen anyone so upset. He practically went berserk, ordering people around, standing guard over you. He was frantic."

Her words ignited a tiny glow of hope in my chest, but I quickly squashed down the feeling. "Well, that doesn't mean much, does it? He would have been that way no matter who got attacked."

"I don't think so. You've been pretty busy trying not to look at him, but anyone else can see the way he looks at you."

I didn't answer. We started up the first long flight of steps, the white stone brilliant in the morning light.

Kyla went on. "I don't know why he's been pretending to be someone he's not, but there might be a good reason. It wouldn't kill you to hear what it is."

I fought against her reasoning all the way through Hatshep-sut's temple, which I did not appreciate properly through a combination of headache and preoccupation. It annoyed me to think that Kyla might be right about something, but in the end I decided I should probably take her advice—which

248

meant I was going to have to start by apologizing to Alan for my rudeness. And after that, if he would listen, I needed to tell him about all the things I knew. Whatever else he was or wasn't, Alan Stratton was not involved in the murders. I'd finally figured out what had bothered me earlier. If he suspected me of being involved, that could only mean that he wasn't involved himself. And if I didn't try to talk with him, I would hate myself forever. The tour was coming to an end. I'd never see him again. Did I really want to leave without knowing what he wanted to tell me?

We had a couple of hours on the ship before our evening excursion. Kyla decided to lie out on the sundeck with a book, which gave me a chance to look for Alan without having to hear her mock me.

Of course I couldn't find him. He was not in the lounge, not in the gift shop, not on the sundeck. Frustrated, I was just crossing the lobby when I saw Anni.

She smiled, radiant and welcoming as always. She actually looked pleased to see me, when she had to have been glad to have a few minutes to herself. I did not know how she did it.

"Hello, Jocelyn. Do you need something?"

"No, no. Not really. Well, yes. Do you know where Alan is?"

Her face retained its usual serene expression, but I thought her eyes held a knowing glint. "Perhaps he is resting in his room." She opened the little notebook she carried and scanned down a page. "Room 207."

"Thank you," I said. I started for the big curving staircase, and then hesitated, wondering if I should call first. But the lobby seemed too public.

Anni just smiled, as though reading my thoughts. "Why don't you just tap on his door? I'm sure he would be delighted."

I gave her an embarrassed grin, then, taking a deep breath, I started up the stairs. I found his room and knocked quickly, before I could change my mind.

The pause, although probably only a couple of seconds, seemed an eternity. I had just decided he must be out when the door opened.

His hair was damp, as though he'd just stepped out of the shower, and he had on a t-shirt and a pair of shorts, probably thrown on to answer the door. His feet were bare and his eyes looked particularly green.

I opened my mouth to say something, anything, but no sound came out.

He rose to the occasion. "Come in. I'm really glad to see you."

He took armfuls of clothes off the chairs by the big picture window and dumped them in a crumpled heap on the unused second bed. We stood and looked at each other.

"I wanted to apologize . . ."

"I'm really sorry . . ."

We both spoke at the same time and then he laughed. "I know it should be ladies first, but if you'll let me, I'd like to explain."

I nodded.

"I own WorldPal Tours," he said.

"What?" I stared at him, my mouth hanging open a little in surprise. Not what I expected, but suddenly his questions, his involvement with the police, his odd comings and goings clicked into place.

He nodded. "I started it ten years ago. I had a lot of experience traveling, and when I got out of school, my partner and I got the idea that we could arrange tours better than most travel agents and that we could provide local knowledge and service by hiring local guides. It worked out surprisingly well. We found a niche, a step above budget tours but still reasonably priced, and we've done pretty well.

"Three or four times a year, I go on one of the tours myself as a guest, just to see how things are going. Usually I don't find anything out of the ordinary at all. Oh, I might notice that too much time is spent on the bus one day, so I'll tweak the schedule for the group. Or one of the hotels has gone downhill, so I'll scout out a suitable replacement. I rely heavily on the local guides that I hire and things are usually pretty smooth. Until recently."

"Millie's death," I said at once.

"Well, yes, but even before that. A few weeks ago, I got an e-mail from Anni, saying that she didn't know how or what exactly but she thought the tour was being used as a cover for illegal activities."

"Smuggling!" I said. "I think it's smuggling."

He smiled at me, his eyes warm. "Exactly. But smuggling what? The most obvious thing here in Egypt is ancient artifacts. In the past, tomb robbing was practically a national sport. But these days, that's not so easy. The government guards the archaeological sites and really monitors imports and exports. However, the only thing more valuable in Egypt than antiquities are tourists. They smooth the way for tourists in every way possible. So, if you were able to use a tour group as a cover, the smuggling part of it just got a lot easier. I decided I needed to come see for myself."

"But if Anni was suspicious, that means this has been going on for a while."

"Yes. Which points to one of my employees."

"Mohammad."

"The obvious candidate, but not the only one. He hires people too, to check out hotels, to make arrangements. To be honest, it could have been anyone with access to the trip itinerary and connections to someone who could appear as an ordinary tourist. An American, for instance."

"Or an Australian," I said slowly.

"True," he agreed. "I did some background checks on everyone on this tour. No phony names or addresses, no criminal records. As far as I could tell, we are all who we say we are. Except me, of course," he added with a grin.

"So you signed up for the tour as a regular tourist."

"Yes, I figured if I just stayed in the background, kept my eyes open, I'd be able to spot something," he said. "And then the second morning, one of the guests, *my* guests, is murdered. And I didn't see a thing. To be honest, I feel responsible. I knew something was going on." He looked down at his hands. "I should have been able to prevent it."

I wanted to throw my arms around him, but I settled for patting his shoulder awkwardly.

"That's ridiculous," I said. "There's no way you could have known that would happen. There was never any reason to think it would turn to violence, right?"

"No, I suppose not. But then there was a second murder. Even though the victim wasn't part of our tour, we were there. And it was the same method used on Millie. Too much of a coincidence. And now you've been attacked." He put his hand over mine. "Twice. I just don't understand it all. And to be honest, I haven't really learned anything more than I knew before all this started. Except that I'm sure now that Mohammad is involved in some way. His coming along is definitely not part of his job."

He didn't seem to notice he was holding my hand. It was now harder to concentrate on what I was saying.

"I've learned some things," I managed. "I don't know what they mean, but not everyone on this trip is who they seem."

"What do you mean?"

"Well, the Carpenters."

He looked surprised. "What about them? They're great."

"I know. They are. They're just about my favorite people on this trip. The thing is, they arrived at the airport just a little after Kyla and I did. We were just heading for the car when they came into the baggage claim area, and I know this is going to sound crazy, but the girl who is with them, their niece? She is not the same girl who arrived in Cairo with them."

His eyebrows shot up. "What? That doesn't make any sense at all. Who else could she possibly be?"

"I have no idea. I can't even begin to imagine what is going on."

"She's been ill. Are you sure she doesn't just look different because she's been losing weight?"

"No. I'm completely sure. If you look carefully, you'll see it too. The clothes she's wearing are too big for her. Not loose, like she's lost weight, but really too big as though they belong to someone else. Probably the girl I saw in the airport. And this girl isn't sick—she's terrified. I mean, she might be sick too, it's hard to tell, but that's not the reason she's spent most of the trip hiding in her hotel room. And Ben and Lydia are afraid too. You should have seen them at Abu Simbel when we found the body."

"I think everyone was pretty scared then," he pointed out.

"Yes, but not of the police. Most of us were just afraid of being detained again. Jane actually crouched down on the seat of the bus, hiding." I gave a little shrug. "I know it's crazy. You don't have to believe me."

He smiled then, a nice smile, full of warmth and genuine friendliness. "I didn't mean it that way. I believe you. I guess I just don't want to believe anything bad about Ben and Lydia. I was trying to think of other explanations."

"I know. I feel the same way."

"So what else have you noticed? I think you make a much better detective than I do."

"Wait here, I'll be right back." I dashed out of the cabin and down the passage to my room. I yanked my suitcase from the closet and found the little blue WorldPal bag, Millie's bag, stuffed in the bottom.

When I got back to Alan's cabin, a bellhop with a linen-covered tray was just leaving. He greeted me and held the door, then departed. Alan beckoned me back to the little table by the window. Outside, the sun sparkled on the Nile, and a felucca glided gracefully over the surface a few hundred feet away. On the table sat two icy beers and a bowl of mixed nuts. My face must have lit up, because he laughed.

"I figured we needed to keep our strength up," he said.

"Well, as long as it's for medicinal purposes," I agreed.

I sat down beside him. He twisted the top off a beer and handed it to me, then opened his own. He clinked his bottle lightly against mine.

"Here's to figuring this thing out," he said.

"Here's to you not being a creepy murdering smuggler."

He laughed, but looked at me searchingly. "Did you really suspect me?" I could tell it stung a little.

I grinned. "Just as much as you suspected me."

He looked sheepish. "At least I had a reason. Anni had told me she'd heard something about sisters being involved. You and Kyla seemed to fit the description."

"We're not sisters," I said automatically. Still, something niggled at the back of my mind, something I thought I should know, but couldn't quite grasp. "Anyway, I had reasons, too. You're a terrible liar, so it was obvious your whole cover story was fake from the start. Then you're running around, speaking to the locals, vanishing at times. What was I supposed to think?"

"And now I'm off the list?" He said it casually, but I could tell it mattered.

"It finally dawned on me that if you suspected me, then you didn't know what was going on either. Besides, I didn't want it to be you."

He smiled suddenly, a blindingly attractive smile that made my heart turn over.

"So what have you got there?" he asked with a nod to the bag.

"Okay, you're not allowed to judge me. Well, you can, but

you have to keep it to yourself. Plus, you can help me figure out what to do with this."

"What is it? And what are you talking about?"

I was embarrassed. "It's Millie's bag."

He raised his eyebrows.

"See? You're judging me. I found it, and then I didn't know what to do with it."

"Okay, fine. I'm not judging you. Why didn't you just turn it in to Anni?"

"I didn't want her to think I'd been snooping. I was going to leave it on the bus, but then there just wasn't a good time."

"Okay, well, what's in it?"

"A bunch of stolen stuff and her travel diary. And probably the reason she was killed, if I could just figure it out."

I dumped the bag onto the table, then held up the items one by one. "Fiona's or Dawn's hairbrush. Lydia's cigarette lighter. Jerry's or Keith's pen. Yvonne's coin purse." I put each item back in the bag as I named it.

He whistled. "What a horrible little thief."

"She had my lip balm, too, but I took that back," I said, glancing at him a little defiantly. "On the first evening in the hotel, I saw her rooting through a bag that I'm pretty sure didn't belong to her. And the next day on the bus, I caught her going through mine. I think she probably went through everyone's things. And I think she saw something that she shouldn't have seen."

We sat in silence for a moment.

"I guess we'll never know what that was," he said, looking grim.

"Maybe not. But look at this." I picked up the red note-book and opened it to the entry about the smuggling.

He read it and sat up straight. He began flipping through the pages. I remembered the entry about the sisters and felt myself blush. It was too much to hope he didn't notice it.

"She was pretty spiteful," I said. "That bit about Kyla and me. Not true."

He had the look of someone who has solved a puzzle, that aha! look you get when you finally get the math problem. Then his expression changed and a little crease appeared between his eyebrows.

"What is it?"

"Nothing. But now I've got an idea at least. We might have another case of mistaken identity." He drained his beer and rose to his feet. "I need to check up on a couple of things, but this is exactly what I needed. You're wonderful!"

I stood too, more out of bewilderment than anything. "What idea? What did you see?"

He didn't answer, and before I knew it, he was escorting me to the door. "Don't worry," he said. "I'll give this stuff to Anni, and she'll be able to get everything back to the rightful owners."

"Wait, what are you going to do?" I asked.

"Check on just a couple of things. I need to make some calls."

"But—" I started.

He interrupted. "I'll see you later this evening, okay? I'll tell you everything, if I get it figured out. And you and I still have a lot to talk about."

We were in the hallway now, and he was closing his door

257

behind us. He started for the staircase, leaving me standing stunned by the door, still holding my half-finished beer. I wasn't done talking. I hadn't even gotten to my suspicions about DJ or the odd behavior of Jerry. He was almost to the stairs when he pivoted back around, grabbed me by the shoulders, and kissed me. A hard, quick, wonderful kiss. Then he was gone before I could move, taking the steps two at a time.

I stood there a moment, still feeling the pressure from his warm lips against mine. What the hell was that? A thank-you kiss, a good-bye kiss, or something else? And how absolutely aggravating. The fact that it was the best kiss I'd had in years, possibly forever, just made it all the more annoying. What the hell had just happened, where was he going, and why the hell did he think he could just scamper off without letting me know what he had discovered? In fact, who the hell did he think he was? I ground my teeth together, then started up the stairs to the sundeck. It was time to wake up Kyla and get ready to go to Karnak.

Besides, I needed to vent.

Chapter 14

KARNAK AND CHAOS

The late afternoon sun cast a burnished ruddy glow over our little group as we gathered at the bus to drive to the ancient temple of Karnak. This was to be the grand finale of our trip, the most massive ancient religious site in the world. Unlike most Egyptian monuments, which were the work of a single ruler, Karnak was the awe-inspiring achievement of over thirty pharaohs, ruling over a period of thirteen hundred years. Much of the history of Egypt was represented in the vast halls of ruined Karnak, and I wanted to see it more than anything else we had seen so far.

My headache, mostly forgotten while I talked with Alan, was back and throbbing dully just behind my eyes. I had gulped a couple of aspirin before coming downstairs, but they hadn't kicked in yet. Nevertheless, I was determined not to let it slow me down or make me less alert. For a reason I couldn't define, I felt I couldn't afford to miss anything tonight. On the other hand, I had no idea what I should be looking for, so I

259

attempted to covertly scan everyone and everything. I bumped into Kyla a couple of times before she pinched my arm.

"What is wrong with you? Watch where you're going."

Mohammad stood beside the bus steps next to Anni, who was counting us off as we climbed aboard. I shivered a little as I went past him. A sheen of sweat on his brow caught the light and his shoulders were stiff with guilty tension. Or, to be fair, he was hot in his heavy houndstooth jacket, and he was just praying to get this out-of-control tour finished before anything else happened.

I tried to reel in my imagination. Although I was practically positive he was up to something, had he really killed two people and attacked me twice? Here, in the air-conditioned interior of our luxury coach, it seemed so unlikely. I turned my attention to my fellow passengers. After all, one of them was a smuggler and possibly a murderer.

The Petersons, with their two teenage sons, were already in their seats midway down the aisle. I considered and dismissed them. They were excited, happy, and just so normal. Besides, I liked the boys, and their parents had their hands full just trying to keep up with their kids. No time for smuggling.

Dawn and Keith Kim climbed up next. Keith was busy with his digital camera, trying to reattach the huge lens as he followed his wife down the aisle. She glanced over her shoulder at him, half exasperated, half amused. I wouldn't give very good odds on their marriage lasting, but they seemed like ordinary tourists, just along for the ride.

Jerry and Kathy Morrison followed. Kathy looked like a jackal about to bite the head off a meerkat, and Jerry's expression was sour. Maybe he was the meerkat. She was still limping a little from her fall at Abu Simbel, and I noticed she now wore a pair of flat espadrilles below her ACE bandage. They sat in the seat right behind Anni's, taking advantage of injury to claim a front seat even when it wasn't her turn. None of us would have begrudged it or even given it a second thought if Jerry hadn't pounced on it with a smug proprietary air as though daring one of us to challenge him.

The Carpenters followed, Lydia, then Jane, then Ben. They moved quickly to the very back seat, which stretched across the aisle so that all three of them could sit side by side. Jane looked pinched and, well . . . frightened. And the way Lydia and Ben always flanked her like bodyguards seemed strange. Were they being supportive or were they actually protecting her? And from what? If she was really just their niece from Australia, then their behavior made no sense. On the other hand, if she was an impostor on the run from the Egyptian authorities, then their actions made sense, but hardly explained who she was and why they were helping her. The fact that Ben and Lydia were so nice and so ordinary made it that much harder to believe that anything criminal was going on.

DJ and Nimmi boarded next, DJ in full flow about the wonders that Nimmi could expect to see at Karnak. To give her credit, Nimmi was responding enthusiastically. In fact, I had never seen her respond to her big husband with less than amused affection. I thought about her shoplifting attempt in the ship's gift shop and of his constant haggling and buying sprees. Was Kyla right? Was there more to it than just exuberant fun? How easy would it be to hide a real antiquity inside a suitcase full of plaster junk? Their kindness and generosity did not necessarily preclude a little smuggling on the side. But violence and murder? I didn't think so.

As usual, Fiona and Flora arrived late and last. Mohammad had to help Flora up the stairs, although Fiona jerked away from him and refused his assistance. She looked as though she'd like to spit on his feet, and I wondered how he'd offended her. We were all tired after seven days of constant sightseeing, but the fatigue of travel had really caught up with the poor ditz duo. Flora's polyester shirt was right-side out for a change, but she'd misaligned the buttons and one hem hung lower than the other. She had an odd manic gleam in her eyes behind the Coke-bottle glasses, and she was muttering to herself under her breath as she tottered down the aisle. On the other hand, she seemed cheerful about it. Fiona seemed less senile, but her black wispy hair stood at all angles as though she'd been pulling on it, and she seemed more stooped and beaten than I'd seen her before. It couldn't be easy trying to keep her sister in line, I thought, feeling suddenly sympathetic. Looking at her, I imagined that she must have been tall and athletic in her youth. Actually, both of them must have been. Contrary to first impressions, they were not really little old ladies. They were big old ladies, now a little stooped and wrinkled, and slowly growing tired and confused. Growing old is a bitch. I hoped when I was like that, Kyla and I would still be giving old age the finger and traveling on buses around the world.

Anni and Mohammad climbed on the bus, the door closed, and we started.

"Where's Alan?" I asked Kyla, keeping my voice low.

She raised up in her seat a little, looking over the headrests. "He must have told Anni he wasn't coming. You know she wouldn't have left without him otherwise."

"Where is he, though? Why wouldn't he have come with us?" I asked. I had a bad feeling in the pit of my stomach that I couldn't explain. Alan should be here.

"How would I know?" asked Kyla. "Besides, I thought you trusted him now."

"Yes, that's true. Mostly." I looked out the window without really seeing. "It just doesn't seem right for him to miss Karnak."

"Maybe he wasn't feeling well. Maybe he had something else to do."

"Like what?" I asked. He was investigating something. Something he had thought of when I showed him Millie's notebook. But what could it be?

"Okay, maybe he didn't have anything to do."

"No, that's just it. I'm worried about him. Why wouldn't he be here?"

Kyla looked at me and shook her head. "You've got it so bad."

I refused to be distracted. "Maybe I do. But that's not the point. I don't think any of us should be alone with all this going on. We've already had two murders."

"Uh huh. Well there's nothing you can do about it now. Too bad. You'll just have to concentrate on your actual vacation."

I ignored the sarcasm. "No," I said slowly, coming to a decision. "I'm going to follow Mohammad. I'm pretty sure he's up to something too. You can stick close to the Carpenters."

She stared at me, appalled. "Tell me you're joking."

I didn't answer.

"Look," she went on. "Even if you're right, it's none of our business. The Carpenters are nice people. So they hang close to their niece, so what? She hasn't been well—of course they are going to stay with her. And Mohammad." She snorted. "For God's sakes. Even if he is running some kind of illegal operation, what is it to you?"

"He might be the one who hit me and stole my necklace," I answered. "That makes it my business. Besides, what if he is smuggling out ancient artifacts?"

"I thought that was DJ. Besides, I'm pretty sure the Egyptians are capable of protecting themselves. And you don't have any reason to believe Mohammad hit you. You suspected Alan of the same thing. They can't both have done it."

That was true. I knew now it wasn't Alan, but I didn't want to go into details on the bus. "Look, just keep the Carpenters in sight," I whispered. "You're right, it's ridiculous, but just humor me."

"I don't want you following Mohammad," she said. "In the unlikely event that you're right, it could be dangerous."

"I just want to know if he meets up with anybody. We'll be in a public place. What could happen?"

About ten minutes later, we were walking toward Karnak from the bus parking lot. I could see the enormous walls of the temple. From here, they seemed very plain and disappointing.

Then we rounded a row of buses and found ourselves on the Avenue of the Sphinxes.

What can I say? For a few magnificent moments, I forgot all about Mohammad, all about smuggling, all about murder. I was at Karnak. Ram-headed sphinxes, sitting in regal silence on low plinths, flanked both sides of the wide promenade approaching the temple complex. They guarded the entryway against all comers, ancient sentries carved of gray stone. Time, it seemed, was the only enemy they could not hold at bay. A few were only mildly worn, regal faces still watching with sightless eyes, but the heads of others had crumbled back into the sand, leaving only the long lion bodies intact. The voices of tourists, the endless camera clicks that filled the air had no meaning or power here. I stood mesmerized, but Kyla gave an exasperated sigh and tugged at my sleeve. We followed the others.

As always, Anni gave us an educated, thorough tour of the place, but for once I could hardly listen. More than anywhere else we had visited, Karnak captured the very essence of Egypt and its immeasurable past. Stopping just inside the first pylon, we turned to see a huge mound of earth pressing against the massive wall.

"Archaeologists were baffled for many years about how the ancient Egyptians built such enormous walls," Anni said. "There were many theories, but no evidence. Considering the tools they had, the task of raising blocks of stone weighing hundreds and even thousands of pounds was unexplainable."

We all nodded in agreement. Even with hundreds of workers, how had they done it?

She continued, gesturing to the pile of dirt resting against the walls. "The answer was here, at Karnak. The ancients used dirt mounds as ramps, pushing the blocks up the slope. They may even have used logs to help roll them up the hill. It was an unbelievable amount of backbreaking work, but easier than trying to lift the blocks, even if they had been able to build a device such as a crane. After the wall reached the highest point, the workers would move the mountain of dirt away. Very simple, but very clever. And for some unknown reason, they did not clear away this last pile, and so we learned their secret."

I smiled at the pride in her voice, pride in the discovery and pride in the cleverness of the ancients who created something lasting in a land that demanded every last resource just to stay alive. The mound of dirt, the humblest artifact in the whole complex, was perhaps the highest symbol of the intelligence and sacrifice that had been required.

We followed Hello Kitty into the hypostyle hall and immediately forgot about dirt piles. Passing the second pylon, we found ourselves in a forest of stone columns, soaring sixty feet above our heads, standing in perfect rows. Each was carved like a papyrus plant, with elaborate leaves at the top, beautiful and mysterious. They looked slender and delicate until you approached more closely and got some idea of their actual size. Ten people joining hands could scarcely circle their bases. The roof they had supported centuries before had long since vanished, although high arched windows in a crumbling wall were evidence that once a second story had existed far above the ground. Remnants of faded paint adorned the undersides of the stones, and carvings of pharaohs and gods, battles and ceremonies, covered the walls. The tourists walking among the columns looked like tiny mice in a very large garden.

I took a few photographs, but I knew I would never be able to capture the beauty and sheer scale of the hall. I glanced around at the group. All eyes were turned up. Except Mohammad's. He was standing on the edge of the group, peering out into the growing dusk, hands in his pockets, shoulders hunched. I thought he looked edgy and nervous. He suddenly looked in my direction, and I hastily turned away to take a picture of Kyla standing by a column.

Anni waved Hello Kitty, and we followed her between low walls, past a huge obelisk, broken and lying on its side, and into an open courtyard. To the left, we could see a rectangular lake, full of blue water gradually deepening to gray and purple in the fading light. In the center of the courtyard, a giant scarab crouched on top of a large plinth. Around it, a dozen tourists walked in circles, some clockwise, some counterclockwise. Bemused, we stared.

Anni smiled. "Legend has it that if you walk around the scarab seven times, you will receive your deepest wish. I highly recommend you try it. After all, it can't hurt."

"Which direction should we walk?" asked Nimmi.

"Ah, you must go counterclockwise. Otherwise it won't work."

Quickly, she pointed out a few landmarks, and then released us with orders to meet back by the scarab in half an hour so that we could sit together for the sound and light show. Most of the group started circling the scarab, talking and laughing as they walked. Chris and David raced each other around, their sneakers throwing dust into the air.

I looked around for Mohammad and spotted him slipping away past the fallen obelisk. I threw Kyla a look and hurried after him. Glancing back, I saw that she hesitated a second, then fell in behind the Carpenters circling the scarab.

Mohammad moved swiftly now, and I almost had to trot to keep up with him. He never looked back. After all, why should he? Even I thought I was being totally ridiculous. Why would he ever think that one of the little sheep he had been guiding all week would take it on herself to follow him? Nevertheless, I kept up, holding back just far enough to have a chance of not being seen should he turn around, yet always keeping him in sight. It wasn't difficult. Karnak was full of tourists, most roving in small packs led by guides, but a good number wandering about on their own, pointing and snapping photographs.

He led the way back through the hypostyle hall, where the forest of columns dwarfed the tiny mortals skittering around their bases. Here he stopped, standing beside a column as though he was waiting. Uncertain, I hesitated beside a wall. Between the columns and the tourists, it wasn't hard to duck out of sight. I decided to wait where I was, behind him, but in the shadow of a wall. I didn't need to bother. He never turned toward me and focused only on the path ahead. Every once in a while he glanced at his watch. The shadows grew longer. I was starting to get bored. What was he doing just standing there? I began glancing away from him for longer periods, enchanted by the ruins around me. Then suddenly he was gone. Sprinting forward a few paces, I caught sight of his broad shoulders again. Relieved, I dropped back, keeping my focus on him.

He turned down a narrow path running beside the great obelisk of Hatshepsut. The twilight was waning fast, and the walls and columns cast long shadows that stretched to greet the night. I glanced at my watch. It was almost time to meet back at the giant scarab, but I couldn't stop now. Mohammad slowed, and I quickly slipped into the shadow behind a pillar.

Just in time. He gave a quick glance around to make sure no one was watching him and then stepped under a chain that said the equivalent of "No Admittance" in about six different languages. I hesitated. Then I did the most foolish thing I'd ever done in my whole life. I followed him.

Someone told me once that your brain knows you are going to do something before you are consciously aware of it. Some study had shown that the brain lights up a significant amount of time before its owner acts on a decision. My friend was pondering what this said about our free will, and whether our conscious decisions were actually all that conscious. I very naturally scoffed at this notion, but all I know is, I was bending under that chain and creeping after Mohammad while my conscious mind was still screaming for me to get back to the group and telling me what an idiot I was.

Behind the high, crumbling walls, away from the tourist paths, the dusk had fallen in earnest, and it took my eyes a moment to adjust. In the soft white light of the rising moon and the distant glow of electric lights, I could see the crumbling walls of the temple forming a ragged honeycomb of rooms beside the obelisk. Fallen rocks and other debris as yet uncleared by the restoration teams littered the ground and made walking hazardous. The deep bass from the sound and light show started vibrating over the rocks, thrumming in the distance. Uneasily, I picked my way along a broken walkway, stumbling a little.

I could no longer see Mohammad, and Kyla would be worried by now, wondering where I was and if I was hurt. I jumped at a scuffling sound near my feet and thought of snakes slithering out to soak up the last heat from the rocks before seeking out the local rodent population. That did it. I decided to turn back.

The sudden sound of voices changed my mind. Off to my right, somewhere beyond a jagged wall, I heard a faint moan and then Mohammad's voice shouting, "What have you done?"

As quickly and silently as I could, I picked my way across the rocks until I could peer over the top of a broken wall. I'm not sure what I expected, but it wasn't this.

Mohammad stood aghast in front of Fiona and Flora, and at their feet lay Alan Stratton, motionless. My heart jumped into my throat. They had killed him.

"What have you done?" Mohammad asked again, his voice hoarse and tight with fear.

The shaft of pain that pierced my heart froze the scream that welled up in my throat. Only a small moan escaped my lips, unheard over the beat of the background music.

Flora gave a girlish giggle and held up something that glinted in the light. I was pretty sure it was a knife.

"He was following us, the bad man." She kicked him none too gently in the back. He stirred a little in protest.

Mohammad lurched forward. "He's still alive!"

My heart started beating again, or at least I became aware of it, pounding in my chest. He was alive! Alan was alive. I crouched lower, trying to think what to do.

"You said we couldn't kill anyone else, MoMo," said Fiona. "So we decided to let you kill him." Her voice was both peevish and dreadfully cold.

"What do you mean? There will be no killing. No killing!" Even from here, I could hear the outrage in his voice.

"Oh, we think you'll change your mind. We've been

watching this one the whole trip. We're pretty sure he's been on to our little plan from the start, probably hired by WorldPal to investigate—isn't that right, Mr. Stratton?"

Alan gave no answer. I wasn't sure he was conscious.

Fiona went on. "He's been sniffing around everyone in the group. He's very dedicated, I must say. Of course, he didn't suspect us. Even after he ran through almost everyone else, he never really gave us a second look. I told you, our cover is perfect."

"Then why couldn't you have left him alone?" whispered Mohammad.

"Wrong place, wrong time. He didn't suspect us, but he seems to have guessed that something was happening tonight. I'm not quite sure how he knew that." She frowned and glanced down.

"He would have ruined everything," added Flora. She was now staring up at the big moon. The light reflected off her huge glasses. "And now you can kill him yourself. If you don't, he'll have us all arrested. We can't have that, can we, MoMo?"

"Don't call me that," Mohammad whispered. "And no. We cannot kill him. Another death? Every policeman in the country will be called in."

Flora and Fiona both laughed. "We've already thought of that for you. You'll have to bury the body in a dune somewhere. He didn't come with us tonight. No one will notice he's missing until we're all getting ready to go to the airport tomorrow, and by then it will be too late. Anni will take us back and leave you to start a search for him. We'll be home and counting our money before anyone notices. And, if you do your job right, they'll never find the body."

271

I couldn't understand the change in their voices. The women standing in the moonlight looked like the ditzy sisters who had plagued us with their inane chatter and constant foolish wandering. But they now sounded sharp and logical and very, very cold.

"WorldPal will know," Mohammad protested. "If they hired him, they'll know he wouldn't just wander off. We have to let him go."

"Don't be ridiculous. He knows about all three of us now."

Mohammad paused, then said, "We can leave the country. If we left right now, we could catch a plane to Cairo this evening."

Fiona shook her head pityingly. "You've lost your nerve. And your head. Leave now? We haven't even made the exchange."

"And we are not leaving without our pay, MoMo," said Flora.

Mohammad sat down on a fallen pillar and put his head in his hands. In the dim light, he looked more like a bear than ever, his huge shoulders straining at the heavy fabric of his jacket.

Alan stirred weakly.

"What did you do to him?" asked Mohammad. "Did you stab him, too?"

"Goodness, no. We used morphine. There was a nice little supply in the ship's first aid cupboard."

"A knife would have been much easier," added Flora. "The morphine took a minute to kick in. He almost got away, didn't he, Foney?"

"Yes, he gave us quite a fright. It's too bad in a way. Such a nice-looking young man."

Mohammad groaned. "You're both insane."

"Now, that's not nice, MoMo. This was hardly our fault."

"Not your fault? Not your fault?" Mohammad sprang up again. He paced back and forth. "Killing that tourist? That wasn't your fault?"

My ears pricked. Millie? *They* were the ones who had killed Millie? My mind reeled. I thought back to that day at the pyramids, Millie's body lying in the sand, Flora and Fiona crying hysterically, then wandering away together. It had all been an act.

"We had to, you know that," said Fiona in a reasonable tone. "She found the statue from Alexandria in Florie's purse."

"So what?" shouted Mohammad. "She was just a foolish American woman. She wouldn't have known whether it was an antiquity or not."

"We couldn't take that chance. If she'd said something to Anni, the whole thing would have been over. Anni would have asked to see it. And *she* would have known what it was immediately," Fiona explained.

"And the shopkeeper in Abu Simbel, Foney," Flora reminded her. "That was MoMo's fault, too."

"Yes, it was. And honestly, you should be just a little more grateful to us, MoMo. After all, it was *your* contact at Elephantine Island who cheated us and gave us those old Sudanese dinars instead of the new currency. How were we supposed to know they'd changed money recently and the old stuff was worthless?"

"Yes, you should have warned us about that," chipped in Flora.

Fiona nodded, then continued. "Now, I grant you, it

273

would have been more fitting to kill him, but we didn't find out that he'd cheated us until that shopkeeper refused to turn over the diamonds. And what would your Cairo backers have said if we'd told them we exchanged their money for worthless old currency? They certainly would not have paid us. And I think they might have wanted to kill you, MoMo."

"Stop calling me MoMo!" snapped Mohammad. "And what do you think? Do you think that my Sudan contacts will be pleased that you killed their man in Abu Simbel? Do you not think that they might want to kill me now?"

"Ah, yes, we did consider that," said Flora, nodding. "But at least we got the diamonds."

"Exactly," Fiona agreed. "And we wanted to talk to you about that little matter. We think there is no need to turn those diamonds over to your backers."

"What do you mean? They paid for them. They will expect to receive them, and they are not the type of people we can cross."

"Well, not more than once anyway," Fiona twinkled. "And once is all we need. After all, Mr. Stratton here is proof that WorldPal is suspicious, and Flora and I aren't exactly getting any younger. This would have been our last trip anyway. As for you, if you're smart, you will be leaving the country as fast as you can. With any luck, your Sudanese friends won't think you're worth hunting down. But it's expensive to emigrate. You could probably use your share of those diamonds."

Silence fell on the little group. In the distance, the music and applause from the sound and light show filtered over the cooling stones. Then Mohammad exploded.

"Are you mad?" he shouted.

"Now don't be nasty," said Fiona, with a purposeful look at her sister. Flora stepped slightly to the side, and I could see her slip her hand into her purse. I thought that Mohammad ought to be very afraid, but he did not seem to notice.

"We've thought this out very carefully," she went on. "Naturally, we should split everything three ways, but Flora and I agreed that if you will take care of Mr. Stratton here, we will give you two-thirds of the diamonds. Those will be easier for you to convert into whatever currency you choose. We will keep the statue, naturally, since we will be able to smuggle it out without question."

There was a brief silence, and then Mohammad rasped out a protest.

"The statue is worth as much as all of the diamonds."

"Only if it could be purchased legitimately. You know very well that we will be lucky to get even half a million for it. Besides, we know you have the necklace."

"Only because I knew you would kill that girl to get it!"

My hand flew to my throat. My necklace. So it had been Mohammad who had taken it after all. About the only one of my suspicions that had been correct.

Flora giggled. "You almost killed her yourself, hitting her like that. Still, it was a good job. I didn't know you had it in you."

"You've ruined my life," he said, almost wonderingly.

I'd heard enough. Too much in fact. But what should I do? If I left to find help, they might kill Alan before I could get back. And screaming wouldn't work over the music and noise from the sound and light show.

I picked up a rock. Somehow, in my head I was thinking

if I threw it and then ran, they would know they had been overheard and would be too afraid to kill Alan. I took careful aim at Mohammad, mostly because I figured they needed him to carry Alan, and threw as hard as I could.

Years of playing ball with my brothers had strengthened my arm, but unfortunately had no effect on my aim whatsoever. Straight and true, the rock whistled through the air and struck Alan squarely on the head. He had been woozily struggling to sit up and now collapsed back down like a punctured balloon. I froze in horror. For a long moment all four of us just stared at Alan and the rock, and then Mohammad spotted my head above the wall and gave a roar.

I fled. Exactly like the old mummy movies. Heroine running through Egyptian ruins, pursued by monsters. Except I wasn't wearing pumps and a dress. I vaulted over a low wall and hit the sand running. Unfortunately, Mohammad wasn't wrapped in linen bandages, de rigueur for most Egyptian monsters. I could hear him pounding behind me, his breath harsh and loud, gaining fast. I squealed and, with a burst of speed, exploded out of the pillars and into the open obelisk court.

I narrowly missed running into Kyla. She, Anni, and DJ Gavaskar stood in a little cluster, talking. I later learned that Kyla, almost frantic about my disappearance, had rallied the troops to come looking for me.

As I shot past the group, Mohammad's hands closed on my shoulders. I felt myself jerked back, and my feet flew out from under me. He stooped over me, reaching for my throat, apparently oblivious to the witnesses. In a shining moment, one that she would recount with pride for the rest of her life and one that I would never tire of hearing, Kyla leaped behind him and kicked him squarely in the middle of his wide stance.

Unlike mine, her aim and execution were perfect. I could hear the solid thud as her pointed Gucci ankle boot connected directly with his balls and watched as though in slow motion as he released my throat and dropped like a stone. That is, if stones curl in fetal positions and writhe in agony.

DJ had also leaped forward to deal with Mohammad, but since there was now no need, he pulled me to my feet. I was gasping, my voice hoarse. "Alan! They have Alan."

"Who? Who has Alan? What is happening? And are you all right?" asked Anni. She was obviously shaken, but instinctively trying to soothe me and calm things down.

I wanted to scream. "They are going to kill Alan," I shouted, grabbing DJ's hand and pulling. This time it sank in and we ran, leaving Mohammad where he lay.

I ran back through the columns and past the "No Admittance" chains and around the crumbling walls. To my intense relief, Fiona and Flora were gone and Alan lay where I'd last seen him, stirring feebly. DJ rushed to his side, pulling out a little flashlight.

"He has a head injury," said DJ. "He's bleeding and may be concussed. We need an ambulance right away."

Anni whipped out her cell phone and dialed rapidly.

"He's also been injected with morphine," I added.

Three pairs of eyes turned to me with a mixture of surprise and disbelief.

"I heard them talking," I explained. "That's how they overpowered him. They lured him out here and gave him an injection before he could stop them."

DJ lifted Alan's wrist to take his pulse. "It's possible. His pulse is very slow. Tell them to hurry," he directed Anni.

"Who did this?" Kyla asked, looking down at Alan. "Mohammad and who else?"

I knew they weren't going to believe me even before I said it. Two senile old ladies, doddering and feeble. Still, they would have to listen after the police questioned Mohammad, I thought. He would surely rat them out.

"Fiona and Flora," I said, trying for quiet and convincing. My throat hurt. A lot.

To my surprise, while DJ and Kyla looked dumbfounded, Anni just nodded thoughtfully.

Catching my look, she said, "I knew they weren't what they were pretending to be. I've been around a lot of elderly women, and they just did not, what do you say? Ring true. How ironic, though, that I asked Mohammad to keep his eye on them."

After that, things happened rather quickly. A team of paramedics arrived and carried Alan away on a stretcher, DJ in tow to make sure that everything was done properly. I felt a twinge of remorse that I'd ever suspected him of anything. I wanted to go with them, but Anni stopped me.

"You can't do anything for him, and I need you to help describe what happened to the police."

She flagged down the police officers when they arrived, and began explaining with a torrent of hand gestures and rapid Arabic, which made me wonder just why she thought my presence was necessary. Two of them peeled away immediately, presumably to search for Mohammad. The remaining officer listened with growing skepticism to Anni, taking notes in a small notebook. He looked over at me when she pointed.

"Jocelyn, come here. I want to show him your neck." Anni beckoned to me.

"What?" I asked, stepping forward.

"Your neck. You have bruises already. Can't you feel them?"

I pulled down the collar of my oxford shirt and heard Kyla's gasp. I could still feel Mohammad's huge hands where they had gripped me, but I didn't see until much later the angry red and purple marks that they had left on my neck. The officer's attitude changed in a flash, and he pulled out a radio and barked instructions.

The sound and light show ended and tourists streamed out of the theater area on their way back to the buses. Anni clicked her tongue in frustration.

"I must meet my group at the bus and see that they make it back to the ship," she said. "And these two must be exhausted. Do you need them tonight?"

The officer hesitated, and then shrugged. "We can come to the ship if we need anything further." He referred to his notes. "The *Nile Lotus* you said, yes?"

I grabbed Anni's arm as a thought hit me. "They'll come to the bus!" I said.

"What?"

"Fiona and Flora. They might come to the bus with everyone else. They couldn't have seen me before. I mean, they couldn't have known it was me that Mohammad was chasing. I could have been anyone—some kid who overheard what they were saying or a security guard. And if they didn't know it was me, they might try to brazen it out and rejoin the tour."

"That would be very foolish," said Anni.

"But how else are they going to get out of the country?"

As it turned out, I was finally right about something. Fiona and Flora turned up at the bus, late as always, looking more confused and bent than ever. Kyla and I watched from the windows as Anni delayed them at the steps just long enough for the police to swoop out of the shadows and arrest them. I thought our bus would flip over on its side as everyone leaped to the windows.

"What are they doing to those old ladies? They can't do that! We're Americans!" said Jerry, outraged. He jumped to his feet. "I'm a lawyer! Let me through. Lawyer coming through!" shouted Jerry. He literally pushed Keith out of his way and went charging off the bus.

It was too much. Kyla and I clutched each other's arms and fell back in our seats laughing. I could see Jerry talking to the police. He tried throwing himself protectively in front of Flora and Fiona, gesturing wildly. Even through the bus windows, I could hear muffled shouts of "American citizen" and "rights." I thought one of the policemen was going to punch him, and I could see another reaching for the handcuffs. Fortunately for Jerry, Anni grabbed his arm and said something in his ear. He deflated like a pricked balloon, or maybe just a prick. He crept back onto the bus with his tail between his legs and snapped at his daughter as he sat down. Still, you had to give it to him. Misguided and arrogant, maybe, but still, surprisingly chivalrous.

As I watched Jerry return to his seat, enjoying the red glow on his face, I noticed the Carpenters sitting in the back. Unlike the rest of us, they were not watching the spectacle from the windows. They weren't even gloating over Jerry's embarrassment. Instead, they had switched seats so that Jane was pressed into the back corner, guarded by both Lydia and Ben. She had even half pulled the curtain and was sunk down low, as if she were hiding. I caught a glimpse of her face and was shocked at the raw fear in her eyes. If I'd had any doubts before, I had none now. Jane was terrified of the Egyptian police.

As the police led Fiona and Flora away, Anni hopped back on the bus, gesturing to Achmed, the driver, to start the engine. Achmed didn't need to be told twice.

Anni took up her microphone as the bus lurched forward. "Hello, is everyone here? I'm afraid this one time I have neglected to count heads."

We all looked around, scanning for faces. Yvonne actually half rose in her seats and did a quick count. "Short four," she called.

"Good," smiled Anni. "Just what I expected."

"Amazing," whispered Kyla. "What do you think it would take to rattle that woman?"

"Just what the hell is going on?" shouted Jerry. He had bounced back into full bluster mode in record time.

"Don't talk to Miss Anni that way, young man," reproved Charlie de Vance in his quavery voice. Yvonne gave Charlie an admiring glance and stroked his arm.

Jerry opened his mouth to say something scathing and then finally noticed a dozen pairs of hostile eyes on him. He pressed his lips together in a thin line and sat back in his seat.

"I know you are all curious. I wish I could tell you what has happened, but unfortunately I know hardly more than you. All I can say is that the police want to speak with Fiona and Flora regarding the murder of Millie Owens." She held

281

up her hand to stop the wondering murmur that arose. "Don't worry, your consulate has been called. They will be given every consideration, and WorldPal will ensure that they are provided with all the resources that they need."

We digested this as the bus rattled back through the darkness toward the Nile.

Dawn Kim looked worried. "Those poor old ladies. I knew they were going to get into trouble, traveling alone like that. I don't see what the police can possibly want with them. They must be so afraid."

"I'm sure they'll be fine," said her husband. "And Mohammad is with them, right, Anni?"

Without skipping a beat, Anni nodded. "Yes, Mohammad is on his way to join them right now."

Everyone on the bus visibly relaxed. Thinking that Mohammad was on his way to the police station made everyone happy, especially Kyla and me. I rubbed my throat, which still felt pretty raw, and then pulled my collar higher. I certainly didn't want to have to answer any questions.

Anni went on. "The most important thing is that tomorrow, we need to be packed and ready to fly back to Cairo at eight a.m. I have arranged wake-up calls as usual."

And she went on to discuss all the logistics of our return. Tomorrow we would start the long homeward journey. In less than twenty-four hours, Kyla and I would be on a plane headed for Frankfurt and then home.

Kyla and I loitered beside the bus until everyone had filed past on their way to the *Nile Lotus*, then turned to Anni.

"What about Alan?" I asked.

"I am going to the hospital as soon as everyone is safely on board. You may come with me."

I threw a glance at Kyla.

"Go on," she said. "I'll start packing for you. I'll do a better job than you would anyway."

I thought briefly about arguing with that and then decided she was probably right. "Thanks."

The hospital was a small, relatively new building on the outskirts of the city. Even at this hour, it was very busy. At least a dozen men sat and stood in the waiting room in various poses ranging from boredom to anxiety. A woman holding a crying child in her lap sat in a corner. All eyes turned on us as we walked in. Anni ignored them and stopped at the front desk to inquire. Hospitals are the same everywhere. Same smell, same overworked staff, same combination of impatience and worry. The woman at the check-in desk seemed to be trying to tell Anni that she couldn't or wouldn't give out any information about Alan. Anni kept the half-smile on her face and spoke gently but rapidly. After a few moments the woman shrugged, pulled out a sheaf of papers, and located the record.

We found Alan in the emergency room, on a bed in a room with several others, hidden behind a white curtain. He looked very pale, his eyelashes dark against his white skin. An IV dripped steadily into his veins, and a white bandage covered his forehead. Somehow, he looked young and vulnerable. I reached out to stroke the hand that lay on the sheets.

A doctor wearing a white coat joined us. To my surprise, he was a sandy-haired young man with prominent front teeth and freckles. He didn't look old enough to have graduated high school, much less medical school, but he was cheerfully competent. His accent marked him as American immediately.

"He was lucky, that's for sure. Another couple of cc of morphine, and he'd be dead. As it is, we've got him on fluids to flush it from his system. He'll sleep it off and probably start coming around in the morning."

"He's going to be all right then?"

"Oh yeah. He'll be completely fine in a day or two. And on the bright side, with all that morphine, he didn't even feel the stitches."

"Stitches?" I asked hesitantly.

"Yeah, right there above his eyebrow. Eight of 'em. I did a great job," he said enthusiastically. "It looks bad now, with the sutures and the swelling, but take my word—he'll only have a tiny white line to show for it. Looks like he was hit with a rock or something else pretty jagged. Must have hurt like hell."

"I'm pretty sure he was already under the morphine when he got hit. Would he have felt much?"

The doctor shook his head. "Nope, he wouldn't have felt a thing in the condition he's in. He'll have a hell of a headache in the morning, though."

I looked down at Alan's unconscious form.

"Those bastards," I said, with only a small pang of guilt. After all, I wouldn't have thrown the rock if it hadn't been for Mohammad and Flora and Fiona. It wasn't really my fault.

"You got that right," he agreed. "Looks like they were trying to kill him. Why in the hell would they have banged him with a rock if he was already doped up?"

I decided to change the subject. "You sound like you're a long way from home."

He grinned. "Baltimore and Luxor are sister cities. We've got a program where our medical folks can come and help out and do some training for a few weeks every year. We get to see the sights, get some of the local flavor in a way you can't as an ordinary tourist. It's pretty cool."

Anni returned. "The best thing will be to return to the ship. WorldPal is sending another agent who will arrive the first thing in the morning and who will look after Alan. I will escort the rest of the group to Cairo as originally scheduled."

I swallowed hard. I knew she was right, that the best thing to do was to continue on with the tour. There was nothing I could do, here in a strange country, knowing nothing of the language, with no influence and very little money. And after all, what was Alan to me? A man I'd known for only a few days, shared a few jokes and a dance with. A man who probably wouldn't even remember my name in a month. The thought was unbearably painful.

Anni caught my stricken look and patted my arm. "Don't worry. He'll be fine. You saved his life, you know. I think that you will see him again."

Saturday and Beyond

Return to Cairo for your final night. Take an optional afternoon excursion to the Khan el-Khalili, Egypt's most famous bazaar, before saying good-bye to your traveling companions and catching your flight home.

—WorldPal pamphlet

Chapter 15

RESOLUTIONS AND REUNIONS

We flew to Cairo on the earliest flight the next morning. Our little group seemed curiously diminished. Not that I missed Mohammad or the ditz duo, murderous old bats, but I hadn't realized how often I'd searched the group for a sight of Alan. His absence removed a lot of the luster from the day. Then, too, my throat hurt, and I felt sore and achy all over. I guess getting thrown to the ground isn't as easy as it looks in the movies.

In the airport waiting lounge, Yvonne drew me aside.

"Well?" she asked, her faded eyes bright with interest.

"We were right about Mohammad at least," I said, and then gave her a brief account of last night's events.

She gave a little whistle. "Fiona and Flora? Really? They had their act down, that's for sure. I never thought twice about them," she added with chagrin.

"Me either. But apparently they weren't good enough to fool Anni. She actually had asked Mohammad to keep his eye on them. Which suited him wonderfully, since that's why he showed up in the first place."

I glanced past her to the rest of the group, so familiar by now. DJ and Nimmi were together at a little shop, haggling again for something.

"What in the world is he going to do with all that stuff?" I asked rhetorically.

"Oh, I finally just asked him that. He works in a children's hospital, and he likes handing out little toys to the kids. He thinks this stuff will be great for the older ones. And plus, he just likes haggling. He says it's more fun than gambling. And cheaper."

I laughed.

She nodded to where Ben, Lydia, and Jane were sitting. Jane was wearing a hat and dark glasses again. "I wish I knew their story. But the sooner they get on a plane to Australia, the better. That girl is going to have a nervous breakdown."

I agreed, and apparently they thought the same thing because they left us at the Cairo airport. Their connecting flight through Vienna was leaving almost immediately, and they were going to skip the afternoon activities scheduled for the rest of us. With a feeling of frustration, I watched them wave good-bye and head to the next terminal. I wished them well, but like Yvonne, I wanted to know what was going on with them.

Kyla and I had to leave for the airport at three in the morning, so we said good-bye to Anni that night. I handed her an envelope containing the suggested tip amount, my twenty-five-dollar bet, plus every Egyptian pound I had left. It wasn't as much as she deserved, although I was pretty sure that Kyla's envelope contained the bonus I couldn't afford. I also handed her a sheet of paper torn from my purse notepad.

"This is my e-mail and other information. Would you let me know how Alan is doing?"

"Of course," she said, her dark luminous eyes full of understanding.

Cairo to Frankfurt, Frankfurt to Chicago, Chicago to Austin. Almost twenty-four hours later, I was back in Texas and due back in the classroom in less than twelve hours. Exhausted and let down, I crawled into bed and prepared to resume my normal life.

As she promised, Anni e-mailed me two days later to let me know that Alan had been released from the hospital. Her note was friendly, but brief. I'm not sure what I expected. "He has a fever and is calling for you," would have been nice. I doubted I would ever see him again. I had no way to contact him and wasn't sure what I'd say anyway. Sorry for hitting you with a rock just seemed so inadequate.

Life quickly returned to the old routine. A couple of weeks later, Kyla and I went to Eeyore's Birthday Party, an annual festival that draws all the magnificent weirdness for which Austin is famous. You just never know what you're going to see there—new age hippies smoking half-concealed joints, a transvestite in neon blue hot pants sporting a mountain-man beard, a couple of anorexic-looking women in fairy costumes.

We also ran into my ex, Mike, and his fiancée. I looked at the two of them, taking in the pressed clothes, the flash of diamonds at the wrist and neck, the manicured nails. And that was just him.

I grinned and said hello, then moved on, already looking forward to the catty things I would be able to say to Kyla as soon as they were out of earshot. I had taken ten paces and was already starting in on the fake tans, when I suddenly realized that the sting was gone. I might be vindictive and bitter, but I no longer grieved for what I'd lost. It felt really good. I saw the look of approval in Kyla's eyes, as she came back strong with an observation about the fake boobs. All four of them.

One Saturday afternoon at the beginning of May, I was sitting on my back porch grading papers and drinking iced tea when the phone rang. I picked it up absently, still concentrating on the pathetic spelling and poor grammar on the page in front of me. My red pen was poised and quivering.

"Jocelyn? Alan Stratton here."

I absolutely froze. My mouth was open, but no sound was coming out.

"Alan Stratton?" he repeated, sounding uncertain. "From the Egypt tour?"

"Alan," I managed, voice a little croaky. "Of course I know who you are. I'm just surprised." I swallowed hard and sat up, scattering papers everywhere. "How are you? I mean, how are you feeling?"

"All recovered," he said, a little more confident. "I'm back in the United States."

"That's great. No side effects? No headaches?" I asked the last a little gingerly. As far as I knew, no one knew I'd been the cause of his head injury.

"Nope, completely back to normal. And I hear I have you to thank for it."

"Oh, I . . . oh, no. I didn't do anything," I said weakly.

"Not how I heard it." He paused, then cleared his throat. "Anyway, I was wondering if I could come by sometime to thank you? Maybe we could even, I don't know, go to dinner?"

"I'd love that," I said. Was he actually going to come to Austin? Just to see me? I was suddenly very excited.

"How about tonight?"

"Tonight?"

"If you've already got plans, I completely understand," he said hastily.

"You're not in town, are you?"

"Actually, yes. In fact, I was going to just drop by your house, but then I decided that was just a little too much like a stalker."

I was now pacing back and forth, unable to sit. I briefly wondered how he'd found my address, but it didn't matter. He was here. In town. And he wanted to see me. I felt like one of my students, and not the brightest one at that.

"Jocelyn?"

"One hour." I squeaked and hung up on him.

I was halfway to the shower before I realized how idiotic I must have sounded, but it was too late. I started the water, then raced to the phone and punched in Kyla's number.

"Hey," she answered lazily. She has caller ID, but I wasn't positive it would have mattered.

"Alan! It's Alan. He's coming to take me out."

"What?" I could hear her sitting up.

"Alan Stratton. He's here." I dropped the phone as I pulled my shirt over my head.

293

"Alan? From Egypt? Are you kidding me?" she was saying as I picked it back up.

"No, really, he just called." I kicked off my shoes. One of them flew across the room and left a mark on my white wall. I didn't care.

"When you say here . . ."

"Here! In Austin. He's coming over."

"What the hell are you doing talking to me, you idiot?"

"I'm doing what we swore we'd never do to each other. I'm canceling with you for a man."

She laughed. "Hell, I'd do it to you in a heartbeat. Just remember, you'll owe me details later. Specific, sweaty, bodice-ripping details."

"I don't think so. Besides, I don't think he'll be wearing a bodice."

She ignored this. "And wear that new sundress. If I find out you met him in those pathetic fat-ass jeans, I'll slap you into the middle of next week."

I laughed and hung up, then paused. What was wrong with my jeans? Nevertheless, the sundress it was.

Alan arrived at my door exactly one hour later, looking different somehow. And it wasn't just the small scar above his right eyebrow. He seemed taller or something. Maybe his eyes were more green than ever. Maybe he just seemed more remote now that he was on my turf and out of the tour setting where I'd come to know him. He seemed to be searching my face, looking for something. I felt suddenly shy.

"Come on in," I said, remembering my manners. I stepped back and held the door wide.

He walked past me then turned to give me a hug. Unfortunately, it was the kind of hug you might give a friend.

"It's really good to see you," he said, but at least he really seemed to mean it.

"You too," I said. "How are you feeling? No lasting effects?"

"None at all. I'm completely fine, thanks to you. You saved my life, you know."

"I don't think so," I protested. "I didn't really do anything." I shot a glance at his scar again, feeling even more guilty.

I led the way to my tiny living room, glad the place was relatively neat. It had taken three weeks, but I'd put away the last remnants of my Egypt laundry and souvenirs the weekend before. On the wall near the kitchen hung the papyrus in its unbreakable glass, the one I'd bought after the saleswoman bounced it off the floor. It was actually a nice piece, the Eye of Horus, and here, where it was not surrounded by hundreds of other prints, it did not look so garish. Beside it, on a small shelf, sat the gold pyramid he'd given me on Elephantine Island. With a smile, he paused to look at it.

A thought occurred to me. "You know, I never even asked if you had my address. I'm not in the phone book. I hope you didn't have trouble finding me."

"Not for someone with my innate and impressive detective skills," he said with a grin. "Also, Anni handed me your contact information."

"She did?" I knew I hadn't tipped her enough.

"She did. And told me she hoped I was smarter than I looked."

"She never said that!"

He grinned. "She might as well have. She certainly implied it."

I went to the refrigerator and returned with two beers. He gave me an approving look. "Shiner Bock. A woman of taste and discernment."

We clicked the bottles together. He was looking at me in the oddest way, as if he wanted to say something but couldn't quite find the words. I'm not sure how long we would have stood there staring at each other, but I decided to break the spell.

"Come on, let's sit outside. It's such a gorgeous day. And then you can tell me what happened after we left."

He followed me to the back porch where I had two lawn chairs and a small iron table. The roses around the patio were covered with small buds and the tomato plants in the raised bed near the back fence were already spilling over their cages. My fat little poodle, hearing the door, lifted her head and leaped to her feet, yapping obnoxiously. I stomped my foot at her and she subsided, tail wagging.

Alan stared. "What is . . . I mean, who is that?"

"You had it right the first time. She's a pest. But a pretty good pest," I couldn't help adding. "Her name is Belle."

He scored points by dropping down on one knee and holding out his hand. Belle waddled forward and licked his fingers, which meant nothing about his character at all. She was not a discriminating dog.

We sat down. Belle leaped into his lap, tried to stick her tongue in his beer bottle, which he jerked away just in time. Then she jumped back down and curled up at his feet. He laughed out loud.

"I told you she's a pest. An old pest. She was a present for my sixteenth birthday, which seemed very cool at the time. Anyway, tell me what happened with Fiona and Flora. I've been trying to find out, but there hasn't been a thing in the news, and Anni hasn't written me."

"Well, it's not exactly something the Egyptians want to advertise. And the press there doesn't have the same freedoms that it has here. But I stuck around long enough to give a deposition."

"So tell."

"Well, Fiona and Flora are being held in jail in Cairo on charges of murder, diamond smuggling, and antiquities theft. Actually, I'm not even sure the Egyptians bothered to file charges for the assault against me, they had so much else to work with."

I leaned forward. "I heard them talking with Mohammad about diamonds, and they mentioned that Millie had seen some sort of statue. Poor Millie. I guess that's why they killed her. You know, that entry in her notebook—where she suspected someone of smuggling? I actually thought she was talking about me and Kyla," I admitted. "I thought she was crazy, when she was really smarter than all of us."

He nodded. "I think she figured out Fiona and Flora right away. She may not have known the extent of their plans. In fact, I don't see how she could have, but having found the statue, she knew enough to ruin their trip and possibly get them arrested. They couldn't take that risk. She was a dead woman the instant she opened their bag."

"And what about Mohammad? Did they ever catch him?"

"Almost immediately. He might have escaped if he'd left

Karnak and never looked back, but he wasn't prepared to do that. He wasn't even carrying his passport, much less any money. He decided to sneak back onto the ship to get his things, and of course the police were waiting for him."

I digested this. "You know, he might have been involved in the smuggling, but he never wanted anyone hurt. He really seemed appalled by Fiona and Flora's activities."

"Yes, murder was never supposed to be part of the plan. And from his point of view, everything that could go wrong did go wrong. He wasn't in the same league with them in terms of ruthlessness, not that it will matter much when it comes to prison time over there."

I thought back to the conversation at Karnak. "Fiona and Flora seemed to know him pretty well."

Alan smiled his attractive smile. I thought he looked exceptionally good on my back porch. "This wasn't the first time they'd worked for him."

"They worked for him? After hearing them talk to him at Karnak, I thought it was the other way around."

"Oh no. This was Mohammad's deal all along. He came up with the plan, he made the contacts, he arranged the transfers. Then all he needed was someone who could play the part of a tourist and collect the items. It was very clever, deciding to use tour groups for smuggling purposes. Very low risk."

"Low risk? You're kidding, right?"

"Not at all. You've seen how tour groups are treated. One big happy family. Luggage scooped up all together, identities vouched for by the tour guide. If the luggage is inspected at all, it's very cursory. And everyone expects to see all kinds of fake Egyptian crap in tourist luggage. How easy would it be to throw in one or two real pieces? It would take an expert eye to notice one authentic item in a load of fakes."

I blushed a little. "I suspected DJ, as a matter of fact. He was buying so much worthless stuff. And once I read Millie's journal and started thinking about smuggling, he moved to the top of my list. I feel bad about it."

"Well, you had company. I thought the same thing for a while." He reached down to pet Belle. "It was an easy mistake to make, or at least I hope it was. Anyway, Mohammad was WorldPal's chief director in Egypt, and he was ideally placed to set up exchanges and contacts. We were even paying him to scout out locations and make local contacts. In fact, if he hadn't gotten greedy, he could have done it for years."

"Greedy?"

"He thought he found the ultimate smugglers in Fiona and Flora. Looking over our records, they've been on at least two other WorldPal Egyptian tours. And from what has come out in the investigation, they were apparently quite good at fencing stolen items. With their abilities, I think Mohammad was planning to repeat his little scam indefinitely. Everyone was getting rich, and it was seemingly foolproof. He had no idea Anni had become suspicious and had contacted me."

"It just seemed so elaborate. All those people involved. I don't see how he could have kept it going without getting caught."

"To be honest, I think the previous trips were on a much smaller scale—I suspect they just took out one or two small items. But Fiona and Flora had decided to retire and apparently they told him this would be their last trip. He decided that he would arrange as many exchanges as he could. If the statue that got Millie killed was the only goal, they would have gotten away with it. But Mohammad had something set up in nearly every place we stopped, and they couldn't handle it. I'm sure you noticed that Flora was getting a little . . . confused at times."

"I wondered about that. I thought it might be part of her act."

"I'm sure it was at one time, but it was becoming all too real. In fact, I'm pretty sure that's the main reason things got out of control. Flora at least wasn't able to make cool judgments anymore. She should have stopped the operation the minute Millie Owens became a threat. In fact, according to Mohammad, that was one of the many scenarios they had worked out in advance. If any of the other tourists noticed or commented on anything whatsoever, the whole thing was supposed to be canceled, and Mohammad himself would swoop in to remove the item and replace it with something similar but very fake. But instead, Flora killed her."

"Flora did it?" I'm not sure why I was surprised. Maybe because Flora had seemed fluffier and softer than Fiona, with her talon-like hands and stringy shoulders.

"Yep. According to Flora herself, she killed Millie, and Fiona took out the vendor in Abu Simbel. By then, Mohammad had joined the tour so that he could prevent that sort of thing, but you'll remember he had to help carry Kathy Morrison to the first aid tent. While he was occupied, the two ladies took the opportunity to retrieve the diamonds. But the vendor refused to take the outdated currency they had."

"Yes, what was that about? I heard them talking about that too, but I didn't understand."

"One of their many operations was a little money laundering. On Elephantine Island, they met with your friend, Aladdin, and traded him a load of Egyptian pounds for Sudanese currency, which they were to use to buy the diamonds at Abu Simbel. That transaction went without a hitch, except that Aladdin double-crossed them. A couple of years ago, the Sudan switched from the Sudanese dinar to the Sudanese pound. The dinars are now all but worthless. I suppose it might be possible to exchange them for pounds, but not without going through the Sudanese banks and certainly not without attracting attention. It was a lot of money."

"So when they got to Abu Simbel, their money was no good?"

"Exactly. And the vendor wasn't going to give them their diamonds. And again, they had a chance to walk away, to contact Mohammad, but they decided to act on their own. Flora distracted him by bursting into tears and when he leaned forward to comfort her, Fiona stabbed him in the neck. Flora was quite proud of her acting skills and was happily describing it all in gory detail. Fiona was frantically trying to shut her up."

"I bet she was." I gave a little shudder. "Horrible."

"Horrible and crazy. Flora especially."

"Did they say anything about my necklace?" I asked. I still thought of it that way. My necklace, heavy and warm against my throat.

"That was the final straw. All through the tour, you must have noticed over and over how strangers were approaching you and Kyla, making odd references to sisters and Utah?"

"Yes! What was that about?"

"That was the code for all the transactions Mohammad had lined up for Fiona and Flora. The parties involved were to

301

look for and contact two sisters on the tour to pass money or goods. What no one foresaw was another set of sisters on the trip. I know you're cousins, but you and Kyla looked more like sisters than Fiona and Flora do. Plus, who would suspect two little old ladies of being involved in anything illegal? The contacts, scanning the group for two sisters, fastened on the two of you every time."

I thought about it. "The guy in the carpet shop—he asked me about Utah and wanted me to go in that back room. He scared me."

"From his point of view, I'm sure he couldn't understand why you weren't cooperating. It must have been very confusing." He gave a little chuckle.

"I saw Fiona with him as I was leaving. I actually felt sorry for her," I remembered. "I thought he was going to con her into buying an expensive rug. What did he actually want from them?"

He shrugged. "No one knows. By the time the authorities tried to arrest him, he had vanished. And Fiona and Flora aren't saying much."

"So, the guy in the rug shop, the guy on Kitchener's Island who called himself Aladdin, and the stall keepers in Edfu who gave me the necklace," I said slowly. "They all thought they were supposed to contact Kyla and me."

"And one tour group owner," he said ruefully, meeting my eyes.

"Ah." My mouth dropped open a little as I processed this. Several things clicked into place. "That's why you were following me . . . us . . . around. That's what you were talking about

302

at the hotel on Elephantine Island. I could not figure out what you were getting at."

He nodded. "I was an idiot. As soon as Anni told me about hearing someone talking about sisters, I was sure it was the two of you. But the more I got to know you, the less sense it made. Give me a little credit, I really couldn't see you as a murderer."

"No, you just thought Kyla had pressured me into a life of crime." I stifled something between a laugh and a sigh. "You know, part of the time, I actually thought you sort of liked me. And all the while, you thought I was a murderer. Or at least an accessory."

He laughed with me. "I did like you. That's why I was trying to get you to come clean about your life of crime."

"Turn in my evil cousin, who'd led me astray."

"Exactly."

"When did you know you were wrong?"

"Well, remember I was questioning my own judgment right from the start."

"Uh-huh."

"But I was positive at the Valley of the Kings. I saw the knife cut on your arm. After I figured out that you'd been handed a necklace you didn't know anything about, things started to make more sense. I looked around for anyone else who might be involved and finally took a look at Fiona and Flora. They seemed too old and senile at first glance, but they were the only other group members who were at Seti's tomb at the right time."

I blinked. "You mean it was Flora and Fiona who attacked me and tried to take my purse?"

303

"One of them at least."

"But whoever it was knocked me down. He . . . or she . . . was strong!" I protested, indignant that he thought one of those old ladies could overpower me.

"Probably Fiona then. She's a big woman, and she's in surprisingly good shape. Very surprising, in fact." He looked embarrassed.

I stared. "Wait, you mean . . ."

"Yup. They popped out of nowhere while I was following Mohammad. I thought they were lost and was actually trying to show them the way back to the group. I didn't want them to blow my cover. Fiona sidled over to me with a map, and while I was pointing out where we were, she knocked me flat. Flora injected me with the morphine while I was trying to get up. I guess I'm just lucky she didn't knife me. And even luckier that you came along before they talked Mohammad into killing me." He took a drink of beer. "Totally humiliating."

I grinned. "You'll get over it. Besides, in a fair fight, my money would be on you."

"So, you think I could take her?"

"I'm sure you could. Well, two out of three anyway."

He gave me a mock glare, and then we both burst into laughter.

"What will happen to them, anyway?"

"The U.S. State Department found a lawyer for them and has filed dozens of protests and appeals, but so far the Egyptians haven't budged. On the plus side, there's enough attention and pressure from the United States to ensure that they aren't mistreated."

I thought about that. "I guess that's good. Do you think they'll send them back here?"

He shrugged. "Who knows? I'm not sure which outraged the authorities more—murder or antiquities theft. I imagine either one normally warrants the death penalty. But in this case, especially in light of their age and nationality, I think they are probably looking at long prison sentences."

Satisfied, I sat back in my seat. The afternoon sun, still filtering warmly through the new leaves of the live oaks, was gently sinking toward the horizon. A bee hovered lazily around the pink petals of the roses in the garden, and two squirrels chased each other down the bole of a tree across a patch of grass and then up and over the back fence. Belle raised her head and uttered a fierce little growl, but she didn't bother to get up. I was intensely aware of the man sitting next to me, long legs stretched out comfortably, the light turning his hair a soft chestnut color and his eyes bright green.

"Another beer?" I asked him. "Or some tea?"

"Maybe tea this time. If it's made."

"The pitcher's on the counter. Do you need sugar?"

"Nope. Straight up for me."

I smiled and went for the glasses. When I returned, he was leaning forward, scratching Belle's curly little head. He took the glass with a word of thanks, his fingers brushing mine and giving me a warm feeling in the pit of my stomach.

I sat, searching for something to say. "You know, the one thing I never figured out. What was up with the Carpenters and Jane? I've never seen anyone so frightened in my whole life. I'm just positive that she was a different girl. Kyla still thinks I'm nuts."

He smiled. "Well, not about that at least. They left before I was out of the hospital, but Anni knew all the details. She was helping them the whole time."

"Anni?"

"She's a very bright person. She's now in charge of all WorldPal tours in Egypt, by the way. I gave her Mohammad's old job and a big raise. Amazing woman."

"That's perfect. She was wonderful. I'm really glad for her," I said with satisfaction. "So tell about Jane."

"Well, the Jane we saw on the trip is actually the daughter of close friends of the Carpenters. Her real name is Barbara, and she and the real Jane Carpenter practically grew up together. About a year ago, this Barbara met and married an Egyptian man from a wealthy and very connected family."

Alan took a sip of tea and went on. "I guess he seemed nice enough as a student in Australia, but after she went to live with him in Cairo, he changed. He became physically abusive, and when she tried to leave him, he took her passport. She tried to get to the Australian embassy, but he had his men follow her wherever she went. This went on for months, but at last, and I'm not sure how, she managed to get word to her parents. They wanted to come and get her immediately, but Egyptian laws regarding women are tricky, and they were afraid that if they tried to go through the regular channels it would alert the husband and he might take it out on their daughter. He might even have killed her—apparently he threatened to do so often enough."

"That's terrible. They must have been so desperate." I couldn't even imagine how helpless and terrified they must have felt.

"They were. But their friends, Ben and Lydia, thought up a great plan. Practically foolproof. Can you guess?"

My jaw dropped a little. "They swapped girls?"

"Exactly. They thought that since their daughters were close in age and close enough in appearance, they might be able to get Barbara out using their own daughter's passport. A really careful customs screener would notice, but they thought that if 'Jane' was ill, they might get away with it."

"According to Anni, it worked perfectly. The hardest part was getting word to Barbara, but they managed, and the Carpenters signed on with WorldPal. You can't beat a tour if you want to be inconspicuous. The real Jane met up with Barbara in the Khan market, and swapped clothes with her in a dressing room. She gave her the passport and money, and told her how to meet up with her parents. The asshole husband was already insisting that Barbara wear the full head covering, what's it called? A burka? Anyway, that certainly worked to her advantage this time. The real Jane, fully covered in Barbara's burka, wandered through the market for several hours, followed by the goons. When enough time had gone by for Barbara to be safely at the Mena House with the Carpenters, Jane ditched the burka and headed for a cab. The husband's men tried to stop her, but she apparently started screaming and caused a huge scene." He grinned at the thought. "She wasn't a cowed little victim, and obviously she wasn't the woman they were supposed to be guarding. Thank goodness, they weren't quick enough or maybe smart enough to realize that she had actually been involved. Anyway, a crowd gathered and it was enough for her to get in a cab and vanish into Cairo before they could stop her."

"Amazing. How clever of them. But how risky!" I breathed.

"It was absolutely brilliant. Barbara joined the tour as Jane. I think the one thing the Carpenters didn't count on, apart from your having seen the real Jane, was how beaten down and terrified Barbara had become. Ben told Anni he hardly recognized her, she'd changed so much. It was a constant effort to keep her playing her part."

"But wait, what happened to the real Jane? She didn't have her passport."

"They had it all planned out. As soon as the tour ended, and Ben and Lydia were safely on their way home with Barbara, Jane reported that her purse had been snatched and her passport was gone. There was a day or two of hassle, but in the end, the Australian embassy came through with a new one and she flew home."

We sat together in companionable silence while I mulled it all over. "Well, I guess that's it then. Everything is all wrapped up."

"Hmmm. Well, not quite." He gave me a crooked smile, his eyes uncertain.

I raised my eyebrows.

"We still don't know whether you've forgiven me for suspecting you were involved."

I laughed. "That sort of goes both ways. Do you forgive me for the same thing?"

"Absolutely. I even forgive you for chucking that rock at my head."

I gasped, feeling my face go bright red. "You knew that was me?"

"Mohammad ratted you out. Not that it mattered. I told

308

you, the police had so much else to work with, they didn't really care about what had been done to me. But Mohammad was desperately trying to tell everyone who would listen that he had never hurt anyone."

"I'm really sorry about that. I was trying to hit Mohammad, but I missed." I looked down at my hands. "I've always been a terrible throw. I don't know why I thought I could hit him."

Alan laughed, a real, happy laugh that made me start giggling a little. "It all worked out. You saved me from them, and you didn't kill me in the process. So what about it? Are we square?"

"Yes," I agreed.

He rose. "So how about dinner then?"

I stood too and reached for my purse. Looking up at him, seeing him again after all this time, he seemed even more attractive than I'd remembered. Part of me had actually hoped that the vacation magic would have worn off. It had not. My mind was shrieking warnings. So I'd go to dinner with him, but then what? He probably was just being nice, just here out of obligation, to say thank you. Even if he wasn't, long-distance relationships never worked. I'd get my heart stomped all over again. I realized I didn't care, as long as I could be with him even for a little. I told my mind to shut the hell up.

"Dinner sounds great. By the way, how long are you going to be in town?" I asked, trying to sound casual.

He hesitated, then reached for my hand and drew me close. Gently, as if afraid I would run, he slipped an arm around my waist and brushed his lips against mine. Then I was in his arms, and he was kissing me as though he would never let me go.

I'm not sure how many minutes passed before he finally answered.

"I can run WorldPal from anywhere I want. So I guess it depends on you. How long do you want me to stay?"

I started laughing out loud. "A very, very long time."

The shouting started just after lunch, angry and loud enough to
make me spring down from the chair that I'd been standing on
to hang posters and race for the door of my classroom. I burst
into the hallway, then stopped confused. Farther down the corridor, a couple of teachers peered out of their rooms like meerkats
on alert, ready to scatter at the first hint of danger. Otherwise,
the hall was empty.

A furious male voice boomed through the air, echoing
along gray concrete floors and walls, coming from everywhere
and nowhere. In the open building, sounds carried from the
first floor to the second and from one corridor to the next
without hindrance. When two thousand kids were on the
move the sound of feet on stairs; the talking, giggling, and
shouting; and the clang of lockers became an indescribable
din. On this day, the last day of summer vacation, the school
was all but deserted, and, until a moment ago, the halls had
been silent.

White-knuckled, I grasped the railing of the stairwell and leaned out ever so slightly, trying to see movement on the first floor far below without really looking. I loathed heights. Even behind a firm rail, the drop made me feel a little queasy. A second shout made me turn. This time I had it. The argument was coming from the classroom directly across the hall. Fred Argus's room. Dashing around the intervening stairwell, I threw open the door with a bang.

Two men turned startled faces in my direction. Fred Argus, my fellow history teacher, stood behind his desk as though poised to flee, open hands raised to his adversary as though in supplication. The other guy was a stranger, a big man with the thick neck of a fighter, black-eyed and red-faced. He turned a malevolent gaze on me, and I felt an unexpected stab of fear. An aura of rage, barely contained and menacing, flowed from him. Alarmed, I stood a little straighter.

"What's going on, Fred?" I asked, trying to keep my tone light but not taking my eyes off the newcomer.

"Nothing that concerns you," the stranger answered for him. His was the voice that had been doing the shouting, a deep bullhorn of a voice, the kind that could carry across a crowded room or shout down a mob.

I ignored him. "Fred?"

Fred gave me a look of mingled fear and hope, like a beaten dog receiving a pat from his master. He didn't quite come out from behind the shelter of his desk, but he did straighten a little from his crouching position.

"Mr. Richards has concerns about the tennis team," he said, shooting a nervous look at the stranger.

"The tennis team?" I repeated blankly.

Of course I knew that Fred was the tennis coach, something I'd always found a little ironic, considering he was on the wrong side of sixty and smoked at least two packs of cigarettes a day. The sight of the white toothpicks that he called legs flashing from beneath a pair of spandex shorts had been known to cause convulsions in even the strongest of women. I also knew that our tennis team, although possibly the worst in the league, was one of the few high school teams which every kid, regardless of experience, was welcome to join. What I didn't know was why anyone would need to raise his eyebrows, much less his voice, for anything remotely related to the Bonham Breakpoints.

Mr. Richards took a step toward me, and again I felt a small flash of fear, so out of place in a bright classroom on an August afternoon. I knew from Fred's return to full flight-or-fight stance that he felt it too—this man was very close to violence.

"Is your child thinking of joining the team, Mr. Richards?" I asked quickly, trying to keep him talking so that he would focus on something, anything other than his anger. He reminded me of a bull at a rodeo. He'd thrown his cowboy and was now waiting for the clown to get a little closer.

His eyes narrowed, and he shot a glance at Fred that could have stripped paint from a wall.

"My son IS the team. The only real player you've got. And this old son of a . . ."

I cut him off. "Did you know Coach Fred started the tennis program here at Bonham, Mr. Richards?"

This distracted him for an instant. He looked at me like I was crazy. I went on in the most cheerful voice I could manage.

"Yes indeed, Coach Fred is the reason we have a tennis team at all. He was the one who lobbied to get the courts built. And he did all the paperwork and lobbying to get us into the league. We wouldn't have tennis at this school if it weren't for him."

I could have gone on like this forever. I was watching Mr. Richards's face, hoping to see the redness vanish or at least fade, but he drew in a deep breath in preparation for another tirade. Where in the world were those other teachers?

"Get out!" he shouted in a voice that practically blew my hair back from my face. He took another step toward me, and I felt a chill run down my spine.

"No." I stood my ground, holding his gaze with one of my own. My best teacher look, in fact, complete with the all-powerful lifted eyebrow. It was a look that could quell thirty teenage boys, and now it made this arrogant bully pause. I seized the moment.

"It's time for you to leave, Mr. Richards. If you have anything further you'd like to discuss about the tennis team or any other subject, I'd suggest you make an appointment with Mr. Gonzales, our principal, who will be happy to address your concerns."

For a moment none of us moved. In the silence a clock somewhere in the room ticked out the seconds. Mr. Richards hesitated another instant, then erupted with a bellow, kicking a desk out of his path. It toppled over with a crash. I jumped but held my ground.

Glaring at me, he halted inches from my face, at the last instant deciding not to strike me. He tried to stare me down. I stared back, partly in defiance, mostly just frozen with shock. Either way, it finally worked. He backed down.

"I'll do that. This isn't the end of this conversation," he said to Fred. "You fucking bitch," he added to me as he stomped by.

"Mr. Richards," I said, my voice quiet.

He half turned.

"Don't come back. If I see you in this hall again, I'll call the police first and ask questions later."

He didn't bother to reply. Cautiously, I followed him out the door, watching to make sure he actually went down the steps and out the double doors to the quadrangle. He did. I heard the crash the double doors made as he slammed through them, sending them banging in unison against their doorstops. He was halfway across the courtyard before the springs drew the doors shut again with a muffled clang. Silence returned to the hall. Not one teacher bothered to look out again, the cowards. I drew a deep, shaky breath, then returned to the classroom.

Fred had collapsed into the chair behind his desk, looking curiously shrunken and defeated. He stroked the smooth wood of his little desk clock with fingers that trembled as though with cold. The clock had been a parting gift from his coworkers when he'd left his original career to become a teacher some twenty years earlier. I wondered if he was feeling sorry he'd made the job switch. Noticing my glance, he set the clock back in its usual place on the corner of his desk, then let his hands drop into his lap.

"You know, I thought he was going to hit me," he said in a wondering tone.

I pulled up a chair and sank into it, taking the clock into my own hands, admiring it. It was a pretty little thing made of polished mahogany, about the size of my two fists held together, standing upright like a miniature grandfather clock. Along the bottom was a small drawer complete with lock and miniature key, and on the back an engraved plaque.

Now that the argument was over, I could feel a reaction of my own setting in. My fingers trembled enough that I decided to put the clock down.

"So what did he want anyway?" I asked.

Fred answered slowly, as though puzzled. "I'm not even sure. Something about wanting his boy, Eric, to be team captain. Which is ridiculous because I don't have anything to do with that. The kids vote for team captain. I don't think Eric even signed up to be in the running."

"What does the team captain do?" I asked.

I didn't care, but I didn't want to leave him just yet. I didn't like the gray hue of his face or the way he slumped in his chair—it made me wonder about the condition of his heart for the first time. For years he had been the head of our team of history teachers, a vibrant, passionate man, completely dedicated to his students and to the school. He and I argued occasionally over things like lesson plans, but I usually deferred to him in the end. I liked to tell him it was because I figured he'd been an eyewitness to most of the things we taught. But until now, I'd never thought of him as being old.

He didn't answer for a long moment. Then finally he looked up as though confused. "I'm sorry. What did you ask?"

I repeated the question.

"Ah, that. It's nothing much. The captain is responsible for little things like maintaining the calling chain and acting as my assistant for the away games. It's mostly just an indication of the other players' respect. I suppose it might look good on a résumé," he added as an afterthought.

I frowned. "Then I don't see what he wanted. If he tries to bully you again, Fred, you need to call someone. Preferably the police."

"Oh, I don't think that will be necessary," he said, not quite meeting my eyes. "A one- time occurrence, tempers getting a bit out of hand. Nothing to worry about."

"Nothing to worry about? Fred, that guy was two seconds from hauling off and hitting you. What exactly is going on?"

"Nothing. No, it's nothing." He rose abruptly, glancing one last time around his classroom, taking in the rows of desks, the whiteboards, the newly hung maps and posters on the walls. Everything appeared neat, clean, and ready for the first day of class tomorrow. Even the air held the scent of lemon polish and new books, the smell of a new school year, sweet with promise. "I'm going home. Nothing left to do that can't be done tomorrow."

Always a gentleman, he held the door open for me, leaving me no choice but to precede him into the hall. He pulled the door shut behind us, locking it and then nervously scanning the hall, then the stairwell.

"Fred—" I started, but he cut me off.

"I'll see you tomorrow, Jocelyn." He walked to the stairs, then turned. "Thank you for . . . well, just thank you." Then he hurried away, pattering lightly down the stairs. Maybe he wasn't getting old after all.

I watched him go, feeling dissatisfied.

There should be a special place in purgatory for whoever had designed James Bonham High School. In the main academic building, the upper-floor corridors were lined with painted metal railings and provided a perfect view of the floor below, which in a high school was just an open invitation to spit. The architecture reminds first-ime visitors of something they can't quite place—I was there a whole year before I figured it out, and then only did because I'd just seen *The Shawshank Redemption*. Contracts to build schools go to the lowest bidder, and in this case the winning bidder's most recent project had been the state correctional facility. And it showed in every loving detail. From the concrete floors to the cinder-block walls to the unheated and un–air conditioned hallways. You could practically hear the clang of the bars and the shouts of the guards.

I suppose to the casual visitor, it might not seem so bad. The campus was spacious, liberally sprinkled with trees and consisting of four main buildings that enclosed a central concrete courtyard. Closer observation revealed that these main buildings were surrounded by what we less than fondly referred to as portables, which were basically double-wide mobile homes, each stripped of appliances and other niceties and divided in half to make two uncomfortable classrooms, poorly heated in the winter, poorly air conditioned in the summer. Of course, this wasn't much worse than in the permanent structures. Only the administrative building had central air conditioning. The rest had individual heating and cooling units in the classrooms only, leaving the hallways to the mercy of the Texas weather. In fall and spring, the heat was stifling. In winter, the cold and damp turned fingers blue and cheeks red.

Now, I fought back the feeling of vertigo that I get from heights and leaned over the rail for a moment to watch Fred's little white head disappear through the same doors that Mr. Richards had barged through just minutes ago. I was just straightening when a number of strangers walked in, led by the principal, Larry Gonzales. I leaned out again with interest.

Larry was doing his Lord of the Manor walk, which meant these were visitors of particular importance. All the teachers could tell the exact status of a visitor by Larry's walk, and my friend Laura and I had set up a rating system. The all-purpose Brush-off was used for students and teachers alike— long quick steps, eyes focused on a sheaf of papers or a cell phone, a pretense of deafness. The Brush-off got him through the halls with minimal interruption and maximum efficiency.

The PTA or "Tight-ass" walk was for parents—short quick steps, arms stiff against his sides, stern gaze focused on a vague point on the horizon. This walk conveyed a sense of mission and importance, although the shortness of the steps allowed a determined parent to keep up without breaking into a trot. The Concerned Administrator was reserved for groups of parents or teachers with actual grievances who needed to be "handled" to avoid unpleasantness, which meant anything from bitter letters to the editor to full-blown lawsuits. It was hardly a walk at all and involved slow, measured steps, a lot of head nodding, and the occasional sensitive touch on the shoulder or forearm, which let you know what a great and concerned guy Larry was. And finally, there was the Lord of the Manor—head thrown back, arms gesturing expansively, voice booming—the walk Larry reserved for visitors who needed to be impressed, which meant visitors who could do something for Larry.

I wondered who they were and what Larry wanted from them. Unlike the usual Lord of the Manor candidates, these three weren't terribly impressive at first glance. A skinny blond guy with a ponytail was holding some sort of electronic device at arm's length and swinging it this way and that. He walked beside an earnest-looking young woman with serious black-framed glasses that she apparently did not need because she kept pushing them down to the tip of her nose and looking over the top of the frame. And finally, a slightly older man in jeans trailed behind about ten paces, making notes on a legal pad. As they moved directly beneath me, I could hear the woman saying, "Yes, this will be absolutely perfect. Just fantastic."

Then they turned a corner, and I decided to go back to my room instead of following them, feeling sure I'd hear about it sometime soon. Anything that rated a Lord of the Manor walk was bound to make its presence known and probably bite the rest of us in the ass.

I picked up the chair, which I'd knocked over when I raced out, and returned to the poster I'd been hanging. I'd saved this one until last, putting it in the corner where it could be seen by all my students. It was a picture of lemmings jumping off a cliff with the words, "Those who cannot remember the past are condemned to repeat it."

Stepping off the chair, I looked around with satisfaction, feeling my room looked almost as nice as Fred's. Of course, mine didn't smell of lemon polish because it would never have occurred to me to dust with more than a damp paper towel, but still everything looked pretty good. Tomorrow was the first day of the new school year, August 24. A little later this year than in past years, but still the height of summer. Long days, cloudless skies, sizzling heat. There wasn't a kid on the planet who wouldn't have rather been at the pool, but at least I was ready for them.

I returned to my desk and started looking over the lists of student names again. This year, my day was made up of four history classes, two French classes, one planning period, and one lunch period. Which meant I had about 180 students. Going through the lists in advance made it easier remembering who was who when I finally met them all. I prided myself on my ability to know every kid's name by the end of the first week. I was just going through the list a second time when the door to my classroom opened, and my best friend Kyla Shore walked in.

Although most people assume we are sisters, Kyla and I are first cousins. Our fathers were identical twins and we look enough alike to be twins ourselves. Maybe not identical twins, but we'd been mistaken for each other before, a fact that drove Kyla absolutely crazy. She would never admit there was anything more than a remote family resemblance. For my part I would have been happy if we looked even more alike, or rather if I looked more like her. Because, although I wouldn't break mirrors, Kyla was drop-dead gorgeous—the kind of beauty that made men stop in the middle of the street to pick their jaws up off the ground. She was no fool either, and was fully aware of the effect she had on men. In fact, she shamelessly used it to her full advantage, telling me once that she hadn't bought a drink for herself in five years. It might have made her obnoxious, but she was also completely charming. And to be fair, it didn't seem to mean much to her other than as an entertaining diversion. She'd graduated with honors in computer programming and now worked as a lead developer for a software company, raking in money and bonuses.

Today she looked glum. And beautiful, of course. And stylish and elegant. August in Austin, Texas, meant the temperature outside was at least ninety-five degrees. It meant that touching a steering wheel could leave grill marks on your palms.

It meant that the thirty seconds it took to dash from an air conditioned building to an air conditioned car could leave your shirt clinging to your back like a professional wrestler's. However, in her white and yellow sundress, Kyla looked as cool and together as an ice sculpture. Even her dark hair curled and bounced around her shoulders with a life of its own. My own hair was pulled back in a limp ponytail, and I looked sourly down at my denim capris and oversized T-shirt. We could have been the Before and After shots in a makeover commercial.

Now, she dropped her purse on my desk with a thud and flopped dramatically into a chair with a groan.

"That doesn't look like good news," I said. "How did it go?"

Kyla had recently had a little trouble with the law.

"Pretty good. I guess. I got community service," she added with a frown.

I whooped. "Hey, that's great! You couldn't have hoped for much better than that."

She looked at me sourly. "The best thing would have been for them to give me a fucking medal for protecting myself and the public in general."

"Well, yeah. But you pulled a concealed weapon on Sixth Street. They couldn't exactly let that go," I pointed out.

A look of outrage lit her sapphire eyes. "I don't see why not. Was I supposed to just let those assholes carjack me? I don't think so."

"No, of course not."

"If it wasn't for me, those little bastards would still be out there, taking someone else's car, maybe hurting someone." Her finger jabbed the air at every word.

Now she was glaring at me like it was my fault.

I held up my hands. "You know I'm one hundred percent on your side. It's just that carrying a gun down in that area is illegal. They had to do something. Think about it— community service is really just a slap on the wrist. It's a good thing."

"I don't see what the good is of having a concealed-carry license if you can't carry around bars. That's exactly where you need to have a gun," she grumbled.

"Yeah, maybe everyone should just walk around with holsters and six shooters on their hips."

I was being sarcastic, but she considered it. "Not a bad idea. An armed society is a polite society."

"Robert Heinlein," I responded, impressed she knew the quote.

She rolled her eyes. "Whatever. Anyway, you'll never guess what I have to do."

From her tone, it was pretty nasty. "Pick up trash on the highway? Clean urinals at the bus station?"

"Worse. I have to teach a six-week seminar about girls in technology. You know, encourage high school girls to go into the sciences."

I stared at her blankly. "You get arrested for carrying a concealed weapon, and the punishment is teaching children?"

My whole life, my whole career, reduced down to a community-service penalty.

Kyla was oblivious. "Yeah, does that suck or what? But here's the good part. I got them to let me do it here."

I choked a little. "Here?"

"Yup. Twice a week for six weeks. And you have to help me. I don't know what to say to the little monsters."